CORRUPT UNION

KNIGHT'S RIDGE EMPIRE
BOOK 15

TRACY LORRAINE

Editing by Pinpoint Editing

Proofreading by Sisters Get Lit.erary

Photography by Wander Aguiar

Models - Liam Black and Joli Irvine

1

———

NICO

"No," I breathe, my hand trembling as I tug the note from beneath her phone and stumble back.

This is a joke.

It has to be a joke.

"BRIANNA," I bellow. My heart pounds, hoping that this is just some sick and twisted game. A way to punish me for being unable to stay away. But my head? My head knows the truth.

Ice-cold fear races down my spine, dripping through my veins.

The note flutters to the floor, and I take off long before it makes contact.

Swinging her bedroom door open, I pray I'm going to find her waiting for me, spread-eagled on the bed. I think of her naked, her hand between her thighs working herself as she impatiently waits for the inevitable.

She fucked up when she gave me her key. She had to know there was no way I'd let the rest of today go without using it.

Of course she knew. She's your good little whore.

The door crashes back against the wall, revealing what I already knew but refused to accept.

Her bed is empty. Hell, it's not just empty, it's perfect. The sheets are in place and all the pillows are propped up just as she likes them.

I scan the room, looking for something, anything that might be out of place.

Lamps sit on each bedside table, her wireless phone charger on her side.

Her e-reader which is always beside her bed is gone, and when I look closer at her dressing table, I find her makeup and hairbrushes both missing.

Pulling open her underwear drawer, I find it mostly empty. Her wardrobe is the same.

"No." I shake my head, walking backward and refusing to believe that she'd pack a bag and leave.

My calves hit the edge of her bed, and I fall down.

Her scent that first hit me when I walked into her space gets stronger, and I have the urge to lie down and bury my face in the pillow to breathe her in more deeply, for all the fucking good that will do.

I give myself twenty seconds to wallow in self-pity, and then I force myself to my feet again, a little of that lingering hope still alive within me as I begin searching the rest of her flat.

There's not much; her home is pretty modest. Just a bathroom and a fairly big storage cupboard off the kitchen. But she could be hiding in them.

But even as I have that thought, I know it's pointless.

Brianna might be a lot of things, but she's not that cruel.

But would she leave?

I guess the answer is right here in front of me when I

find, as expected really, that the flat is empty. There's even more evidence that she's packed up and gone when I find her toiletries missing from the bathroom.

Pulling my phone out of my pocket, my hand continues to tremble as I unlock it and find the person who will hold all the answers.

All the breath rushes out of my lungs as I think about her going back to be with Jodie.

It makes so much sense. Jodie wouldn't have wanted her here just as much as I didn't.

But then my eyes lock on that simple, heart-stopping note at my feet and reality hits.

This isn't a joke. She's not hiding with her best friend, waiting for me to find her.

This is serious.

She's gone.

Refusing to accept the hurt that slices through my chest like a jagged knife, I jab my finger into my phone screen, hitting call on Jodie's contact.

"Good to know you've come up for air," she teases the second the call connects. "Is my bestie still able to stan—"

"Where is she?" I bark, cutting off her taunts.

"W-what?"

"Where the fuck is she, Jodie?" I spit harshly.

There's a beat of silence as my words filter through her brain.

"I-I don't know what you're talking about. She's with you."

"No," I state. "She's not. And you're the only one who can know where she is," I bellow, my sanity beginning to falter.

There's some shuffling down the line before my best friend's voice fills my ears.

"I don't give a fuck who you are, no one talks to Jodie like that," he growls possessively.

"She's gone, Toby. She's fucking gone."

"Where are you?" he asks, sounding way too fucking calm.

"In her flat. She... she left a note. She's... g-gone."

I press my palm against my chest as I stumble back, colliding with her wall. My knees give out, sending me crashing to the floor.

My chest heaves, each breath heavy and painful as I rest my arms on my knees and hang my head in defeat.

This is punishment.

Karma.

Every single bad thing I've done in my life has led to this moment.

And fuck if it doesn't hurt.

Just when I pulled my head out of my arse and figured out what I wanted and needed in life, it all comes back to bite me.

Wasn't losing my parents enough?

Clearly not.

I guess whatever higher power has decided to fuck my life up even more than it already was thought I deserve more pain than the image of my dad lying there lifeless in the remains of that destroyed country club.

My thoughts flicker to my mother. The reason we were all there in the first place. She might be a selfish cunt of epic proportions, but he wanted to do it for her.

For whatever reason I'm still trying to figure out, he loved her something fierce. He never denied her of anything. And as much as the boys like to tease me, I know it's not just because of what's between her legs. *Shudder*.

There was more to it. Maybe she was a different person

all those years ago when he first fell for her. Maybe she grew into the cold bitch she became.

She was never meant to be a mother, I know that for a fact.

Did we break her?

And did he even see it?

I have so many questions. So many that I wish I'd had a chance to ask him. So many things I wish I'd been able to tell him. To share with him.

By the time the door crashes back against the wall once more, I'm a fucking wreck. And I don't even care to try and cover it up.

Lifting my head from my arms, I stare up at my best friend and his girl through tear-filled eyes.

"Where is she?" Jodie asks, clearly forgetting the first fucking thing I asked her when she picked up her phone.

A bitter, sad, and hopeless laugh tumbles from my lips.

"You're meant to know the answer to that question," I seethe, earning myself a warning glare from Toby.

"Nic—"

"Don't, okay? Just fucking don't."

Climbing to my feet, I stalk over to the abandoned note and swipe it from the floor.

Thrusting it at Jodie, I wait as her eyes scan those three little words.

Three tiny, should-be-insignificant words that shouldn't have the power to bring me to my knees like this. Just like the woman who wrote them.

I shake my head.

This is why I wasn't interested in anything but one-night stands.

Women. Love. It makes you weak.

Right now, all I'm thinking about is her, about how much it fucking hurts that she basically shoved her hand inside my chest, ripped my heart out and took it with her.

I haven't even considered the fact that her front door is wide open and we could be ambushed by an Italian or two.

I'm weak. Weak and vulnerable. And if anything were to happen to me now, it's all going to be her fault. Not that she'll give a shit.

She left.

After everything she said this weekend—the promises we made, both out loud and silently as caved to what we've both been denying for too long—she's just upped and left.

"No, I don't believe it," Jodie states confidently. "She wouldn't do this."

Ripping my gaze from the note in her hands, I find her eyes.

"What part of that note makes you think she's joking, Jodie? She's gone, she left me, and all I've got is that bullshit note in her place."

Didn't she have any more to say? Even a, 'thanks for the ride' would have been fucking nice.

"She wouldn't do this," Jodie repeats, her dark eyes urging me to believe her. "I know her, Nico. I know her better than she knows herself. She wouldn't leave. She..." Averting her gaze, she looks at her best friend's handwriting pinned between her fingers. "She wouldn't leave me."

Her unspoken words twist the knife that's already buried in my chest harder.

She wouldn't have left Jodie. But she would have left me.

Deep down, I know she's right. I've been nothing but a prick to her since we met, but I thought we'd turned a corner.

I guess I was naïve to think she'd suddenly change her mind and take a chance on me. Since the night we met, she's told me over and over that she doesn't do serious, that she has no interest in a future with me or any guy.

Then, I nearly killed her. What woman in her right mind would suddenly do a U-turn and decide they want everything they've vehemently refused as a possibility before?

I was kidding myself, thinking this weekend was the beginning of something. It wasn't the start. It was the end, and I was too fucking pussy blind to see it.

We weren't embarking on the next chapter of our relationship. We were ending it. She was saying goodbye and I had no clue.

I know I've accused her of being a liar, but I never thought she was capable of playing me quite so easily.

"I'm so fucking stupid," I bark, unable to keep this inside. "I believed her. Every fucking word. I believed her, and all of it was lies. Ugly lies from her pretty, pouty lips."

"No," Jodie argues. "Brianna isn't a liar. She's the most trustworthy, honest person I know. If she's left then—" Jodie swallows nervously.

"Then?" Toby asks, reaching out and pulling his girlfriend into his side when she begins to break down.

"It wasn't by choice," she whispers, her voice cracking.

I blink at her as my brain fights to decipher the words.

"You mean she was taken?" Toby rationalises before I get a chance to.

"Makes sense, doesn't it? She was with you this weekend, Nico. One hundred percent. And if you push this bullshit pity party aside, you'd know it too. You know Bri better than that."

"Ricardo," I breathe. His name alone makes my blood run cold.

The image of what Daemon and Ant looked like when they defied the odds and returned from the Italians' clutches fills my mind and bile churns in my stomach.

It doesn't matter that Brianna is a woman. He'll use her to deliver his message.

First my dad, and then my girl.

Motherfucker has one serious death wish.

"Let's go. We need to get the others and take this to the boss."

My body moves of its own accord, my legs taking steps toward the front door before Jodie cries out.

"Wait. You've tracked her, right?" she asks hopefully. "Like we all are." She lifts her hand to her necklace.

"No." Tracking her would mean claiming her, and until recently, I was adamant that wasn't going to happen. "Haven't you?" I ask, my eyes lifting to Toby's. As his girl's best friend, cousin, hell, sister, for all intents and purposes, I'd have thought he'd have done it.

"No. She refused to allow anything but her phone to be tracked. She's as stubborn and hard-headed as you," he states, holding my eyes firm, reminding me of all the times he's brought this conversation up over the past few months.

"This wasn't meant to happen," I argue, unsure if I mean this situation or the fact I went and fell for her.

"We know. Now let's go find her," Toby says confidently, gesturing for me to continue to the door.

I move toward it, but before I pass through, I pause and look back.

Her presence might be gone, but this is still her place, and I feel some weird kind of comfort being here. Even if everything inside me is rioting at the thought of her being in our enemy's clutches.

I want to wonder, why her? But the answer is obvious. While I've been refusing to accept what she means to me, others have been able to see it. They knew she was our weak link.

If I'd just locked her down sooner...

2

BRIANNA

y body aches and my head is fuzzy as hell as I come to.

Rolling over, I groan into the pillow beneath me, wondering why I allowed myself to drink so much on a school night.

There's only one person to blame for this lapse in judgement.

Nico Cirillo.

The reason for all my bad decisions this year.

Shame I can't also blame all the previous ones on him too.

Sadly, they're all on me. I never even learned most of the names of those previous mistakes, so I can hardly blame them.

As I shift my legs, my core aches, sending little after-shocks racing to my nerve endings.

This weekend was... well, pretty sextacular.

A smile twitches at my lips as I recall all the places we fucked, all the ways he bent my body to his will, and just how loud I screamed for him. Those places are soundproof

—probably for a very good reason, knowing those boys and their skills—but it still wouldn't surprise me if all of them heard me.

It. Was. Just. That. Fucking. Good.

Tugging the sheets up higher, I snuggle into the soft pillow beneath me and allow myself to drown in thoughts of Nico and the things he can do with his insane body.

Damn, that dick should be illegal.

Maybe I'm not even hanging from alcohol. Maybe I just got so dick drunk that I'm now suffering the after-effects.

Sleep claims me quickly, and I forget all about reality and let myself drown in my salacious dreams.

"Babe," a deep voice growls in my ear, stirring me from my slumber.

I stretch my legs out, my muscles aching in the most delicious way as I remember Nico recently pinning my thighs to my chest as he railed me.

My pussy clenches as I remember just how he feels sliding that magnificent cock inside my body. A moan rumbles deep in my throat as his lips kiss down my neck and across my injured shoulder.

"What are you thinking about, Siren?" he whispers, his voice rough with his own desire.

"You," I confess.

"Hmm," he groans. "Now that's something I could get used to, babe. Are you sore?"

"Deliciously so," I confess as his hand slides over the dip of my waist and to my hip.

"You think you can go again?"

A quiet laugh spills from my lips.

"Is that a serious question, Nico?"

He shifts closer and pulls my hips back for a better angle, his hard dick pressing up against my arse.

"Whore," he murmurs quietly, almost lovingly.

"Yours," I confess. The word feels right. After all the time I've spent denying the truth behind it, now I've embraced it, I can appreciate just how right it is.

"Fuck, babe. Is this real?" he asks, hooking his hand around my thigh and opening me up for him.

I gasp as his fingers find my clit and gently begins circling it.

"I can't help feeling like I'm going to wake up and all of this will have been a dream."

The head of his dick presses against my entrance before he pushes in gently.

It stings for a beat, but it quickly gives way to pleasure. So much fucking pleasure.

Nico doesn't need to do anything fancy when we're together. There doesn't need to be any sex toys or special lube that's meant to add to the sensation. He. Is. Everything.

My body responds to his as if it was made for him.

We align and fit together perfectly.

It's terrified me in the past. The thought of being the other half to someone's whole was not a concept I was willing to admit existed. But lying here now, none of that seems quite so scary.

"Nico," I breathe when he pushes deeper, filling me in only the way he can.

"Right here, babe. And I'm not going fucking anywhere."

He rocks into me slowly as his fingers play with my clit.

My release grows quickly, but his almost lazy movements mean that he never builds me high enough to fall, and I end up riding the crest of that almost-in-touching-distance orgasm for the longest time.

His lips continue kissing my shoulder, paying attention to each laceration left behind from his reckless behaviour.

Knowing that he's not turned off by the mess of my skin does make me feel a little better about it, but until the stitches are finally gone and I can see the true mess of what I'm left with, I'm always going to think the worst.

"Addicted to being inside you, Siren. Your pussy is fucking spectacular," he whispers against my skin. The heat of his breath sends a shudder of desire down my spine.

He might be inside me, he might have his hands on me, but it's not enough. And I fear that it never will be when it comes to Nico Cirillo.

Quite how fiercely I want him, even that very first night, is all-consuming. But it's only getting worse now that I've allowed myself to have him.

"Your cunt is practically strangling my dick, babe. My girl sure is hungry for it, huh?"

"Nico."

"Fuck yeah, it's me. And from here on out, it'll only ever be me," he says possessively. His words make me think of Brad briefly. But I quickly stomp on those thoughts. We're long over. I was only ever keeping him around for selfish reasons. But after what happened last weekend, I think it became very obvious to both of us—at last—that there was nothing of any substance there. He fulfilled a need I had— scratched an itch, so to speak. And I... well, fuck knows what I fulfilled in his life. He wanted more from me than I was willing to give. That was always more than obvious. Maybe pretending, taking me out on dates and showing me off was enough for him.

Whatever it was, it doesn't matter now. It's done. That chapter of my story is firmly over, and I'm ready to embark on this new one.

"Yes," I groan, agreeing with him. "Just you, Nico."

A filthy groan rumbles in his throat, and it's enough to push my release a little closer.

"Are you going to come all over my dick, Siren?"

"Yes."

"Tell me what you need," he demands, torturing me with his sexy, deep voice as he continues his slow, measured strokes.

"More. I need more."

"More how?" he asks, playing with me.

"Faster. Harder. I need... I need you at your worst."

"Well, that's a real shame, babe. Because right now, you're getting me at my best."

Pushing up on his elbow, he looms over me.

"Now, give me your lips. I need more too."

"I've been sleeping," I say with a wince, but I should know better.

"And? You could have been licking the bathroom floor and I'd still want those lips on mine."

"Gross," I mutter a beat before he moves my head exactly where he wants me and brushes his lips against mine.

The kiss is just as slow and sweet as what he's doing lower down my body. He kisses me with reverence and love, making my eyes burn with tears. I can honestly say that it's not something I've ever experienced during sex. Sure, there have been more than a few times that I've wanted to cry mid-act, but that's more because it's been so shit and I was craving being alone with my vibrator instead of the dead fish who was trying to rock my world. Honestly, some men can't even cause a wave let alone make the Earth move in any way.

Nico's tongue licks into my mouth as he fuck me as deep as this position allows. Each of his thrusts grazes my G-spot *in the most mind-blowing way. He knows it too, but he doesn't give me any more. He just keeps me right on the edge. And as much as I want to beg for more, I never do. I just give myself over to him, knowing that when he's ready, he'll make sure my world is more than rocked.*

I have no idea how much time passes, or if it's day or night as we continue to... make love?

It's a heady thought that we could be heading into that territory.

I watch the others daily, how much they care about each other, how they've promised forever to each other.

Is that where this is going?

After all the denial, all the ignored feelings and desires, are we racing toward the illustrious happily ever after?

"Babe," he groans into our kiss. "I'm gonna blow. You ready?"

"So ready. Make me shatter," I demand.

And boy, does he fucking deliver.

His hips pick up speed, his fingers working my clit like a pro as he ups his pressure, pinching that little bud of nerves until he throws me right over the edge.

The release is different, although no less powerful. Hell, if anything, it's more so.

Instead of slamming into me, it rolls through me. Each wave gets increasingly intense until I cry out, my eyes slamming shut as I embrace the heat and pleasure rising within me.

I am utterly consumed.

And it only gets even more powerful when he roars my name and his cock jerks inside me, filling me.

"Fuck, babe. Everything. You're fucking everything."

My eyes pop open the second I wake and discover that I'm not mid-orgasm and that Nico isn't inside me.

The disappointment is real.

"Shit," I hiss, staring at the white ceiling above me. "Nico?"

Twisting my head to the side, I search for him, more than ready to make use of his body after how vivid that dream was. But I quickly discover that he's not lying beside me a beat before I realise I don't recognise the sheets that are covering me.

"What the—"

I sit bolt upright, scanning my surroundings as my heart begins to pound.

I recognise nothing.

Panic starts to rise within me.

This isn't Nico's bedroom, or either of his guest rooms.

It's—

I'm on my feet before I've registered the move and I race toward the door.

The second I twist the handle, it swings open, revealing a bathroom.

It's a beautiful white bathroom with teal accents. But I don't appreciate it for long, because my confusion ramps up the second I spot all the products lining the counter around the basin and the shelf in the walk-in shower.

They're all mine.

My brows pinch as I wrack my brain for where I am.

I know we fucked a lot this weekend, but I'm not sure it was enough for me to black out and not know where we were going.

It was a school night, a little voice says inside my head.

Why would he have taken me anywhere on a school night?

Spinning around, I search the room once more. And

just like the bathroom, I find that I'm surrounded by my things.

My Kindle sits on the bedside table beside a glass of water.

My make-up is on the vanity unit, and when I pull open the huge walk-in wardrobe, I find my clothes.

Confused as fuck, I head for the final door in the room.

But unlike the previous two, when I twist the handle of this one, nothing happens.

I pull harder, thinking it's just stuck, but it quickly dawns on me that this isn't a sticky, swollen door. Not in a place this expensive looking.

It's locked.

"NICO," I scream, my fists pounding on the door as my heart beats so fast it makes my head spin.

But it doesn't matter how loud I scream for help or pound on the door. Nothing happens.

No one comes.

3

———

NICO

"Why the fuck did you let her go home?" Theo barks, his eyes wide with disbelief after Toby's explained why we barged in on him and Emmie mid-fuck on the sofa.

"I was trying to do the right thing. She wanted some space before going back to school tomorrow and—"

"SO?" he bellows. "Fuck that, Nico. You should never have let her out of this building, let alone leave her there unprotected."

"I made sure she locked the door after me."

"Oh good, that makes it all fucking better, doesn't it?"

"I don't need your fucking attitude," I snap at him. "I fucked up. Again. Trust me, I fucking know that."

"If you don't want my attitude, then I don't want your fucking pity party. Yeah, you fucked up again. Own it." He lifts his hand, pushing his messy sex hair back from his brow.

"Where's the fire?" Alex barks as Theo's door opens and he, Ant, Daemon and my sister join the party.

"Nico, what's wrong?" Calli asks the second her eyes land on me.

"Bri's gone," I blurt, the words slicing me up once again.

It doesn't seem to matter how many times I say them; they're not getting any easier to swallow.

"What?" she shrieks, pulling her phone from her back pocket and tapping the screen. "It's ringing," she says the second she puts it to her ear, but much to her disappointment, the phone she's calling lights up on the coffee table.

"Calli," I breathe, pushing to my feet and closing the space between us. "She's gone," I whisper, wrapping my arms around her, needing her warmth and support as much as I think she needs mine right now.

"She wouldn't," she breathes, her voice cracking with emotion. "Not after this weekend. Not after she told you—" She hiccups, cutting her words off.

"We think Ricardo has her," Jodie says, her voice freakishly calm.

Since breaking on the drive back here, she seems to have found some strength from somewhere and is purely focused on finding her best friend.

I look up just in time to see Daemon's jaw tense. It's not often he shows any kind of reaction or outward emotion, but remembering what he went through is enough to crack his mask.

"I haven't heard anything," Ant says regretfully.

"Is that really a surprise after Friday night?" Theo snaps.

He's got a point; things with the Italians are at breaking point.

They know we set them up, which means they have the

confirmation they need that we've got someone in their ranks, or more so they we've got some of theirs in ours.

"Well, you need to find out," Calli begs, twisting out of my hold and looking at her friend with soppy, pleading eyes.

"It's not that easy, Cal. I can't just pick up the phone to Enzo. I need to wait for him."

"Have we heard from him yet?" I ask. The last time we were up here, there had been no communication from Enzo, and although no one said anything, unease rippled through us all.

If Ricardo and his loyal men suspect Enzo, then... well, it doesn't really bear thinking about. But safe to say that we won't be getting any more intel on what the cunt is up to.

And we fucking need it. Now more than ever.

We need an opportunity to hit them once and for all.

"No. Nothing," Ant says nervously.

"He's just keeping a low profile, right?" Emmie asks hopefully.

"That would be the ideal situation," Theo states coldly. "Where the fuck are Seb and Stella?"

Silence.

"Someone fucking call them. I'll get onto Dad and hope for a fucking miracle."

Pushing from the sofa, he turns his back on us and heads for his office.

Unable to just sit there and wait like a good little minion, I take off after him.

"What the fuck?" I bark, catching the door he tries to swing closed, making him pause halfway across the room.

"I just need a fucking minute," he snaps.

"Oh, I'm sorry that my missing fucking girlfriend put

pay to you nutting in yours," I hiss, irritation rolling through me in angry waves.

"It's not that," he says, waving me off. "I just..." His words trail off as he falls into his massive, pretentious chair that sits behind his equally ostentatious desk.

"Just what? Brianna is... fuck. And you're hiding in here like you don't care."

His cold eyes snap up from his desk and hold mine. Danger comes off him in waves, not that I give a shit. I'll go toe to toe with him time and time again if needs be.

"Is that really what you think? That I don't care?"

I throw my hands up. "I don't fucking know. All I do know is that we're all sitting in here like idiots while someone has my girl. I need her, Theo. I fucking need—"

"I know, Nic. And we'll get her. I'm just... processing. Getting shit straight before talking to Dad. There is so much shit that's going on it's—"

"I'm sorry," I blurt, making his brows shoot up.

"Trust me, Nico. I fucking care. And we will find her. And if she hasn't already killed that motherfucker herself, then I'll do everything I can to ensure you get to do it."

I nod, accepting that he means that before falling into one of the chairs opposite him and giving him a second to get his shit together, all the while wishing that I could do the same thing.

But something tells me that nothing will be right in my world until we find her and I have her in my arms.

To say Damien was angry would be an understatement.

Of course, he didn't go all red in the face and start shouting his irritation through Theo's iPad—that's not how our boss rolls. But those who know him best, his son and nephew, we see it. The way his already dark eyes turn murderous and how his fists curl on top of his desk in his home office.

He was incensed.

But just like us, he also didn't have any answers.

Really fucking helpful.

He told us that he was sending men out to known Italian locations, but honestly, while we don't know who we should be trusting, that might just be making the situation worse.

"This isn't helping," I whine like a little bitch a few hours later as I stand in the middle of Brianna's flat once again.

"Well, do you have any better ideas?" Jodie snaps impatiently.

Images of watching the Italian compound and every business they own go up in flames fill my mind, and apparently, I'm not the only one able to see it.

"Once we've got her back, yeah. Then, we bring them to their knees," she promises, able to see the bloodlust shining bright in my eyes.

"Motherfuckers," Theo grunts from where he and Toby are sitting side by side on Brianna's sofa with their laptops on their knees.

"What?" I bark when he just continues tapping instead of explaining.

"What time did you get back here with her?" he asks without looking up.

"Uh... dunno, about seven, maybe eight. Why?" I bark when he doesn't respond and instead continues tapping.

"Fucking. Fuck."

"What?"

"They've hacked into the security footage. The film is on loop. There's no sign of you coming back here or anyone entering after."

My teeth grind as I stare at my cousin in disbelief.

"When did they do that?"

"I'm just looking. But this was planned. They were waiting."

My blood turns to ice at the thought of those fucking cunts sitting outside her building, just waiting for her.

"They couldn't have known she'd return."

"No," Toby agrees. "But she's the only one who doesn't live with us, so there was a higher chance of catching her returning than the others."

Regret floods me.

I knew letting her come here was the wrong move. But I didn't want to be that controlling prick she was accusing me of. I agreed with everything she shouted at me.

I don't want her to sit back, accept my money and just look pretty on my arm. I love that she has dreams, desires, a drive to help people. I'd never stop her from doing any of that. But fuck, I should have stood firm on this.

Or I should have refused to leave. Every inch of my body was begging for me to stay. I should have listened.

If I did, I could have been here when—

"There's no sign of forced entry," I say, cutting off my own thoughts by vocalising my fears.

Jodie and Calli are right. Brianna being taken does make the most sense, but still, there's a small part of me that thinks she's run.

And the only person she could possibly have to run from is me.

My stomach knots, pain once against twisting up my chest as I stare down at my cousin and best friend in the hope they have some actual factual answers instead of us just guessing what happened here tonight.

"That doesn't mean anything, and you know it. How many locks have you picked and left no evidence behind?" Toby asks me, knowing my skills with a lock well.

"That's not proof, though, is it? She could have still packed a bag and walk—"

"She didn't," Theo states firmly. "This is not Brianna's doing. She wouldn't do it to Jodie. To Joanne. To you."

I shake my head, unable to believe the words that fall from his lips.

With a pained sigh, I spin on my heels and walk toward Brianna's bedroom.

The second I stop in the doorway, a million images of times I've spent here with her fill my mind.

"Nico," she cries as I suck on her clit.

"Louder," I demand, aware that both our best friends are out in the living room and more than ready to prove that we're having way more fun than they are.

I spear two fingers inside her tight cunt and curl them to make her scream.

We may not have been together all that many times, but I already know exactly how to play her.

She burns up with every single one of my touches. No matter what I do, no matter how innocent, it's like she can't get enough.

It's a fucking heady feeling.

I've been with plenty of women before, but never has one reacted quite this strongly to me.

Not that I'm about to tell her that.

As far as she's concerned, she's just another hook-up. Although, one that's good enough to require repeat performances.

I've already broken so many of my own rules with her. Just like I know she has with me. That makes me feel a little better about these reruns, because something tells me she's just as addicted to my cock as I am her pussy.

She might vehemently disagree when we're clothed and she has appearances to keep up, but the second I get her naked, strip everything away, she's just my needy little whore who can't get enough.

"NICO, FUUUCK," she screams louder, exactly as I demanded when I brush her G-Spot over and over.

I lick and suck at her clit, too fucking addicted to her taste as her body climbs toward her release.

But I don't let her have it.

Just before she falls, my fingers still and my tongue stops.

"You fucking cunt," she cries, kicking her heels into my back.

"Fuck, I love it when you get all angry, Siren. Makes my cock so hard."

"I fucking hate you," she sneers.

"Yeah, keep telling yourself that."

Releasing her, I lean over the side of her bed to the box of toys she helpfully pulled out earlier, my fingers curling around some rope.

Her eyes follow my movement as I loom over her, looping it around the wooden bars of her headboard and securing it before I reach for her arms. But at no point do I meet her frustrated-yet-excited gaze.

Without question, she allows me to tie her to the bed, and the second she's secured, I crawl down the bed, wrap my fingers around her ankles, and drag her down until the rope is taut.

She gasps as her body reaches maximum capacity.

"Look at you," I murmur, releasing her ankles in favour

of running my palms up her smooth, curvy legs. My fingers dig into her muscles, massaging them. She might not need it now, but something tells me she will after I'm done with her.

"Please," she whimpers, her eyes begging for more.

Her skin is glistening from her almost release, her chest is glowing with desire, and her nipples are so hard they could cut glass.

The only time she looks better is when she's on her knees with her make-up streaked down her cheeks.

"Please what, Siren? You'll need to beg better than that if you want something."

"Please," she gasps when my thumbs brush dangerously close to her pussy. "I need to come."

"Is that right? You'd better be a good little whore then, shouldn't you, Siren?"

A shriek rips from her lips as I grab her hips and flip her onto her stomach.

Placing her on her knees, I pull my hand back.

"Hold on," I command, aware that she has fuck all to hold onto before my palm cracks against her arse cheek.

"Fuck, yes," I whisper under my breath as my handprint blooms on her flawless skin.

Mine, *I think before realising just how fucked up that is.*

Needing a distraction, I reach for the butt plug I pushed inside her before I even touched her.

She screams like the perfect whore she is as I play with it.

"Nico, please," she pants, pushing her arse back, trying to get more.

An amused chuckle falls from me.

"You still haven't told me what you want, Siren."

"Your dick, Nico. I want your fucking dick."

"Where?"

"Pussy first."

"First?" I ask with a smirk.

Hell yes, she's always as hungry as I am.

"Nico."

"I think first," I say, climbing off the bed, leaving her arse up and ready for me.

I take a second to study her with her glistening cunt on full display for me.

Reaching down, I palm my aching dick as I imagine how she'll look in a few minutes with her red-stained lips wrapped around it as she deepthroats me.

"Nico," a voice snaps, dragging me from the filthy daydream of my siren.

I blink a couple of times, my vision coming back to me.

My boner that I'm rubbing through my jeans quickly sinks when I find Jodie staring at me with her brows raised.

"Sorry," I mutter, feeling weirdly embarrassed. "Anything?"

"No. I can't find anything that might help. It's all... as it should be," she confesses sadly.

Unable to do anything else, I spin around and plant my fist into Brianna's bedroom wall. It might not help, but at least the pain comes from somewhere other than my chest.

4

———————

BRIANNA

Despite knowing that no one is coming, my fist continues to rain down on the door until I can't stand the pain anymore.

With a terrified sob, I fall back against the wall. My legs give out, leaving me in a heap on the floor.

Tears continue to fall from my lashes as my body trembles.

I like to think I'm pretty strong. But waking up and discovering this has broken something inside me.

"Nico," I sob, squeezing my eyes closed as I think about him.

This is all my fault. If I weren't so stubborn about going back to my flat, then I would never have ended up here.

I'd still be...

My head pops up in the search for a clock.

I have no idea what time it is, what day it is.

The only thing I know is that it's daytime, because the sun is streaming through the window.

The window.

In a rush, I fly toward it and rip the curtains open.

Greenery greets me. Beneath the window is the most perfectly tended-to garden, before trees spread out into the blue sky in the distance.

Safe to say that I'm no longer in London.

Pressing my nose to the glass, I look down and swallow nervously. I'm not scared of heights. What I said to the girls the other week is true; I'm scared of wet cotton wool. But really, my biggest fear in life is similar to Emmie's. I'm terrified I'll turn into my mother and be a complete waste of oxygen and a drain on society. But still, trying to scale that vertical does send a wave of anxiety up my spine. Although, something tells me it'll be easier than whatever I've got waiting for me here.

Wrapping my fingers around the handles on the sash windows, I pull as hard as I can.

"NOOOO," I scream when they don't budge.

Of fucking course they don't.

My fist collides with the glass.

It hurts like a bitch, but it gives me another idea.

Spinning around, I grab the stool sitting in front of the dressing table. Holding the padded seat against my chest, I run at the window, images of the glass shattering before me filling my mind.

"Motherfucker," I grunt when that doesn't play out and instead, I'm bounced backward, falling painfully on my arse with the stool still in my arms.

Who the fuck puts indestructible glass on bedroom windows?

People who don't want their captives escaping.

With an exhausted and frustrated groan, I relax back before curling up with the stool like the pathetic woman I don't want to become.

I don't remember falling back to sleep on the floor, but I must have, because I have no recollection of getting up.

I wake with a start and push myself up on my elbows, staring at the bed.

How the—

My stomach rumbles, and when I suck in a breath through my nose, I discover why.

Food.

Looking to my right, I find a tray sitting on the bedside table.

There's an empty bowl with a flask beside it, what looks like a fresh crusty roll, and not one but three dessert options. A chocolate brownie, a fruit salad with meringue nests, and my personal favourite, a slice of strawberry cheesecake.

My stomach growls loudly as I push myself up so I'm sitting back against the headboard and I reach for the tray.

My movements falter when a handwritten note captures my attention.

Eat well. You'll need your strength.

My brows pinch in confusion while my stomach convulses at the barely veiled threat in those words.

Picking up the square of paper, I study the script, desperately trying to recognise it.

As I stare at it, a memory slams into me.

A scream rips from my throat as fingers twist in my hair, dragging me back into a hard body.

Without hearing his voice, or even looking at him, my body instantly knows it isn't Nico who's just walked into my flat.

Pain shoots down my neck as my head is ripped back until a hot pair of lips brushes against my neck.

My stomach knots, bile burning up my throat as his hot breath tickles over my skin.

Goosebumps erupt across every inch of my body, but they're not the good kind. Exactly the opposite.

"You're going to regret this," I breathe, trying to sound as strong as possible while my entire world seems to fall from beneath me.

"We'll see about that," a deep voice rumbles.

I lift my foot, ready to swing it back as far as I can in the hope of catching him in the nuts, but he predicts the move a mile off and instead of causing him any pain, I'm slammed up against the wall of my flat.

My cheek collides with the exposed brickwork, grazing my skin.

"Behave, Brianna, and this will be much easier for you."

"Never," I spit, bucking against his larger body in the hope of... fuck knows, but I'm not going to take this lying down.

"Now, I need you to do one thing for me."

"Fuck you, I'm doing nothing. Get the fuck out of my flat."

His deep chuckle rolls through me, making all my hairs stand on end.

"They'll kill you," I warn. "When they find out what you've done, they'll hunt you down and kill you for this."

He laughs again, letting me know just how deranged he is. "I'll look forward to watching them try."

"Now, are we going to do this the easy way, or the hard way?"

I can barely get control of my breathing as I come back to myself, the tray on my lap trembling with my body.

The image of that man holding my head over a scrap of paper and thrusting a pen at me to scrawl out the note he wants me to leave, all the while holding a syringe to my neck.

He promised me that if I followed orders, it would be easy. I guess in some ways the fact he stuck whatever was in that plunger into my neck the second I finished writing was the easy way.

I have no idea what happened next. No clue how he treated me or what state he might have left my flat in.

Did he fuck it up, leaving Nico and Jodie to find it and believe I put up a good fight? Or is it perfect, as if I just walked away?

Would they even believe I would?

Jodie wouldn't. She has to know that I'd never leave her. No matter how bad shit got, I would never just walk away from her.

She's my sister. Maybe not by blood, but in every way that counts.

And Nico. Things had been intense between us over the weekend, but surely, he wouldn't believe I'd been playing him?

When I told him I was his, I meant it.

I'm done fighting and ready to figure out if this connection we seem to share can be something.

That thought is terrifying, but it's not scary enough to make me run.

I'm not a pussy. I don't run from my issues or my fears.

I fight. Just like they do.

I want to think they all know that.

Hell, I never would have killed that man if I weren't serious.

I push thoughts of that prick aside. I've got more pressing issues to be thinking about right now. But as much as I try, I can't help wondering if this has something to do with that.

Do the Italians know that I was the one who killed him? Is that why they targeted me? Or was I just easy prey?

I'm not trained like Stella or Emmie, and now Jodie. And I'm not as protected as Calli.

I stare down at the food before me. My stomach hurts, it's so empty, but the thought of eating doesn't fill me with much joy.

But the note is right. Whatever the future holds for me here, I will need my strength.

With trembling hands, I twist open the flask and the scent of fresh tomato soup hits my nose.

My stomach growls louder as I pour some of it into the bowl.

I'm sure it tastes amazing. Homemade soup is usually far superior to the canned stuff, but as I push the first spoonful into my mouth, it might as well be cardboard for how much of it I taste.

I eat on autopilot because I know I need it. But I don't enjoy any of it.

After managing half the soup and a few mouthfuls of the bread, I give up and place the tray back on the bedside table.

My eyes linger on the door, willing it to open with just the power of my eyes. It's hopeless, and I wonder if I'm already going crazy from knowing I'm locked in here.

Just in case whoever has me in here didn't double check behind him, I walk over and test the door. Unsurprisingly, it doesn't budge.

I make use of the bathroom and brush my teeth. But despite how much I might want to shower and wash that man's touch from my body, I don't do more than imagine how amazing it would feel with all the jets that are embedded in the tiles. Then, my eyes linger on the huge bathtub, my muscles aching to sink down into too-hot water covered in fluffy bubbles.

But the thought of stripping down and being vulnerable when anyone could walk in and see me doesn't sit right with me. So, after splashing my face with water and washing my hands, I walk back into the bedroom.

I spend a few minutes staring out the window before I curl up on the bed once more.

There is no TV, no radio, no way for me to access the outside world. And I don't need to remember him putting my phone next to that note he forced me to write to know I don't have that either.

Reaching out, I grab my Kindle. Turning it on, I stare at the black and white screen for a few minutes.

The battery is full. Thank fuck. But what I really wanted to see isn't there. There's no WiFi signal.

I guess this is one way to make a dent on that TBR list.

Without the internet, I'm seriously limited with how I can make use of this device other than to lose myself in my favourite fictional worlds.

But just thinking about trying to focus on reading is enough to make me want to go back to sleep.

Placing it on the other side of the bed, I pull the covers up, turn on my side, and lift my knees to my chest, as if curling up like a child will help in any way.

I lie there for the longest time, straining to hear something, anything.

I can only assume that someone else is here, because they brought food. But is it just one person? Or many? Is it all men, or are there women too?

But other than my own racing heart and ragged breathing, I hear nothing.

There is no sign of life, and because it helps to settle my racing thoughts, I convince myself that I'm here alone and that Nico and the others are already casing the joint, ready to rescue me like in the movies.

I fall into a fitful sleep. Whatever drug he pumped into me is clearly still having an effect, assuming I wasn't given another weaker dose when my visitor delivered the food. It wouldn't surprise me if they wanted to keep me somewhat sedated. I might not be a real danger like Stella and Emmie, but they have to know that I killed a man at least double my size only a few days ago.

A moan rips from my lips as something tickles down my cheek. An image of Nico brushing a lock of my hair from my face fills my mind and I relax for a beat.

Fighting to pull my body from the depths of sleep, I shift closer to the warmth of his hand.

Eventually, I manage to get my eyelids to flicker open. The first thing I notice is that it's dark. The second thing is that it isn't Nico that's touching me.

"No," I breathe.

"Hey, baby. How are you feeling?"

5

———

BRIANNA

"W-what are you doing?" I ask, my body suddenly more than awake as very familiar grey eyes stare down at me.

Jumping back away from his touch, I scramble across the bed to get away from him.

But as I try to stand, the world around me spins as I crash back onto the bed.

"What have you done?" I ask, unable to miss how my voice slurs.

Clapping my hand over my neck where that man stabbed me with a needle, I try backing away again.

"Baby, please calm down," he says, twisting around to watch me as I stumble toward the wall.

"You," I breathe.

How? How didn't I recognise his voice?

"It's okay, baby. You're where you're meant to be now. You're safe."

"Where I'm meant to— Safe? Are you fucking kidding me? You attacked me. You abducted me. You locked me up like I'm a weak princess who needs protection. And I'm not safe here. You're fucking insane, Brad. You need to let me go."

At some point during my tirade, he climbed from the bed and moved closer. And when I blink again, he's right there in front of me.

"No," I cry, a beat before my palm collides with his cheek.

His eyes widen, anger immediately darkening them, allowing me to see a side to him that I never have before he grabs my wrists and restrains them behind my back in one of his hands.

"You can't do this."

He chuckles, the sound sending ice through my veins. It's the exact same chuckle from Sunday night. It's unhinged, maniacal, and nothing like I've ever heard coming from his lips before.

"Oh," he says, stepping into my body and pinning me back against the wall, showing me just how much more powerful he is than me. "But I can."

Mimicking the move I woke to, he reaches out his free hand and tucks a stray lock of hair behind my ear.

His manic eyes hold mine, studying me as if he can read all my thoughts.

"So naïve, baby. You thought I didn't know, didn't you?"

"D-didn't know what?" I ask, my voice more slurred than before. "W-what d-did you g-give me?"

"Just something to keep you relaxed. Is it kicking in?" he asks, amusement glittering in his eyes. "Good."

"W-w-what are y-you—"

"Nico Cirillo," he spits, making the hairs on the back of my neck stand on end. "Really? Out of everyone in this city, you went and fell for him?"

My lips part, but this time I can't find any words.

Whatever he's drugged me with is stealing everything but his touch from me.

Revulsion rolls through me as I stare back at him, wondering who I spent all that time with in the past.

He was so normal. So... boring.

"Ah, it looks like she's starting to understand," he states happily, as if this is some crazy-arse game show. "Do you have any idea how long it took for me to find you, Brianna Andrews?" The way his eyes narrow as he asks that question makes me think there's so much more to it, but as my brain is barely able to keep up with his words, it's a thought I can't hold on to.

"Lemego," I slur, jerking against his body. Although I instantly realise my mistake when I feel him hard against my stomach.

Bile burns up my throat. He's fucking getting off on this.

Releasing my arms, he grips me by the back of my neck and guides me across the room.

"Geoffme," I cry, or at least, I try to as he pushes me into the bathroom, my legs barely holding me up.

The scent of lavender hits my nose, and I try and turn away from it. I fucking hate lavender. It's the scent of grandmothers. I mean, I assume. It's not like I've ever had one to know for sure. By the time I arrived at Joanne and Jodie's, it was too late for all that family bonding.

"Please, no," I whimper, my eyes landing on the bathful of bubbles.

My body wants it, craves it. But my head, no matter how fuzzy from the drugs, knows that nothing good can come of this.

"Aw come on, baby. I need you nice and clean. I've got a gift for you, after all."

I don't want anything from you, I scream, although I quickly realise the words didn't actually leave my lips.

"Arms up."

I want to fight. I try to fight, but I don't have the strength. My limbs are like jelly, and before I know it, I'm slumped against the wall before him naked.

His eyes are glued on my shoulder.

"He deserves to die for hurting you, baby."

"I'mnoyourbaby."

"You were always mine, Brianna. Always were and always will be."

I scoff at that.

"We'll get through this. I've already spoken to the best doctors who will be able to fix that ugliness."

All the breath rushes out of my lungs at his words.

I might have hated the mess left on my shoulder from that accident, but I never once thought about seeking plastic surgery to get rid of it.

It might be fucked up. But that night, the injuries and the scars are all part of our story.

I hold his stare, fighting against my own body to stay strong, to keep my fight.

Sucking a deep breath, I drag something up from the depths to say what needs to be said.

"They will find you. And they will kill you."

"Baby, even if that were possible, they're currently chasing the wrong enemy."

I shriek when he lifts me off my feet as if I'm nothing more than a doll, placing me in the bath. The water is the perfect temperature. Damn him for getting that right.

"They're going to do us all a favour and get themselves killed by the Marianos long before I even have to consider doing it myself. See, that's why my plan is so brilliant.

"I hated having to wait. But as they say, patience is a virtue. And it paid off.

"Now, sit back. Relax. We've got all the time in the world."

I have never hated myself or my life more than in the minutes that followed as I had no choice but to let him wash me.

The way he looked at my injured shoulder with abject hatred ensured that my body continued to tremble, no matter how warm the water was surrounding me.

My only saving grace, I guess, was that whatever he'd given me didn't make me lose consciousness. Not this time, at least.

The thought of being this vulnerable and completely at this lunatic's mercy sent fear searing through me like I'd never known.

I'd take those old days of having awful, violent men in the house while Mum 'worked' over this any day. At least there, I could lock myself away and pretend it wasn't happening.

I know, without a doubt, this is happening right now.

Every single touch disgusts me.

My skin prickles with disgust as what feels like a million knives slices through it as he 'cares for me', as he put it.

"Everything is going to be okay, baby. I've got you now; you're safe."

I'm in such a daze that after a while, his words start to sound almost sincere.

Maybe to a point, he's even right. He's not hurting me.

He's gently washing me, although pointedly avoiding my shoulder as if it disgusts him.

Maybe it does.

Fuck it, I hope it does.

I hope it's a reminder to him every time he sees it that he's delusional.

He can lock me up like this for as much as he likes, but it won't last forever.

It can't.

By now, I should have some of the city's fiercest men and women hunting for me.

Or at least I hope I do.

Fear makes its way through me as I consider the possibility that Brad really has planned this. What if he really has made it look like I chose to leave? And worse, what if they believe it?

If they're not coming for me then—

No. I refuse to accept that as a possibility.

They are coming for me.

They have to be.

"Lie back," he coos, as if he's talking to a child, not a fully grown woman.

Unable to do anything but what he says due to the fact my body is like putty, I sink lower, allowing him to wash the shampoo out of my hair that he just massaged in like a pro.

"Conditioner. We don't want these curls drying out," he mutters.

If he's expecting some kind of response, then he's going to be disappointed. I can barely keep my eyes open right now, let alone find the strength to speak.

He wanted me under his control, and it seems he's got it. And there's nothing I can do about it.

He finishes up and then pulls the plug, allowing the water to drain away before he grabs a massive towel, scoops up my sopping-wet body and wraps me up.

"Now, let's go and get you dressed up pretty, ready for your gift."

I'm carried through to the bedroom where he pulls out a dress I don't recognise from the wardrobe along with a set of lingerie and a pair of heels.

He works diligently, dressing me and polishing me up as if he has plans to take me out and flaunt me around town like he's so keen to do.

"There," he says, putting the cap on my lipstick before taking in every inch of my face, assessing his handiwork.

"What do you think?" he asks, spinning me around on the stool and allowing me to study myself in the mirror.

I suck in a quick breath as my reflection is revealed to me.

I'm not sure what I was expecting really. But I'm pretty sure it isn't what I find.

My make-up is... perfect.

He's... really fucking creepy.

Has he been studying me so closely over the previous few months that he knows exactly how I do it? How I flick my eyeliner, just how I use my lipliner to make my lips look fuller?

My heart races and my hands tremble in my lap as I hold my own eyes in the mirror.

"Do you like it?" he asks, lowering down so he's hovering over my shoulder, seeking out my approval.

Unable to do anything else, I nod once.

There's a part of me that wants to make him angry, that wants to fight. But right now, with my energy in the pits, I know it's pointless.

From what he's said, he seems to think this is a done deal, that I'm here and it's where I'm going to be staying... alive. So I figure I've got some time.

That will either allow for my rescue party, or for me to regain some strength and figure a way out of this myself.

"You look beautiful, baby. Your gift is going to be so happy to see you."

I blink at him in the mirror, my head spinning with sluggish thoughts. But the mention of someone makes an image of Nico appear in my mind.

No.

Surely, he wouldn't have been able to overpower him like he did me and drag him here.

Or Jodie.

Vomit climbs up my throat, that little bit of soup I ate earlier—which I'm now assuming was laced with something—threatening to make a reappearance.

If he's got my girl, then I'll kill him even more painfully and slowly than I'm already planning.

Standing back to full height, he grabs my hand and pulls me to my feet.

My legs barely hold me up, and I hate that I'm grateful in any way when he pulls me into his side and allows me to use his strength to keep me up.

The second he walks toward the door, hope floods me.

The thought of getting out of this room after fuck knows how long is a relief in itself, but the possibility of finding an escape is even more exciting.

When he reaches for the handle and pulls, it does the opposite of what it has when I've tried it and the door swings open smoothly. It's almost as if my previous experience wasn't even real.

Was it?

I have no idea what he's drugging me with, so I could easily have been hallucinating.

He guides me out into a pristine hallway. The only thing out here is a small side table with a lamp and a weird looking elephant thing on it.

My eyes narrow as we pass. Questions whirl around my mind faster than I can compute.

We're right at the very end, and the number of doors that line the walls before me makes my head spin even more.

It would be impossible to count them even if I wanted to.

"Come on, baby. We're only going a few doors down."

My heart is pounding, blood racing past my ears in anticipation of what I'm about to discover when he stops in front of an identical door to mine.

He pushes his hand into his pocket and pulls out a key, sliding it into the lock.

The click of it releasing rocks through my entire body before he pushes it open.

The room is in darkness but Brad quickly corrects that when he presses his hand to the switch and floods it with light.

There's a mound in the huge bed that sits in the centre of the room, and after a beat it moves.

My breathing is erratic, but I have a little hope that this isn't going to be as bad as I first thought. He's clearly not torturing whoever this is if he's letting them sleep in a luxurious super king-sized bed.

"Sweetheart," Brad coos like a creep, "I've got a present for you. Wakey wakey."

He moves me closer to the bed as my confusion ramps up.

Time seems to slow down around me as the person turns over and flips the covers off.

A pair of tired blue eyes locks on mine the second her head is revealed, and despite the lines around them that never used to be there, recognition hits me like a fucking truck.

"No," I breathe, finding some strength from somewhere and ripping myself from Brad's hold.

I don't stop moving until I collide with the wall.

By this time, she's sitting up, pushing her wild curly hair from her face as she blinks at me, almost as confused and shocked as I am.

"B-Brianna?" she chokes out in complete disbelief.

"No," I repeat. "No."

She stares at me for a few more seconds before her shock morphs into something else entirely.

Anger.

It's so strong, so potent that I'm sure it sends a chill through the air.

"What the fuck are you doing with my daughter?" she sneers at Brad, pure hatred in her tone.

For a moment, I'm almost proud of how fierce she sounds. In the past, the only thing I've ever thought my mother as is weak. Weak, pathetic and easily led.

Maybe the wrinkles on her face aren't the only change since I last saw her.

"I brought her for you, sweetheart. I know how much you missed her."

All the air rushes out of my lungs as I watch Brad—the man I've been fucking for months—move toward my mother and take her hand in his.

Her anger doesn't faze him in the slightest.

Instead, he lifts his free hand to sweep a stray curl from

her cheek—just like he did to me back in the other room—before he cups her jaw.

"I just want to make you happy, *mi amor*."

6

———

NICO

"NICO," Toby bellows as he throws his weight against the bedroom door, trying to force his way inside. "Stop being such a fucking pussy," he grunts before trying again.

The door rattles, the dresser that I've pulled in front of it like the pussy he's accusing me of being shifting forward an inch.

I knew it wasn't going to be a foolproof plan when I locked myself in here. But I figured it might be a big enough challenge to make him give up on me. If I was lucky.

Clearly, I underestimated my best friend's tenacity, because he's been at this for a long fucking time this morning.

"I'm not letting you fuck everything up more than it already is. You've got a fucking exam."

He crashes against the door once more, roaring out with either pain or exertion, I'm not sure.

The dresser shifts farther from the door, allowing Toby to get his hand inside and somehow shove it even more until he's slipped into the room with me.

His chest heaves, his hair is a mess, his uniform dishevelled as he stands there breathlessly, glaring at me.

"You're a dick," I mutter from my position on the edge of Brianna's bed, wearing the same pair of boxers that I have been for days.

"And you fucking stink. She's gonna be pissed when she comes home and finds that your sweaty scent has permeated every inch of the place."

My lips press into a thin line at the thought of her never returning here.

It's been four days. Four fucking days and no one has found anything of any fucking use.

Toby and Theo have run her through whatever systems they've got, and they're confident that she's still in the country.

As reassuring as that is, each day that has passed, the pain, the desperation has only gotten worse, and I'm drowning in a whole new way.

I thought the grief in the days after losing Dad was bad. But at least I knew the outcome of that was final.

Right now, there are so many unknowns that I don't know whether I'm coming or going.

Is she alive? Is she suffering?

And if she is still breathing, does she hate me even more now than she ever has because I didn't protect her? Because I haven't come for her?

"Stop it. Just fucking stop it," Toby demands as he drags Brianna's dresser back into place before throwing the window open and stalking out of the room.

When he returns, it's with a pile of clean clothes in his hands, my wash bag sitting on the top.

"Go and sort your shit out, Nico. Don't let those motherfuckers think they're winning."

"They are," I hiss. "They've taken too much from me." I hate how vulnerable I sound, but I can't help it. I'm fucking broken.

"We don't know that. She could be waiting for you to find her right now."

"Then she needs to tell us where the fuck she is."

"It'll happen. We will get her back," he states confidently.

I sigh, hanging my head in defeat.

It's a mistake, because the stench he mentioned when he first walked in hits my nose and I groan in disgust.

The pile in his hands is thrust in front of me.

"And for fuck's sake, have a shave. That is not a good look on you."

I look up, glaring at him, wishing he'd just fucked off to school without me like he has every day this week.

So what if we've got an exam this morning?

What's the fucking point when everything is crumbling around me? What fucking good is an A Level or two going to do?

But despite those thoughts spinning around my head, my body defies my brain and I find myself on my feet and padding through Brianna's flat to her bathroom.

Swinging the door closed behind me, the bang of it echoes through the silent flat as I dump the clothes on the counter and turn to take a piss.

Reaching up, I rest my free hand against the wall before me and hang my head in defeat.

The vodka I've been drinking like water the past couple of days makes it pound like a motherfucker. I'm not in any kind of state to be heading to school to sit an exam. But I don't think I'm going to have much of a choice.

I guess I just need to pray for a miracle. Not that I've had much luck with them recently.

I thought Brianna agreeing to be mine last Friday night was the beginning of things turning around for me, not the start of everything getting even more fucked up.

Jade has been blowing up my phone ever since I didn't show up for our Monday night session. She wants to talk, wants to listen to me confess to fucking up again and losing the best thing in my life. But I can't do it.

Talking about it will make it even more real that it feels right now.

"Fuck," I bark, tucking myself away and pushing from the wall.

I step in front of the basin and stare down at the porcelain for a few seconds. I've been in here more than a few times in the last few days since I decided to move in, but I haven't once looked at myself.

I couldn't.

I knew that all I'd see staring back at me was a man who's lost everything, and I couldn't deal with seeing that as well as feeling it.

I suck in a breath and lift my head.

A bitter laugh spills from my lips as I take in the dark bruising around my eyes. Most of the evidence of last weekend has faded now, only leaving behind the exhaustion and devastation of the past few days.

With my pale complexion and the dodgy beginnings of a beard covering my chin, I look like I've aged about twenty years in four days. Toby is right. It's not a good look but—

"ARGH," I roar, before throwing my curled fist into the mirror before me, watching with sick fascination as it shatters. The glass immediately rips my knuckles apart and blood trickles down through the shards.

"Nico," a concerned female voice calls from the other side of the door.

For a second, the briefest fucking second, I think it's her. My siren.

But then the door flies open and instead of my hot-as-hell girl, my sister stands there, looking utterly wrecked.

Seeing her pain only makes mine worse.

She loves Brianna like the sister she never had. I knew that before this situation, but it's even more obvious now as she suffers right alongside me once more.

The only difference this time is I'm not shutting her out.

I learned from my mistakes, at least some of them, after Dad.

I've spoken to Calli every day this week despite locking myself inside this flat. Although looking at her now, I'm not sure it's really helped all that much.

Her eyes shift from mine to take in the destruction I've caused before they drop down my arm to my hand, which is undoubtedly dripping blood all over the floor.

"Sit down," she demands, pointing at the toilet.

I move on autopilot, lowering the lid and then my arse.

Without saying another word, she pulls the cupboard beneath the basin open and emerges two seconds later with a first aid kit.

"It's fine, Cal. I'll just—"

She fixes me with a look that cuts my words off immediately.

"You've been spending too much time with Daemon," I mutter as she opens the box and pulls out what she needs.

"This glare? That's not Daemon's influence. It's Stella and Emmie's. So's my right hook, if you want to test that out too."

She drops to her knees beside me, places my hand on my thigh and gently starts cleaning my knuckles up with a wipe.

I hiss in a sharp breath when it stings.

"Don't be a pussy, Bro," she teases, trying to lighten the mood.

"Why are you here?" I ask. I regret the words the second they roll off my tongue.

But when she glances up at me, her eyes show no hurt. Or at least, none that I caused. The fucking Italians, however...

"We thought Toby might need backup," she confesses.

I nod, unable to come up with a response to that.

"I'll bandage this up after you've showered. Seems pointless to do it now."

She sits back in her heels and just watches me as I sit there slumped on the toilet.

"I know it hurts, Nico. Trust me, I really do. But the world is still spinning outside this flat. And when we get her back, she isn't going to want to see this. She wants to see you strong, fighting for her. Not falling apart."

"I know," I confess quietly. "I... I just don't know how to."

"I don't have the magic answer to that. You just have to dig some of that inner strength you harbour inside and harness it. Stop focusing on the now and think about the future, when she's back in your arms."

"But what if—"

"Not an option, Nico. No matter where she is, she won't give up fighting. Not for you, not for Jodie. Not for any of us. Just look at last weekend. Those weren't the actions of a weak person. She's got this, Bro. And she's relying on you having it too."

She climbs to her feet as my mind spins with her advice. I don't even realise what she's doing until a soft buzzing fills the air around me.

I startle when my shaver is pressed against my neck.

"Cal—"

"There's not much I can do to help, Nico. But I need to do something. So we're gonna get you fixed up and get you to school. You're gonna smash that exam, because that's what Dad wanted, and then we'll spend the weekend doing whatever we can to find her. Plus, you've fucked the mirror, so you'll probably make yourself look even worse if you attempt this blind."

Unable to argue, I sit there and humour her as she works on the mess of my face.

Once she's done, she orders me to get in the shower before walking out and closing the door behind her.

Knowing that one of them will only bust back in and throw me in the shower themselves, I push to my feet and shove my boxers down my legs.

I groan in delight when the water first hits my shoulders. I don't even notice it's cold until it begins to warm up.

Without thinking about anything outside of this small, steamy space, I focus on what I need to do—washing until I no longer smell like a hobo. And when I walk out, admittedly, I do feel a little better.

It's by no means fixed anything, but I don't feel like I'm drowning quite as badly.

I drag my uniform on, hoping that it might act like some kind of armour, before pulling the door open and discovering who Calli was talking about when she mentioned backup earlier.

The strong scent of coffee is the first thing that hits me

before the conversation that was going on halts abruptly when I move closer.

"Holy shit, Nico was actually under that beard," Toby teases while Alex and Calli study me as if I'm about to explode or some shit.

"One of those for me?" I ask, gesturing to the mug in his hands.

"Yeah, here," Alex says, pushing a mug that's sitting on the counter they're standing around closer to me. "And these." He drops a couple of pills into my hand as Calli places a glass of water beside my coffee. "Figured all those empty vodka bottles in the bedroom had to hurt."

"Like you wouldn't believe," I mutter, instantly throwing the pills back. But instead of the water, I reach straight for the coffee.

"Shit, your hand," Calli says in a rush when she notices I'm bleeding through the tissue I wrapped around it when I got out of the shower.

"Get that sorted, then we need to leave," Toby says firmly.

Despite not having an exam this morning, Calli and Alex walk with us toward the exam hall.

Their support doesn't falter, and part of me wishes that they could come inside and sit beside me the whole time. An added benefit would be them whispering the answers to me, because fuck knows I'm totally unprepared for this.

I haven't studied since...

Figures standing beside the door catch my attention, and I immediately recognise them as Mr. Davenport, Mrs. Piper, AKA Emmie's step mum, and Mrs. Hendrix.

All of them have their gazes locked on me, concern pulling at their brows and darkening their eyes.

I hate it. My skin prickles with what feels like a million knives as their worried stares continue.

"You've got this, Bro. I believe in you. And I know they do too," Calli whispers, not making this fucking situation any better.

The only way I can do it is to compartmentalise. I need to put Dad and Brianna in a box and force myself to think about the task in hand instead.

Admittedly, it has been getting easier to do that with Dad. It could be time, or it could be Jade's influence. But Brianna? Yeah, good luck getting her out of my head anytime soon.

"Nico," Mrs. Hendrix breathes, stepping forward. "No news?"

It's a rhetorical question. If we'd have heard something, if we'd have found something, then I wouldn't be standing here right now.

"Okay well, I have every confidence that you'll smash this," she says softly as other students begin to arrive around us.

Not wanting to make a scene or give anyone a reason to talk about us more than they already do, I drop a kiss to my sister's cheek, give an appreciative nod to Alex, and then walk into the exam hall with my head held high and Toby right on my heels. It doesn't matter that my heart is in tatters; no one can see that. I hope.

I quickly find my desk, pull my pens from my pocket and lower my arse to the seat as more and more students spill into the room.

But I don't look at any of them. I can't.

So instead, I keep my eyes focused on the clock, counting more hours of my life that she isn't beside me.

Thankfully, the minutes tick by quickly and an exam paper lands on my desk, followed by an encouraging shoulder squeeze from Mrs. Hendrix. Any other time I'd think it's creepy as fuck. But not today. I'll take all the support anyone is offering.

I don't hear the words that Davenport says to start the exam, but the second everyone around me shuffles and opens their papers, I get the gist.

I've sat in here enough times now to know the drill.

Sitting forward, I grab my pen, scrawling my name and candidate number on the paper before opening the first page.

I scan the question, my heart rate picking up with each word. It's almost identical to one of the questions Brianna gave me that day in the library.

Closing my eyes, I take myself back there.

I picture her sitting across the table from me, her wide blue eyes studying me as she wondered what I was going to do next. The way she'd tucked her hair behind her ears, the way her lips were parted and her chest heaved.

Fuck, my cock swells just thinking about her.

It should do. What happened in that small room was pure fucking fire.

With my head full of memories of better times—okay, so she might not describe anything that happened in there as that—my pen begins to scratch over the paper, words pouring from my hand with little thought from my brain as I focus on her, the things we discussed, on the answers I gave. She told me they were almost perfect. And that's exactly what I need right now.

7

BRIANNA

I wake sobbing. My entire body trembles with the strength of them, and the pillow beneath me is soaked.

I have no idea why. I don't remember what I was dreaming about. My head is too fuzzy. It's like that motherfucker has ripped my brain out and replaced it with nothing but damp fucking cotton wool.

I shudder at the thought alone.

I have no idea what day it is, and without opening my eyes, it could be night or day. Not that it really matters. Nothing changes.

I'm still locked in a room by my... ex fuck buddy while he what? Rails my mother in another room?

My stomach turns and I suck in a deep, slow breath through my nose in the hope of settling it.

How did I get him so wrong?

I've always thought I had a pretty good sense of character. I knew Nico as a prick the first time I laid eyes on him. I knew he was good for a wild night. And man, did he fucking deliver.

I lose myself in memories for the briefest of seconds before a sound hits my ears.

It's... singing. But it's so soft, so quiet that I almost think I'm imagining it.

I listen harder, recognising the lyrics to the nursery rhyme before realisation hits.

I flip over, sitting up so fast that my head spins to find my fucking mother sitting in a chair in the corner of the room, singing to me as if I'm still a child.

"What are you doing?" I snap, that coldness in my tone shocking me as well as her.

"You were having a nightmare. I could hear you screaming from down the hall."

"So you thought you'd come and have another shot at parenting me. Newsflash, Jennifer, you fucked up the last time you tried it and lost your chance at ever doing it again."

She sucks in a sharp breath at my words, her eyes filling with tears.

"No," I bark, jumping onto unsteady legs. "You don't get to sit there pretending that just because we're stuck here, I'll forgive you and we can move on. That shit isn't happening. I would ask if you remember what it used to be like, but I very much doubt you have any memory of it."

When nothing but guilt flickers through her eyes, I know I've hit the nail on the head.

"Right, well. Think of your worst day. Now times that by about ten and make yourself a child in the memory. You might be somewhere about close."

"I know I screwed up, Brianna. I know, and I live with those mistakes and regrets every day but—"

"Good," I spit. "You should. And I hope it fucking hurts."

I surge past her, storming into my bathroom and swinging the door closed with a floor-tremoring crash.

I wince at the thought of that bang dragging Brad up here to see what's going on, but as my hands tremble with pent-up aggression toward the woman sitting out there, looking the picture of innocence, I soon discover that I don't care.

For the first time since I woke up here, I realise that my thoughts are pretty clear, my movements less sluggish.

Whatever he's been dosing me with is wearing off.

After I discovered he was lacing my food, I stopped eating. But when that achieved nothing aside from being hungry and him still finding a way to drug me, I started again. I was a mess. Starving right alongside that wasn't going to help me escape.

Because that is what I'm going to do. If the guys aren't coming, then I've only got myself to rely on. And I'm sure as shit not staying here any longer than I have to. The second I get an opportunity, I'm making a break for it.

I don't care where we are, I'll run for as long as my legs will carry me to get me away from this fucking psycho.

I pee and brush my teeth to freshen up before once again eyeing up the shower. My skin is itchy. I haven't washed properly since he bathed me. But I've refused to voluntarily strip down and shower.

What if he's watching? Waiting for an opportunity to get me vulnerable?

I have no clue what's going on in his head, what he's trying to achieve, but I refuse to give him any more of me than I already have.

A bang and then voices on the other side of the door prove that I was right to regret slamming it.

There's a part of me that wants to curl up in the bathtub

and try and hide. To be fair, yesterday, I might have done that. With that drug pumping through my veins, I wasn't good for much else. But I'm stronger today.

So with some renewed strength, I rip the door open and storm out.

"GET OUT," I bellow.

Both of them still, but Brad recovers first.

"Baby, you need to calm down. Your mother was only trying to—"

"Stop it," I spit. "Just stop it. I am not your baby. And she"—I point at the woman still sitting in the chair—"is not my mother. I do not have a mother. Now, unless you're going to do something useful like let me walk out that door" —I glance over at it, noticing it's closed and probably firmly locked—"do me a favour and fuck off."

It makes me wonder how she got in. Did he allow her entry, or does his *mi amor* have more freedom than I do?

She sure didn't give the impression in her room that she was happy about this whole setup. But was that just because I've crashed their little party, or because she's as stuck here as I am?

A shriek rips from my throat as Brad rushes me. His eyes are wild as his hand collars my throat. My back collides with the wall as he looms over me, giving me little choice but to appreciate just how much bigger, stronger than me he is.

But then, so was that arsehole I killed with a champagne bottle. All I need is the right moment. One slip of focus, one distraction, and I could turn the tables. And despite not seeing that opportunity yet, I have to keep believing it will happen.

"Bradley," Mum screams, finally leaving the safety of the chair to come to my rescue.

I guess there's a first time for everything.

As she claws at his shoulders, I go for the bare skin of his forearm that's holding me hostage.

I dig my nails in until there's no doubt that I've broken the skin. But I don't look down for confirmation; I keep my eyes firmly trained on his.

"I always knew you'd have this fire in you, Brianna Andrews." The way he sneers my name makes unease trickle through my veins.

Narrowing my eyes at him, I fight to keep the black spots from my vision and drag in as much air as I can through my nose.

"You have no idea, do you?" he taunts.

"Brad, no. Stop it. Please."

Mum is wild behind him, tugging at his shirt, shoving him in an attempt to get him off me.

"Shut the fuck up, *mi amor*," he spits before releasing me for a beat to backhand her across the face.

My chin drops in utter shock.

Before this, I had no idea that this man had a single violent bone in his body.

But as I stare down at the woman who birthed me, I watch a trickle of blood run from her bottom lip and notice that she doesn't look as shocked as I feel.

He's done this before.

"Motherfucker," I roar, curling my fist and throwing it at his face while he's distracted.

Pain explodes through my hand and down my arm as my knuckles collide with his cheek.

A grunt of shock, and I also hope a little pain, erupts from him a beat before I lift my foot from the floor, slamming my knee right into his balls.

This time, the cry that rips from his throat is definitely full of pain.

He stumbles back with his hands clutching his junk, and tears fill his eyes.

"Run," Mum screams, not that I fucking need it.

With my gaze locked on the door, I bolt for it.

I still have no idea if it's locked or not, but Mum's words make me think that maybe it's not.

Sadly, I never get to find out.

Just as my fingers brush the metal of the handle, fingers twist in my hair and I'm dragged back.

"No," I scream, thrashing my legs as I'm hauled backwards, desperately trying to find some traction.

"Brianna," Mum cries, but as she reaches for me, Brad stops and warns, "Don't."

I have no idea what he's got over her, what he knows, but the second he delivers that order, her arms fall to her sides and she freezes.

"Good girl, sweetheart. Good girl."

Bile rises, burning up my throat as I watch her fall under his command.

She always had a weakness for controlling, narcissistic men. I guess that's something that hasn't changed.

Brad, however, doesn't freeze. Instead, he continues dragging me across the room before I'm thrown like nothing more than a rag doll on the bed.

I fight. I fight harder than I ever fucking have before, but the second he jumps on top of me, straddling my waist, it's hopeless.

But still, I don't give in. Not like the fucking statue of a woman who's standing, watching and allowing her... 'boyfriend?' to assault me.

"Fuck, this fire gets me so hard," he groans as he finally

captures my flailing arms and pins my wrists to the bed above my head.

"You disgust me," I sneer before spitting in his face.

His top lip peels back in fury while I try to fight him.

"Should have fucking known you wouldn't give up easy like your bitch of a mother."

Gathering both of my wrists in one arm, he leans over me, allowing his hard cock to grind against my stomach. I swallow the vomit that rushes into my throat at the thought of him being turned on by this.

I knew he had a few kinks, but this? Kidnap? That's further than I ever thought he'd take things.

Something is bound around one of my wrists, securing me in place, and then he quickly does the other.

"ARGH," I scream when he sits back and studies his handiwork.

"Look at you, baby." A violent shudder rips through my body as he trails his fingertips down the length of my arms.

He stops when he hits my chest and glances over at my mother.

I do the same, shocked to find her eyes glazed over. It's as if she's not even here. If she weren't standing, I'd think that she was fucking dead.

"This is what you wanted, wasn't it, *mi amor*? Your baby back. She's all you've talked about, all you crave. Other than my cock, of course."

I heave, terrified that I'm going to throw up on myself and be stuck lying in it.

"That's right, baby. Mummy here is just as good of a whore as you are. Like mother, like daughter."

"You're sick," I spit.

"She's here, *mi amor*," he says softly, almost as if he's

talking to a child. His ability to switch his demeanour is a serious head fuck.

He is the purest form of a psychopath that exists.

I just can't get over how I didn't see it. Not even a hint of things being off in all those months we were fucking.

His fingers finally move again, brushing over my breast, lingering on my nipple, making it pucker for him.

I hate myself for reacting. But I can't help it.

It's a natural bodily reaction. It does not mean you want him.

"Get your fucking hands off me, you creep."

He chuckles menacingly. "It's cute you think anything you say will change my plans. I need you, Brianna. So does she. Although, not quite as much as I do. I have plans. So many plans that she couldn't help me with. So it's fallen to you. You hold the key."

My brow wrinkles.

The only key I care about right now is the one he holds to my door. Fuck anything else.

When he's happy with my reaction to his touch, he crawls lower down my bed, ensuring he has my legs pinned at all times.

In only a few minutes, he has each of my ankles bound with rope on each corner of the bed.

He stands back, assessing his handiwork.

"Beautiful," he murmurs, his eyes running up my bare legs, over my sleep shorts and my breasts covered by my tank. "You did good, sweetheart." The second he lifts his arm, Mum rushes to his side and curls into him.

"What the fuck have you to done to her?" I ask, staring at the zombie of a woman.

She was so quick to fight for me earlier. Then one look

into his eyes and she turned into this... this shell of a person.

"Power, Brianna. More power than those stupid pricks you've been running around town with will ever experience.

"Together, the three of us can have more of it than you ever dreamed of.

"One day, you'll understand. And you'll crave it just like you were born to do."

I shake my head.

"No, I don't want this. I don't want what they have, I don't want what you want. Just... just let me go. I won't even tell them it was you. They can go after the Italians for it. Hell knows they deserve it."

He shakes his head, a devilish smile playing on his lips.

He looks like a totally different person from the one I thought I knew. Every single thing about him is unrecognisable. I want to think that maybe I stumbled upon his evil twin, but I know it's not. This is Brad. The real Brad. The one I thought I knew was just playing a game. A very, very convincing game. And it seems that I fell hook, line and sinker for it.

"Nice try, baby. You're mine now, so I'd get any thoughts of Cirillo scum out of your head."

"Fuck you," I spit.

"Yeah, baby. All in good time." All the air rushes out of my lungs as he confirms what I already knew. He might be openly fucking my mother, but he's not done with me. All he's doing is biding his time. But why? "Come on, sweetheart. Brianna needs to rest. I'll pop back and check up on her later."

Without another word, he leads her from the room, proving that I was wrong about the door being unlocked.

The cunt didn't need to try and rip half my hair out dragging me away from it; I was never going to get through it.

The second silence falls around me, I begin pulling at my restraints, praying to anyone who will listen that he hasn't done them tight enough, that somehow, I'll be able to slip free of them.

But it's pointless. And if anything, the knots only get tighter as I try to wriggle free.

Only a few minutes after I give up, my hands and feet begin going numb.

"MOTHERFUCKER," I bellow, my chest heaving with anger and frustration. "I'm here, Nico. I'm fucking here. Please, come and get me."

Tears streak down my face, soaking into my hair as my body trembles with fear and exhaustion.

Maybe that drug wasn't so bad. It numbed me to a point. And right now, I'd take that over this terror.

8

____

BRIANNA

I lie there for hours. If it weren't for watching both the sunrise and the sunset, then I might start to think it was days.

I'm not sure if I should be grateful or not that it isn't actually that long.

The more days that pass, the more chance Nico and the guys have of finding me. But also, while I'm stuck here, starving and more desperate for the bathroom than I've ever been in my life, I'm achieving very little of my mission to free myself. If anything, I'm going backwards. Now there isn't only a locked door or window in my way, but unforgiving rope bindings.

The pain from my overfull bladder is making me want to curl up, but I can't. And I refuse to lower myself to that. He wants me weak, humiliated, and I won't allow him to see that.

I haven't been able to feel my hands or feet for hours. Thankfully, with how I'm lying and how he's tied me, I can't really see them, so I have no idea if they've turned blue yet. The only thing I know is that they're still attached.

Quiet, uncontrollable sobs fall from my lips as I try to relieve the pain that's spreading through my body.

If this goes on any longer, I'm just going to have to pee. There is no other option, unless he returns and helps me out. Doubtful.

This is probably what he had in mind. Leave me here so that I'm a weak and dirty mess when he returns.

He's turning out to be quite the sick fuck.

I'm starting to understand why I could never get rid of him. He didn't fall for me, and he was willing to share me with others just so he could keep a part of me. He was grooming me, or attempting to. Something tells me that I wasn't as easy a target as my mother.

I might have dropped to my knees for him a few times, but that is very different from what he has going on here.

The sound of a door closing somewhere outside my room hits my ears, and I have to slam my lips shut to stop from crying out for help. I will not ask that twisted fuck for anything. Even if that results in me peeing myself.

But as it turns out, I don't need to call for him. I quickly discover that he had every intention of stopping when the lock clicks open and he slips inside the room.

"Ah, just where I left you. That's what I like to see," he murmurs.

Closing the door behind him, he makes a show of locking it so I know I don't have an easy escape before pocketing the key.

"How are you feeling, baby?" he asks as he moves closer. "Comfortable?

Refusing to give him any of my attention or energy, I look to the opposite side of the room.

"I thought you might be a little hot, so I took the liberty

of lowering the temperature. Hopefully, you'll feel the effects soon."

A whimper rumbles in my throat, but I keep my lips smashed shut in the hope he can't hear it.

I'm already cold; I don't need him turning the damn air con up.

It took me a while to realise what the constant low hum was, but with all the time I've had here to think, I figured it out.

I still don't acknowledge him, but I don't need to be looking at him to know my defiance is pressing his last nerve. I feel the electricity in the air. It's crackling, warning me that I'll be the one who comes out worse by defying him. But I refuse to cower or do as I'm told.

Not to a crazy dick like him.

A loud, frustrated huff comes from him a second before the side of the bed dips. I just get a chance to suck in a deep breath before his fingers wrap around my throat.

The second my air is stolen, my body takes over, and the relief I've been desperate for floods my body as I soak the bed.

His eyes hold mine before narrowing in suspicion. He's probably wondering why mine rolled back in pleasure as he robs my air.

Yeah, I've been known to dabble with a little breath play, but I'm going to need different foreplay than this twisted bullshit.

The moment the scent hits his nose, his entire expression morphs into one of pure disgust.

"Dirty bitch," he roars before backhanding me across the face.

Lights flash behind my eyes as the pain from his hit

explodes across my face and down my neck before the taste of copper fills my mouth.

"Fuck you," I hiss, still refusing to look into his eyes when he grasps my chin and forces my face toward him.

"Not yet," he grits out.

"What are you waiting for, Brad? Aren't you man enough to take me while I'm here at your mercy?" I taunt, finally finding his dead eyes.

He laughs.

"So what is it? I thought my fire turned you on. Or have you changed your mind? Do you want me as weak and pathetic as my mother?"

My need to ask exactly what he's done to her sits on the tip of my tongue. But I don't want him to think I care. I don't. He can do whatever the hell he wants with her. It's what she did with me as she dragged me from one hellhole to another. Exposed me to drink, drugs, and violent and abusive men long before I ever should have known they existed.

His face shows nothing. Gives me no clues as to what he's thinking. Although, something tells me that I don't really want to know.

He's cooked up some twisted plan, and I think the element of surprise might be better than learning my fate beforehand.

"You've always been so inquisitive. It makes me wonder why you never found out."

"What? That you're a fucking psychopath? Can't say I was suspicious, no. So well done." If I were able to, I'd clap. "You had me totally fooled. Is that what you want to hear?"

A small smile twitches at his lips, telling me that stroking his ego is a way to get through to him.

Typical fucking man.

"I already knew that. I don't need to hear it from your pouty lips."

I breathe a sigh of relief when he releases me, but it's short lived as he shoves his hand into his pocket and reveals a flip knife.

I swallow nervously as he exposes the blade and looms over me.

"Filthy whores deserve to be treated as such, don't you think?"

I cry out as he pulls the fabric of my sleep shorts from my thigh and shreds them, but not before nicking my skin with the sharp tip.

Pain burns down my leg as the wet fabric covering me is ripped away. The cool air that rushes between my spread thighs is the evidence I really don't need that he sliced through my knickers too.

With his lip curling, he balls up my underwear before grasping my face again, forcing my jaw to open.

My scream is cut off when he stuffs my urine-soaked knickers into my mouth.

I heave as the taste hits me and tears spill down my temples as I desperately try to push them out. But the motherfucker clamps his hand over my mouth, ensuring I fail and forcing me to suck in greedy lungfuls of air through my nose.

My body convulses with my need to vomit. It burns up my throat, but I fight it. I have to.

His previously unhinged laugh turns manic once more as he stares down at me, thrashing about as much as I can with my bindings pulling tight.

"Filthy whores should be used and not heard. Didn't your momma teach you that, baby?"

I scream, but it has very little impact.

"She's always been such a good little slut for me. Always doing exactly as she's told, spreading her thighs whenever I want. There's just one thing she can't give me. Because I need it from you."

Fear turns my blood to ice. The violent tremors wracking my body only get worse as his gaze drops to my bare pussy.

My muscles clench with my need to close my thighs, but nothing happens. He has my ankles bound too tightly.

"Now it's your turn to be a good little slut and give me what I need, baby."

Without releasing my mouth, he leans over and lifts a bag I didn't see him carry into the room to the side of the bed.

The sound of him unzipping it fills the air before he pulls out a roll of tape.

I try to shake my head in the hope of convincing him that I don't need it, that I'll be good. But it's not enough.

He rips off a length and pulls his hand free.

"No, please. I—" I scream against the tape, the tears that were already soaking into my hair coming faster.

I don't want to be the weak woman he's trying to turn me into, but I can't help it.

Why won't he just medicate me again? This would be so much easier if I were seeing this through a drugged-up haze. Why does he want me fully alert for his torture?

"Better. It should help muffle your screams. Not that anyone would hear you anyway."

Picking up the knife again, he makes quick work of slicing through my vest, exposing the rest of my body to him.

"I always loved these tits," he says absently, almost as if he's talking to himself, as he grabs a handful, making me cry out when he squeezes too hard. "Fuck you. You always did like it rough. I bet a whore like you is already wet and desperate for my cock."

I shake my head, refusing his comment but also trying to stop myself from hearing any more.

He could have done me a solid and wrapped that fucking tape around my ears to cut off his vile bullshit.

The bed dips as he climbs beside me before throwing his leg over my waist. Apparently, his disgust is long gone. With me naked and the promise of taking whatever he wants from me, he's willing to forget that I'm lying in my own piss.

I stare at him with wide eyes as he holds his knife in front of him, letting the light glint off the razor-sharp blade.

"It's a good job you like a little pain, baby. I think this is going to hurt."

I can't move an inch. With his entire weight sitting on my body, there is literally nothing I can do to stop whatever he's going to do.

"At least the scar will blend in with these other ugly ones. Such as shame to fuck up such a pretty thing. He deserved to die that night for damaging what belongs to me."

Reaching into the bag once more, he pulls out an antibacterial wipe, which shocks me.

But the second he pulls it from the packet and presses it to my skin, I know exactly his intentions.

"No. No. NOOOOO," I scream behind the tape, trying as hard as I can to buck him off, but it's pointless. Totally fucking pointless.

"You might want to lie still," he informs me after he's finished wiping the skin on my inner arm.

Tears and snot cover my face as he holds my arm down

with one hand, adjusting his position so he's sitting over my ribs to get a better view.

"I've waited so long for this."

The second the tip of his knife slices into my skin, this weird sense of calm settles over me. I don't know if it's the pain or the trickle of blood as it runs over my pale skin, or just the fact that there is nothing I can do about this right now.

He wants that implant in my arm gone, and there can be only one reason for it.

"I need you, Brianna. I have plans. You hold the key."

His words from earlier come back to me. This is what he needs me for. What he planned.

But why me? What do I have that is any more special than any other woman?

My mother is a waste-of-space junkie who, as far as I ever saw, didn't have any redeeming qualities.

It can't have anything to do with her. He has her; he could do whatever he wants to her. He does, by the sounds of it.

Which means it must be...

I suck in a deep breath as realisation hits at the same time he hooks his blade under the small device planted in my arm, sending pain like I've never felt before shooting through my entire body. I swear I even feel it in my toes.

"Bingo, baby."

He grins like the psychopath he is, holding it between us like it's some kind of prize.

My head gets heavy, my sight blurry as I stare at the blood-covered device and the room starts to spin around me.

"Oh, we're going to have so much fun."

The last thing I remember is him groping my breasts once more while he laughs like a deranged lunatic.

9
———

NICO

I'm feeling all kinds of nostalgic as I descend the stairs that lead to The Spot, the dive bar across town that Toby dragged me to all those months ago where I first laid eyes on Brianna Andrews.

It's Sunday night, and while it's not the busiest night of their week, the place is still pretty packed as I emerge into the bar.

There's a band playing that seems to have drawn quite a crowd; almost everyone is watching the show.

After ordering myself a drink—okay, five—I take the tray over to a free table in the back. It's perfect. It's hidden from everything and everyone.

I bet all kinds of things have gone on back here. I know they would be if my siren was here with me.

Thoughts of sliding my hand up her thigh and getting her off while everyone partied around us, blissfully unaware that she was coming all over my fingers, makes my cock swell.

It's been a week.

A whole fucking week without her.

The worst week of my life. Hands down. By a mile.

Reaching for my first drink, I lift it to my lips and throw it back. The whisky burns down my throat. But it's nothing I'm not used to at this point.

The second it hits the table, I reach for the next one.

We spent this afternoon at the hotel with the boss. He's done everything he can to get some intel on where Brianna is, but there's nothing. No breadcrumbs.

Enzo has been just as useless.

Ricardo is keeping his cards very close to his chest.

I mean, I don't exactly blame him. We've tried to keep Ant and Daemon's presence locked down. But fuck, this is my girl we're talking about. Not just a soldier.

The third drink goes down even easier than the first two, giving me a nice buzz.

Uncle Damien tasked the others with jobs tonight. He failed to give me anything to do. He didn't even allow me to hang around long enough to hear what my boys are doing.

I hope they're out searching. But honestly, it could be anything.

My phone is on loud just in case they find anything and I'm needed to go rescue my girl. That's why I'm not going to drink myself into a coma here either.

I've done that plenty this week. Each time I've woken up with a hangover, I've regretted it. If she needed me and I wasn't able to get to her, I'd never forgive myself.

I've already let her down in so many ways. I can't do it again.

If I'm lucky to get the chance, that is. It might already be too late.

I slump back in my booth seat and rest my head against the old, battered leather.

The bass from the band up on stage thrums through me.

It's easier to focus on the beat of that than my shattered heart.

Pulling my phone from my pocket, I open my photos and scroll through the ones I have of her from the past few months.

It's pathetic, but it's the level I've been reduced to.

Sitting that exam on Friday was weird. Reading questions that were so similar to the ones we worked on together... It felt like she was there with me. Helping me.

It's fucked up, but it gave me some kind of comfort as I answered them, just like I did when she was watching me. I just have to hope the examiner thinks my responses are as good as she did.

Passing any of these exams seems like a possibility that is out of my reach right now. The chance was already pretty slim after all the time I lost after Dad's death, but add this on top, and I'm not sure why Toby, Calli and Alex bothered. They should have just left me to fester in Brianna's bed.

The fourth and fifth drinks vanish over the next hour. The band finishes its set and the Sunday evening crowd returns to the bar and its tables, everyone, apart from me, enjoying themselves.

My eyes are locked on the battered, old table before me, so I don't notice someone join me until they're sliding across the seat to get closer.

Glancing up, I find a man I've never seen before staring back at me.

His dark hair is cropped close to his head. His eyes are dark, deadly. His nose—well, that's even more bashed up than mine. That motherfucker has been broken more times than I can count, I'm sure. He's got a vicious-looking scar that runs diagonally across his cheek and cuts through his bottom lip. But that's nothing compared to his knuckles when he rests them on the table, showing me he's no threat.

"Nico Cirillo," he states. It's not a question.

I might not have a fucking clue who he is, but he sure knows me.

"I need you to come with me." This time when he speaks, I register his American accent and it makes my brows pinch.

"You?" I ask, crossing my arms over my chest, giving him a blank stare.

"I know someone who might be able to help you with a little issue you have."

My heart jumps into my throat long before he's finished talking.

"Let's go," I state, sliding from the booth, more than ready to follow this dangerous man anywhere if it'll lead me to Brianna.

No one pays either of us any mind as we cut through the people loitering in the bar, and the man quickly overtakes me as we climb the stairs. And with little other choice, I trail him around the corner of the bar where I find a blacked-out SUV hiding at the curb.

It's dark out, but the heat of the day has barely burned off, the stars shining bright above us as he pulls the back door open and gestures for me to get in.

I expect him to close it behind me, so I startle when his hand collides with my shoulder, shoving me to the other side so he can get in as well.

"No offence or anything, but I'm going to need you to put this on."

I rear back when he hands me a black blindfold.

"Anyone would think you don't trust me," I mutter.

"I don't. I'm going to need your cell phone and any weapons you're concealing."

I stare at him, waiting for him to tell me that he's joking. Not that I think he's capable of a joke. Honestly, I'm not sure he's capable of smiling.

If I were anyone else, I'd be fucking terrified sitting in the back of a car with him right now.

"Okay," I agree, passing over my phone and flip knife from my pocket, and then my gun from my waistband.

His brow lifts as I place them in his palm.

"What? You're not packing?" I ask.

He doesn't respond, just pockets my shit and then demands the driver to go the second I place the damn blindfold over my eyes.

"This seems a little over the top, don't you think?" I mutter as we speed through the city.

"You can never be too careful. Who knows who I just picked up in a bar."

"I think you're fully aware, seeing as you know my name," I sneer, much to the driver's amusement. "Where are we going?"

"Asking too many questions will get you killed."

"Great," I mutter, crossing my arms over my chest and waiting patiently.

Really, I have a real good clue who these motherfuckers are. I did the second he spoke; the over-the-top security only confirmed it.

I'm hardly surprised they're in town after the hit they took at The Manor last weekend. I just would have thought they'd go to Damien first. Maybe they have. Maybe they've got that cunt Ricardo, too, and we're going to be able to get all this cleared up once and for all. And by the end of this meeting, Ricardo will be dead, and I'll have my girl back in my arms. Maybe.

The journey to wherever we're going feels like the longest of my life. Seeing as they could be sitting on the intel I need to get my girl back, you'd think they could fucking hurry up a bit.

The car is brought to a stop, and the engine is cut.

"Thank fuck," I mutter, reaching for my blindfold before the seat belt.

"I don't think so, Cirillo," the yank grunts. "We don't want any more locations compromised by your little London organisations."

"Little?" I bark.

"Yes, well, this mess is due to the two of you not handling business. We were happy to leave it that way until you decided to bring it to our doorstep."

"We didn't hurt anyone at your establishment. We merely asked for some protection for our girls. Which you failed to deliver, I might add."

All I get is a grunt in return as his hand presses between my shoulder blades and shoves me forward.

"No one likes a smartass, Nico."

I roll my eyes at his sulking. Not my fault that some people can't handle the truth.

The constant hum of traffic and the scent of the city are both cut off as we enter a building. The air is instantly different. Fresher, clean smelling.

He certainly hasn't brought me to some dump on the wrong side of town, that's for sure.

If I didn't know what had happened at The Manor, I'd think maybe we were there. But something tells me that we didn't actually travel that far; more that they wanted to throw my senses off.

Dickheads.

I refrain from commenting though, aware that the motherfucker less-than-gently shoving me from behind could pull his—or my—gun at any moment and stop me from hearing whatever it is they have to say.

The floor moves beneath me a little, and I can only assume he's walked me into a lift.

That's confirmed a beat later when his hand wraps around my shoulder, bringing me to a stop, and the whoosh of doors closing sounds out behind me.

We begin a long-arse climb through the building, making me more than curious.

It goes on for so long that I'm convinced he must be taking me right to the top of the Shard.

Fucking fine by me.

I'll play their games. Do whatever it is they want if they're going to help me locate my girl.

My fists curl with my need to do something to drag it out of them faster, but I continue to keep my mouth shut.

His attention makes my skin prickle, but I refuse to acknowledge it, keeping my chin raised as I stare forward. Okay, granted, I'm staring at absolutely fucking nothing. But I've got a good imagination.

My body jolts the second the ding for our arrival fills the small space. Something erupts within me. It's akin to excitement, but it's not that. It's more... desperation.

They could hold the key to getting everything I need, and I'm fucking done with their theatrics already.

"Go," the guy grunts, giving me a sharp shove toward the doors.

We walk, and walk, and keep fucking walking until I'm pulled to a stop by a hand on my shoulder again a second before a door opens before me.

The guy greets someone. Someone who grunts in exactly the same way he does.

Eloquent lot. I thought they had more brain cells than your average organisation. Unless that's just the top tier. The minions are nothing if not just well-trained mutts from the street.

"Sit," the guy barks, dragging me, none too gently, into a chair before finally ripping my blindfold off.

I blink a couple of times as the harsh lights burn my eyes before the surroundings clear.

We're in a hotel room. A really nice fucking hotel room with a view of the entire city spilling out before us from the floor-to-ceiling windows.

On the other side of the massive, empty desk is a huge leather chair. A backward leather chair with a high winged back, giving me no chance of seeing who's sitting in it.

The rustle of fabric beside me forces my eyes away from the mystery person I'm here to see.

A small gasp passes my lips when I find out who is sitting next to me.

"Evening, son," Uncle Damien says, a small smirk playing on his lips.

"B-Boss?"

My lips part to ask any one of the million questions that are dancing on the tip of my tongue, but the second Damien nods, indicating that my attention should be elsewhere right now, I look forward once more, just in time to see the chair spin.

I'm not going to lie, I was expecting a man.

Chauvinistic of me? Yes, probably. But it's what I know. Our world... it's run by men. It's all I've ever known.

But the person staring back at me... most certainly is not a man.

Bright red—not the dyed kind, the natural ginger type—waves hang sleekly around her angular face, making it appear softer. She has high cheekbones, a perfect nose, full crimson lips, and the biggest, all-seeing eyes I think I've ever seen.

She's hot, no doubt about that.

She's also... fucking terrifying.

I've learned a lot since Emmie and Stella crashed into our lives, and the most chilling realisation is that they don't need us. Not really.

Women have the power to take on the world and bring any man, no matter how strong, to their knees.

And something tells me that this woman... she's done just that.

"Luciana," Damien says, his voice commanding and firm, not that she's going to let him command anything.

She has control of this entire room. And she hasn't even said a fucking word.

She rests back in her chair, looking casual as fuck as she studies him.

Glancing to my right, I find Damien frozen under her stare. It takes a lot to shake his foundations, but it seems that this woman might just have the power.

I understand it when she turns those dangerous green eyes on me.

Holy shit.

I'm pretty sure I'm staring into the eyes of the Grim Reaper. Who knew there was a woman hiding under that cape?

Finally, when I'm almost convinced she can't talk, she leans forward, rests her elbows on the desk, and levels Damien with another, almost bored, stare.

"It seems we have an issue," she states.

"You can say that again," Damien adds, much to the woman's irritation if her raised brows say anything.

"When I want your feedback, I'll ask for it."

I can't help but snort in amusement, but I quickly cover it with a cough, not wanting her stare to turn my way.

"The problem is, I have better things to be doing than running around, getting my hands dirty in your little war." She pauses, allowing the tension in the room to get heavier.

"So," she says. "I have an offer for you. Something I really don't think you're going to want to turn down."

My heart pounds so hard in my chest that it makes my head spin. My need to demand answers dances on my tongue, but I know that demanding anything of this woman isn't going to get me anywhere. Honestly, I'll probably leave this hotel in pieces if I were to even speak right now.

"I'll give you the intel you need, in return for you wiping out our little rodent issue."

"What intel?" I bark before I manage to swallow the words. "Do you know where she is?"

Luciana turns those wicked eyes on me, and a shiver runs down my spine.

"I didn't bring you here to question me, Mr. Cirillo." My fingers curl around the arms of the chair I was dumped into.

I swallow thickly, desperate for her to get to the fucking point.

"You're missing your girl, am I correct?" Her words are slow, measured, and irritating as fuck.

Why is she wasting time if she knows where she is?

"And you idiots are running around town, going after the wrong enemy."

"The Italians have her," I state confidently.

"Do they?" she asks, something akin to amusement glittering in her previously dead eyes.

She's mocking us. Usually, I wouldn't stand for it. Damien wouldn't either, but Brianna's life could be on the fucking line here.

"So who does?" I bark, my patience more than runs out.

"You seem to be forgetting that there is someone else out there who is as obsessed with your girl as you are."

My chin drops as one man's face fills my mind.

"No," I breathe. "No, he wouldn't. He—"

"Who?" Damien barks.

"Fuck," I bark before dropping my head into my hands and screaming, "FUCK."

Why didn't I think of him before?

All week, I've been so fixated on Ricardo having her. Terrified of all the things he could do to her.

"Bradley Whitlock," I spit. His name tastes like poison on my tongue.

I knew that fuck was too boring for his own good.

It was a cover. Of course it was a fucking cover.

Pushing to my feet, I send the chair I was sitting in toppling to the floor with a loud crash.

Footsteps close in on me. And when I look over, the man who found me in the bar reaching for his gun.

"Angel," Luciana snaps, forcing him to stand down.

"Bradley is an... associate of ours."

My fists curl, my short nails digging into my palms. But the pain isn't enough.

Why didn't I fucking think of him? All this time, she's been stuck fuck knows where with that fuck, and it didn't even fucking occur to me.

"Where is he?" Damien asks, speaking for me.

Luciana pauses, tapping one perfectly manicured nail against the glass desk she's leaning on.

"Why is Ricardo still breathing?" she asks, flatly.

Damien sucks in a frustrated breath.

"I will lead you to Bradley. But—" She pauses, holding his stare, allowing her unspoken threats to fill the silence for a few seconds. "You will take out Ricardo and his inner circle. He's causing me issues. And trust me when I tell you that you do not want me sending my men onto your streets to sort this out."

"Just tell us where she is, and we'll get it done," I assure her. Fuck knows how when we've failed this far, but I'll figure out a way to do just about anything if it means getting my girl back.

Luciana looks at Damien, and I see him nod out of the corner of my eyes.

"I don't know where your girl is. But I can tell you where to find him, and from there, I'd like to think you're smart enough to figure it out."

10

NICO

For the first time since I found that note, discovered that my girl had gone, I forced myself to return to my own flat and sleep in my bed.

Sleep.

Chance would have been a fine thing.

The reality of the situation is that I've laid here staring up at my stark white ceiling since the moment I was dropped back at my flat by Luciana Rivera's henchmen.

Just like on the way in, both Damien and I were blindfolded.

Totally fucking bullshit show of power, if you ask me.

Neither of us is stupid enough to spill the Rivera Cartel's location, or worse, send our men after them.

We're in charge of this corner of the city. We hold the purse strings, and therefore control the gangs and organisations around us because they need us to clean their dirty money. It works perfectly for us, it gives us final say in everything.

But we're never likely to forget that the entire city. Hell, almost all of the south-east of England is ruled by the Riveras.

Our paths hardly ever cross.

We usually run a tight ship and have no reason to bother them. But the Italians fucked up last week when they hit The Manor.

One of the Rivera's properties on our land.

It should be a safe haven, because no one should be stupid enough to put out a hit on anyone on their property. Only they have the power to do that.

But Ricardo...

He made himself an even bigger, scarier, and deadlier enemy than us last Friday night.

He pissed off Luciana Rivera, one of the organisation's most notorious lieutenants.

She might be female, and she might not have ruled over this territory for all that long, but make no mistake: she is five times more lethal than her late husband who held her job until his untimely death a few years ago.

I don't want to gossip or spread rumours about the Riveras. Just letting their name roll off the tongue is risky enough to keep schtum. But I'm pretty sure his death wasn't some freak accident.

She wanted power that her blood alone couldn't provide.

But marriage into the Rivera family? Well, that would do it.

Blinking, I drag my eyes from the ceiling to the window. I didn't bother closing the curtains when I got in last night. I just stripped down to my boxers and crawled into bed.

Damien said he was going to feedback to Theo and come up with a plan for this morning, and all I could do was nod and lock myself in here.

I craved the comfort of Brianna's place, her scent, her belongings. But I didn't feel like I deserved any of those things.

All I've done since I've met her is let her down.

And not only did I immediately assume she'd left me when I first saw that note, but I was then so convinced that it had to be Ricardo who'd taken her that I didn't even consider another option.

But... it was Brad the bellend.

Of fucking course it was.

The red flags have been there all along.

His bullshit, obviously fabricated persona. His reluctance to leave Brianna despite her telling him time and time again that they were done.

I called her a whore for allowing him to buy her designer clothes and parade her around like a toy, but she was right—obviously, she's always right—she didn't want any of it.

Brianna is strong. Stronger than almost everyone I know. If she wanted rid of someone, then she would get rid of them. It just shows his determination if he was able to break her down.

What the hell has he been filling her head with?

And what does he want from her?

Does he just want her? Or is there something bigger at play here?

Does he know something that we don't? That she doesn't?

I let out a sigh as the very beginning of the sunrise begins to illuminate the sky.

Lifting my arms, I curl my fists, cracking my knuckles as hope fills my veins.

By the time that sun sets again, I'm going to have my girl

in my arms once more. And fuck if I'm not going to hold her tighter than I ever have before. And if she thinks she's going anywhere again, then she's going to seriously need to reconsider. The temptation to tie her to my bed and never let her leave the room is fucking strong right now.

I won't, of course. I like my wild, free-spirited woman. But fuck, if it kept her safe, then it would be a serious consideration.

I don't allow any doubts to enter my head.

If Luciana Rivera said she knows where he'll be this morning, then that's where he'll be.

All we've got to worry about is what we do once we've found him.

An unusual bolt of nerves rushes through me, knotting up my stomach.

I'm never apprehensive before a job. Ever. But then, I've never had one that was so personal before.

I'm still lying there a few minutes later when the sound of my front door opening and closing again fills my flat.

Heavy footsteps thump my way before my bedroom door is thrown open and six guys march inside.

Each one is suited and ready to go to war for my girl.

I'm not going to lie; the sight has a messy ball of emotion crawling its way up my throat.

My eyes scan each of them.

My cousin, looking as cold and determined as ever. My best friend, his eyes soft with compassion but his jaw locked with a fierce need to spill some blood for the pain that motherfucker has caused both me and his girl. Alex, well... he's Alex and looks as carefree and easy-going as usual. Seb has a dark need for violence filling his eyes. Daemon is as focused as ever, but since learning the truth about his feelings for my sister, I'm able to see a softer side to him.

And then there's the addition to the group.

Ant stands there dressed in his own black suit, ready to stand right beside us and fight.

I want to ask him why. But I know why.

He might be Italian, and when all this is over, I have no doubt he's going to return to where he really belongs, but the blood that runs through our veins doesn't matter in the face of anyone who wants to cause us harm.

And, of course, we saved him. We've kept him safe. He must feel like he owes us something.

"Emmie and Stella will be here in a few minutes. Get your arse up and get ready, soldier," Theo demands.

I push up until I'm sitting, desperately trying to suck in the air I need as the weight of what we're possibly going to walk in on today presses down on my shoulders.

"The girls are coming?" I ask, my voice raspy.

"It's just us, Nico. No one outside of our circle is going to know anything about this. We don't trust anyone with it."

As much as I appreciate us locking it down, the fact that Uncle Damien has decided our leak could even be as close as the guys' fathers is unnerving as fuck.

Stefanos has been monitoring the situation with the Italians for months. If he—

The thought sends a violent shudder ripping down my spine.

No. There is no way that Alex and Daemon's father is behind this.

Galen either, for that matter.

He didn't fight as hard as he did to return to the fold to fuck it up so soon.

But as confident as I want to be in that, I'm not risking Brianna's safety for anything.

"We don't need anyone else," I state confidently, pushing to my feet. I feel entirely underdressed, standing in just my black boxer briefs with all of them suited and ready to go.

"Get dressed, cuz, then I'll run through the plan."

With a nod of agreement, they all file out of my room. Well, everyone aside from Toby, whose concerns get the better of him.

"Have you slept at all?" he asks when the sound of footsteps fades out.

"I'll sleep when I've got her back in my arms," I tell him, stalking into my bathroom to take a piss.

"She needs you on top form," he says, not put off in the slightest by what I'm doing.

"Do I need to remind you how you dealt with the whole situation with Jodie and—"

"Don't. Don't even think about saying his name," he spits venomously.

"Fine by me," I mutter, reaching for my toothbrush. As far as I care, that motherfucker can rot in hell right alongside the one we're about to send there with him.

I freshen up, throwing myself through a quick shower before pulling on my armour.

Toby watches my every move. If I weren't one hundred percent sure he was straight, I might start getting worried as his eyes remain locked on me. But it's concern. And honestly, I love it. I love that all my boys are here—Ant included—because getting Brianna back is just as important to them as it is me. Okay, so maybe not quite as important. But they're here, and they're ready to fight right beside me. I couldn't ask for better fucking friends.

The scent of coffee fills the air as we emerge from my bedroom at exactly the same moment that Stella and

Emmie come strolling into my flat, looking like the bad-arse motherfuckers that they really are.

"Holy shit," I breathe, unable to keep quiet. "Are you sure this is a good idea?" I ask, ripping my eyes away from them in favour of Theo and Seb. Who, incidentally, are drooling all over my fucking floor.

"Couldn't you have worn those stupid onesies you've all got?" Alex asks.

"Because you all don't look hot as shit?" Stella sasses. "We're only trying to keep up with our men."

"Keep up?" Theo asks. "You far surpass us." He practically devours Emmie with his eyes. And if I were to look down—I'm fucking not—I know both him and Seb are hard as fuck and about five seconds from forgetting it all in favour of fucking their women.

I get it. I do. But also, no.

"Right, what's the plan?" I bark before any public fucking commences.

"Come here, Hellion," Seb growls, holding his hand out for Stella, pulling her onto his lap the second she's in touching distance.

Emmie slides into Theo's side.

"Okay so we've confirmed what Luciana said. Brad's father is in a home about ninety minutes away. And after hacking the security, we can see that he religiously visits every Monday morning at eleven AM."

My eyes lift to the clock hanging on my wall.

Five AM.

I knew it was early, but fuck.

"The second we're done here, we're heading out and getting into position. We're going to drop a GPS tracker on his car while he's inside, then follow the best we can."

"Fuck that, let's just jump him in the car park," I grunt,

my need to get my hands on this motherfucker almost too much to bear.

"No," Theo barks. "If he's an associate of the Riveras, then there is every chance he's had full training. We're not risking him taking Brianna's location to the grave because he's not into Daemon's fucked-up brand of torture."

Daemon scoffs. "You questioning my skills, Cirillo?" he teases.

Theo ignores him.

"Once we've found the location, he's all yours. But can I suggest we keep him alive, at least for a little while?"

My brows lift.

"He clearly knows things. Things that could well be useful to us. To Brianna. He's smart. Smart enough to hoodwink her all this time, not to mention completely cover up his identity. We need to know what he's hiding."

"Fine, as long as I can be in on it. I want to watch that cunt bleed."

"Sure."

Reaching forward, I grab the mug that I assume is sitting here for me and swallow a mouthful down. I barely taste it, but I know I need the caffeine in my veins.

"What are we waiting for? Let's go."

Theo nods before turning to Emmie and planting a kiss on her temple.

"You look hot as fuck, Hellcat," he growls quietly, much to her delight.

"Jesus. Keep them four separate at all times. We're not fucking this up because they can't wait to get their dicks wet."

"Dude, we got this," Seb says confidently. "Stella can just blow me on the way to this place and all will be good.

Ow," he complains when she smacks him upside the head, although I can't help but notice that she doesn't refuse.

"We're getting food on the way," Alex announces, jumping to his feet and clapping me on the shoulder. "And I'm not going in a car with them."

Rolling my eyes at him, I down the rest of my coffee and head toward the door, more than ready to get this show on the road and get back here with my girl in my arms.

"I thought you said the weather was going to be good," Alex grumbles through the—thankfully functioning—comms in my ear.

"Stop being a pussy, Bro. A bit of rain won't hurt," Daemon mocks. "And we don't care if it flattens your hair. It's not like you have any chance of getting laid, anyway."

A series of chuckles follow. But I don't join in. I'm too amped up waiting for this prick to show his face to think about laughing.

"Aw, A. Come see me later, I'll sort you out when Seb is sleeping," Stella offers, making both the men in question splutter in surprise down the line.

"Like fuck you will, Hellion," Seb growls while Alex happily sings, "Hell, yeah, Princess. I've heard all about your skills."

"Go anywhere fucking near her, Deimos, and I'll cut your little dick off while you're sleeping."

"Fuck you, it's not—"

A car indicating to turn in catches my eye, and I shut everyone up with two single words. "He's here."

I have no idea how I know. The black Ford Focus he's driving is nondescript as fuck, but I know.

I lower down in the undergrowth, lifting a pair of binoculars to my eyes as he pulls closer.

The second I catch sight of the side of his face, all kinds of red-hot fury explode within me.

"Got you, you fucking arsehole," I grunt.

"Positive ID?" Theo asks, all business.

"What in that statement made you think otherwise?" I scoff.

"Fuck you, just checking. He sure is a fan of routine; he's pulling into the exact same space he's parked on every security feed I pulled."

"For a smart man, he's pretty fucking dumb," Emmie mutters, saying the exact words we're all thinking.

My eyes are laser-focused on him as he climbs from his car and walks toward the building.

It's too easy.

Is this a set-up? A weekly visit he knows we'll get a sniff of? Or is he just so arrogant that he thinks he'll get away with it?

I really fucking hope it's the latter.

"He's gone. Do you have eyes?" I ask, fear of fucking this up making my blood run cold.

"I got him," Toby says. "He's signing in."

As he moves through the building, one of us always has eyes on him. And for the longest hour of my fucking life, Theo and Emmie watch him in some summer room with his father.

I have no idea what is wrong with the old guy, and honestly, I don't really care. But I hope he's an arse to his son. Brad's religious weekly visits would suggest otherwise, but I like the idea that he's in there getting all kinds of abuse for being nothing but a disappointment, and that it's nothing more than guilt that keeps bringing him back.

By the time Theo confirms that he's on the move after his dedicated sixty minutes with his father, my entire body is aching.

But the second I watch him walk through the electric doors and dip his head, attempting to hide from the drizzle that's still soaking us to the bone, a fire erupts in my belly, filling my veins with everything I need to see this through.

"Toby, is the tracker live?" I ask, watching his lights illuminate as he starts the engine.

"Yep. We're good to go. You ready to get your girl?"

"So fucking ready."

The second we're all confident the prick is far enough away that he can't see us emerge from the trees and hedgerow surrounding the expensive home he's put his father in, we move.

Theo and Emmie make a bolt for Theo's bike, and the second he's seated, she throws herself on behind him—something I'm not sure he's entirely happy with—and the two of them take off in chase.

He figured that they were less likely to look suspicious if they tailed the bellend at a distance than us in the recognisable cars that we'd hidden out of view.

Seb, Stella and Daemon climb into Stella's car, and she takes off like the little pocket rocket that she is while I drop into my own driver's seat, Toby climbing in beside me, Alex and Ant behind.

"Let's fucking go, bitches. We've got a cunt to catch," Alex sings in delight, rubbing his hands together.

"Hell yes," Emmie squeals in my ear from somewhere up ahead.

"Careful, you picked up some of your brother's crazy for a moment there," Ant deadpans as I wheelspin toward the main road.

Alex chuckles. "Nah, you're all usually just distracted by my pretty face and humour. Deep down, I'm just as fucked up."

My eyes catch his in the mirror as something dark passes through them.

Unable to focus on anything but the task at hand, I push those thoughts aside and join the traffic.

"Are you going to tell me where the fuck I'm going?" I bark at Toby as I quickly overtake Stella, much to my amusement when she flips me off.

"Fuck you, Cirillo," she snarls in my ear.

"Get a more useful passenger and you can take the lead next time, Princess," I taunt.

"Just keep going. I'll tell you when he turns off."

The tension in the silent car is unbearable. And as the time on the display before me continues to tick by, the more agitated I get.

"He's shifting into the left lane," Theo informs us.

Toby nods and both Stella and I shift over.

"Left at the roundabout," Theo confirms.

"Looks like we were right," Toby mutters, his eyes locked on the tablet before him.

As the guys chatted around me this morning, they all agreed that he'd have taken her out of the city. We have too many eyes looking for my girl for him to risk keeping her too close. The location of this care home helped to confirm that too.

Theo continues giving us directions as we trail at a safe distance.

My eyes are fully focused, my knuckles white with my grip on the wheel. But the sight of a car darting out of a side road a little ahead makes my heart jump into my throat a beat. We're blinded by brake lights as the lorry he pulled in front of fails to stop, and from the chilling crunch of metal that sounds out around, I assume ploughs right into it.

"Stella, look out," I bark, slamming my own brakes on before I rear-end the car in front.

"Got it," she confirms.

"Theo, you still on that cunt?"

"Yeah. What's going on?"

"Accident," I snarl, slamming my palm against the wheel in frustration.

"Can we get around?" Stella asks hopefully, but everything has stopped.

"Doesn't look that way," Alex says over my shoulder.

"Shit," she hisses.

Glancing to my right, I stare at the central reservation barrier, and then the rows of houses to our left.

We're fucking stuck.

My heart pounds and my hands tremble as any hope I was feeling for getting my girl back today slips through my fingers.

"We'll get her," Alex says, reaching over and squeezing my shoulder.

"Theo, don't you dare fucking lose him," I warn darkly.

"Have some faith, man."

"ARGH," I bellow, throwing myself back in my seat as more flashing lights descend around us.

11

____

BRIANNA

The first thing I feel when I wake is pain, and I have to fight not to sob as memories from before I passed out come back to me.

I don't move for the longest time as I lie there, just focusing on my breathing and the fact I'm alive.

If I'm still alive, then there is a chance I can find a way out of this hell.

Hopefully, before he...

I heave as his intentions come back to me.

But why?

I need to know why he's so set on getting me pregnant. If I do nothing else before I find a way to either escape or kill him, then I need the answer to that question.

Why me?

Forcing my eyes open, the skin around them stinging from the tears I've shed, I'm surprised to see the sun streaming in through the window. But not as shocked as when I move both my arms and legs and discover they're free.

He released me.

Lifting my hands in front of my face, I rub at the angry welts from the rope he used to restrain me that mar my wrists.

But the sight of them is nothing compared to the huge bandage that's wrapped around my upper arm.

Am I meant to feel grateful that he made the effort to clean me up after cutting my implant out like a fucking psychopath?

I really fucking hope not, because I don't feel anything but pure hatred for the monster who's doing this to me.

Pushing myself so I'm sitting, I blink back the tears that still want to fall over this entire clusterfuck of a situation.

I don't know for sure how long I've been here. But it has been more than long enough for Nico to find me.

I'd hate to have to give Brad the credit for outsmarting the fucking mafia. But then, I still don't actually know who he is.

An idea hits me upside the head.

Is he their leak?

No. That wouldn't work.

As far as I'm aware, neither Nico nor any other knows who he is.

He could be connected, though.

He's not Italian, I already know that. But...

I drop my head into my hands as my thoughts spin at a million miles an hour.

I guess I should be grateful. At least I'm not drugged up and don't know my arse from my elbow.

I guess that would be bad for the bab—

I'm off the bed and running to the bathroom before that thought grows roots in my head.

If I wasn't aware of him untying me and patching me up, then he could have...

I retch until my stomach screams in pain, but I can't stop.

Tears race down my face, dripping onto the toilet seat as I hug the bowl, my body trembling with my need to get out of here, away from him before he does something I have no control over.

Standing on weak legs, I stumble toward the shower, and for the first time since I found myself locked in this room, I actually turn it on.

I put the temperature as high as it goes before stepping under the torrent of water.

It burns immediately. But as much as it hurts, I don't move away or try and turn it down.

I need it. I need to hope that it has the ability to burn that cunt's touch from my skin.

My stomach revolts again as I think about having his hands on my body, the things he might have done to me while I was unconscious last night.

Reaching for the shower gel, I squeeze a huge blob onto my palm and I scrub at myself. I need him off me. I need the memory of his filthy hands on my body gone.

I don't stop scrubbing between my legs until it starts to hurt; then, I start on the rest of my body.

When I finally step out, my skin is bright red and raw, but I can't find it in myself to care.

Wrapping a towel around my body and then another around my sopping hair, I pad through to the wardrobe to find something to wear.

But when I pull the door open, I don't find all my clothes like I have previously; instead, all that hangs before me is Brad's shirts.

I take a step back, clutching the towel tighter around me. I'd rather stay damp than dress in his clothes.

It's a show of ownership that he's desperate for for some fucked-up reason, but one to which I refuse to lower myself.

Unsurprisingly, my underwear drawer is empty, and when I turn to the dressing table, I find that he's even stolen my make-up.

I stand there in the middle of the room with nothing but defeat racing through my veins.

Nico isn't coming, and I have no freaking idea how I'm meant to get out of this.

There's an old glass of water sitting on my bedside table, along with some fruit and granola that he must have delivered at some point while I was sleeping.

It's nowhere near appealing, but as my stomach growls angrily, I know I have to eat it.

Starving to death because of my stubbornness isn't all that high up on my to-do list right now.

I sit in the middle of the bed, still wrapped in my wet towel, and munch down as much granola as I can manage, all the while praying that today will be the day I find a way out.

The crash of a door slamming somewhere in the house sends a bolt of fear racing through me.

Despite being determined to hold my head high and refuse to wear his clothes, the room around me seemed to get colder and colder, and I had little choice but to shed my damp towel and reluctantly pull on one of his long-sleeved shirts.

I hate it. The lingering scent of his cologne turned my stomach, but my teeth were chattering even under the covers, thanks to him deciding to force another form of torture on me.

There are voices, but I recognise the rumble of both of them.

Brad and my mother.

I shake my head, wishing I knew what the hell he was playing at.

How long has he been playing her? And did he really believe that he was going to reunite us after all these years?

I scramble so I'm sitting when the lock clicks and my door is thrown open.

He walks in with a manic grin on his face and a tray of food in his hands.

"I've been out and bought your favourites, baby," he coos as if he's talking to an actual baby.

It immediately makes me suspicious.

Kicking the door closed, he prowls closer, making my skin prickle.

Lowering the tray, I find he's right. But even the scent of the freshly cooked steak and chips does little to stir any excitement in my stomach.

"It's a good source of iron," he explains, cutting a piece off and offering it up to my lips.

He pokes hard when I refuse to open my mouth and allow him to feed me.

"I cooked this especially for you," he growls, a red haze of anger beginning to descend around him.

But I can't focus on the food; the only thing I can think about is that he didn't turn around and lock the door.

He didn't lock the fucking door.

"Brianna," he growls, and finally, my lips pop open, giving him the distraction I need to think.

Come on, Brianna. You need to get through that door.

"Good girl," he praises, making the piece of meat I'm chewing on taste like nothing but rubber.

"We need you nice and strong. You've got a very important job to do."

"Why?" I manage to force out through my mouthful.

"Why?" he asks, looking almost confused. "Because I love you, baby."

What I really want to do is throw my head back and laugh.

Love?

Is he for fucking real?

"And together... together we're so fucking strong, baby."

"I'm nothing. A girl with a junkie for a mum and no prospects other than what I make for myself. I have nothing to offer you."

He reaches out and cups my cheek, staring right into my eyes.

I have to fight my reaction to jerk away from him, and instead, I lean into his touch, hoping like hell that he's falling for it.

"Oh, baby, you're so far from being nothing. You have no idea."

I shake my head, reaching my hand out and running it up his thigh.

My teeth sink into my tongue so hard, I'm surprised I don't bite a chunk off as I try to play him just like he has me.

"So tell me," I beg. "Make me understand how we're going to rule together."

The words are like acid on my tongue and dripping down my throat, but I can't come up with any other way to find out the information I need and make the most of the chance of freedom he's provided me with.

I've been called a whore and a slut more times in my life than I care to remember. Now seems like a good time to make use of all those skills I've learned and try to put them to use.

"No one takes me seriously," he confesses. "My heritage is too weak in my blood. I've tried. I've proved myself over and over again, but they all cast me aside as if I'm nothing.

"I am not nothing," he roars as if saying it louder will suddenly make it true.

"Of course you're not," I whisper, trying to stroke that ego.

"I've been working the streets for years," he confesses, making my brows pinch in confusion, "but I'm always kept on the outskirts. They use me for my skills and then cast me aside.

"But someone fucked up when they gave me this job. That stupid fucking Luciana didn't know what she was opening up when she decided to trust me in helping her bring down the ring those who went before her had built."

"What information?" I ask, getting more sucked into this story than I was intending.

He shakes his head. "Dangerous information that has the power to destroy lives."

I consider those words as he pushes another piece of steak past my lips.

"Lists and lists of names. Names of those who have provided stock over the years. It was exactly what I'd been asked to dig up."

Drugs. He's talking about drugs, but where do I fit into that?

"Of course, most are dead now. Some by their own choice, others... not so much. Shame really. Such a waste of good life. But that's how it goes, I guess," he mutters absently as he spears a chip and holds it out for me.

I'm desperate to push him, to demand more information, but I'm terrified one wrong question will force him to lock it all down once more.

This is the closest I've seen him to the man I came to know before all of this. It makes me wonder if it was all an act, or if he really is in there somewhere.

"I saw my father this morning. I see him every single Monday without fail."

"Lucky you," I mutter under my breath.

"He's the reason I took on this job. The thought of reconnecting families... I guess it spoke to the small parts of my soul that haven't been tarnished over the years."

My heart begins to pound even harder as the words he isn't saying ring loud in my ears.

I was right yesterday.

This has nothing to do with my mother. She's just been really un-fucking-lucky in all this.

Or is she? Is it fate kicking her arse for being such a shitty mother?

"You know who my father is," I breathe. It's not a question, it's a statement. As the seconds tick on, it's the only explanation for all of this. "Who is he?"

Brad's lips curl up in an evil smile that shreds all my hope for answers.

"A man who makes me look like a pussy cat," he confesses. "He groomed your mother. Poor young, innocent little girl she was. He groomed her. And do you know why?" he taunts.

I shake my head, too terrified to speak. I'm desperate to hear the answer to that question but equally as petrified to know the truth.

Brad leans in, his eyes holding mine as his hot breath washes over my face.

"Because he was going to sell you, Brianna. You were destined to be nothing but a filthy whore from the day you were conceived, baby."

Before I realise I've moved, the glass of water that was sitting on the tray between us shatters against the side of his head.

His eyes widen a beat before they darken and his expression turns feral.

A shriek rips from my lips as his hand wraps around my throat and he slams me back on the bed.

Any sign of the vulnerable, not-quite-good-enough man who was confessing his secrets moments ago is gone, and I only have myself to blame.

If I could have just kept my cool, then I might have got the rest of my answers.

His breath comes out in rough pants as he glares down at me. Spittle and blood from the cuts down the side of his face cover mine, making me want to vomit again.

"I should be thanking your mother," he sneers. "If she didn't run, if she didn't have someone helping her, coming up with ways to cover for you, I may never have got this chance."

His fingers dig into the sides of my throat, cutting off my air and making lights flash behind my eyes.

I desperately want to ask more, but I'm unable to get the air I need, let alone manage words.

Thankfully, he must read them in my eyes.

"What? You didn't think Andrews was your father's name, did you? You're not stupid enough to believe your mother would name you after a man who fucked her as a child and abandoned you. Oh no, your whole identity is fake," he spits. "You are fake."

My head spins as black spots begin to dance in my eyes.

If he doesn't loosen his grip, he isn't going to be able to make use of me for anything.

"Your mother was too scared to give you a name that would allow anyone to find you. But she never banked on me being given the job to find any of those little whores who were bred for the marketplace."

His words make me sick and have bile burning up my throat.

"You couldn't be Brianna Walker, and you certainly couldn't be Brianna Harris."

A bone-chilling scream pierces through the air as he lands that bombshell, not that it means much to me, before something catches my eye as it collides with Brad's head.

His grip immediately loosens on my throat, and I'm able to suck in a hungry breath before the entire weight of his body lands on me.

I stare at my manic mother who's standing behind him with her chest heaving and an... an elephant in her hand.

Something warm trickles over my neck, and I quickly realise it's blood.

"Get the fuck out of here," Mum screams. "Run, please."

I hesitate just long enough for the prick to come to, but he's still dazed from the elephant to the head and I manage to slip out from beneath him—although not before he reaches for me.

His fingers twist in his shirt and he pulls, ripping it straight up the centre, sending buttons pinging off in all directions.

I scream as I claw at his hand to make him release me,

but he's recovered faster than I was hoping for, and when he does, it's in favour of throwing me against the wall.

My head smacks back against it, sending pain shooting down my neck and making my eyes water.

"Sit the fuck down, Jennifer," he snarls, holding her eyes and waiting for her to submit.

And to my absolute horror, she does.

"NO," I cry as he prowls toward me, ripping his belt open as he eyes my naked body beneath his shirt.

"We can do this the easy way, or the hard way, baby. You get to choose."

The moment he's close enough, I swing my leg up, aiming for his balls, but he sees it coming a mile off and he drops his weight onto me, flipping me over and shoving my face into the carpet.

"I'm more than happy with the hard way. I've always liked a challenge."

With his hand on the back of my neck, he drags my hips up with his free arm, pinning my legs down with his.

"No, please. No," I scream as I try and fight him.

His responding chuckle is enough to tell me that my begging is having the opposite reaction to what I was hoping for.

"Been waiting a long time for this."

The blunt head of his cock brushes against my entrance and I put even more effort into fighting, but it's pointless. His hold on me is too tight, too secure.

"You're going to give me the most fearless heirs, ba—" The final word turns into what I can only describe as a gargle before his grip loosens once more.

The second I can lift my weight from the floor, I find him with blood soaking his white shirt from... it doesn't fucking matter where from.

"Go, please, Brianna. Run. And never look back."

He drops to his knees, his weight knocking her with him.

There's a weird, twisted part of me that wants to grab her and take her with me.

But then she looks up at me with those cold eyes, and I remember that while she might have just saved me, she's still almost as bad as him.

Turning my back on them both, I run from the room, and I don't look fucking back.

The hallway seems endless as I wrap the ripped shirt around my bare body and run toward the end, praying I'll find a set of stairs.

My heart pounds so hard I can feel it in my ears.

Fear like I've never experienced before licks down my spine.

And it's only made worse when shouting erupts from the direction I'm running from.

I swallow down the vomit that rushes up my throat at the thought of him hurting her before coming after me.

The hallway turns at the end, and I breathe a sigh of relief as stairs emerge.

I fly down them. Literally. I don't register my feet hitting the steps, and before I know it, I'm racing across the wooden floor of another hallway. Doors line the walls on each side as footsteps pound above me.

"Please, please," I beg no one as I keep going looking for a sign of a door to the outside world.

I don't care where we are; surely there's going to be somewhere to hide.

There has to be. I refuse to let this sick fuck take whatever he wants from me.

I don't give a fuck who my father is or the reason I was born.

I am a fighter, and I will not bow down to a psycho like him.

Footsteps race down the stairs behind me just as I find a door that will give me freedom.

Please, please, please, I silently beg as I fly toward it. *Be open. Please be fucking open.*

I crash into the wooden door, cursing myself out for giving my location away.

"Brianna," Brad calls. "You can't run from me."

"Fucking watch me," I mutter as the handle turns in my grip, allowing me to pull it open and slip outside.

Fresh summer air fills my lungs as I take off running once more.

The small stones surrounding the building cut into my feet, but I ignore them. What's a little pain compared to saving your own life?

The afternoon sun is blinding as I run aimlessly.

I hit the grass and relief floods me when the pain ceases, but that doesn't mean I stop.

Blood is whooshing past my ears, cutting off anything that might be happening around me.

For all I know, he's right behind me, about to grab me, but I daren't turn and look.

I just need to keep going.

My muscles scream in pain. The wound in my arm burns as I pump my limbs harder than I think I have in my entire life.

My vision clears enough for me to see the tree line in the distance and I run harder, faster, or at least I try to.

Everything is a blur, reality slipping away as I focus on moving.

The softness under my feet vanishes the second I slip into the shadows beneath the trees.

Sticks, stones, and chunky roots make my progress slow as I continue forward.

Branches and thorns snag on the fabric of his shirt that I'm still wearing, tearing at my skin beneath, but it's not enough to stop me.

Nothing is.

Well, not until a pair of arms wrap around me from behind and everything comes crashing down.

12

———

NICO

er blood-curdling scream rips through the air, making my heart race dangerously fast.

"Brianna, Siren. It's me," I say as calmly as I can manage in her ear.

But it doesn't cut through her panic and need to fight.

Her arms flail and her legs kick out as she tries to slip from my hold.

She thinks he's caught her. She thinks I'm him.

It fucking wrecks me.

"Brianna," I say more firmly as I finally manage to pin her arms against her sides. "It's me, babe. It's Nico. I've got you. Okay? I've got you, you're safe. Please, babe," I beg, hating that I can't get through to her. "It's over. We've got you."

I know the moment she hears my voice because her entire body freezes. For the briefest moment, she relaxes back against me. But then it all changes again when she begins trembling violently and her screams and cries fill the silence around us.

I swear my fucking heart rips clean down the centre at the pain in those cries.

Spinning her around, I drag her against my chest and hold her as tight as I possibly can, allowing her the time she needs to work through whatever it is she's been through.

The whole time, I don't stop talking.

It's utter nonsense, but it's all I can think to do that might help.

"I'm so sorry, babe. I'm sorry it's taken us so long. We've had men in every inch of the city looking for you. Fuck, babe. It's okay. You're okay. I've got you and I'm never letting you go ever again. You're mine, Brianna. Mine. Have you got that?"

I ramble on and on until her body begins to still and her screams get quieter.

"I'm going to lift you, okay?" I ask when silence falls around us.

She nods softly, and the second I sweep her feet from the ground, she tucks her face into the crook of my neck and continues to sob silently. Her tears soak through both my jacket and my shirt. I wish I could take them away, both those and her pain. But I can do fuck all but carry her to safety and take her home. I just have to hope it's enough.

With her safely in my arms, I spin around and begin the walk out of the trees.

She ran a long fucking way, and fast. If I weren't so terrified when I saw her burst from the house like the hounds of hell were on her heels, then I might have been impressed. But one look at her and my only thought was getting to her.

Theo and Emmie had been here a while, but we'd arrived only a few minutes earlier after finally getting free from that fucking traffic. Theo began barking orders the second we arrived, sending us to different spots around the perimeter of the house we'd tracked him to.

She was inside, I knew that from the moment we got close to the building. I felt her presence. It was fucking weird. But I was so fucking relieved.

Even more so when she made our jobs easy for us by bursting out of the house, ready to be rescued.

"I've got her," I screamed, taking off after her as the others descended on the house, going after the prick who's been keeping her here.

"Here," Toby says, shrugging off his jacket as I get closer to where he's standing in the middle of the garden, watching us with concern filling his blue eyes.

"Thanks, man. I've got this. Go and make sure the others don't need you."

"Okay. I'll meet you at your car in a few and take you both home."

He takes off running toward the house where I assume everyone else is.

I'm halfway down the driveway, heading toward where I hid my car on the track that led us to this place, when a blacked-out SUV comes to an abrupt stop in front of me.

The sun gleams off the windscreen, hiding the driver from view. My heart jumps into my throat, knowing my gun is tucked into the back of my trousers. But the second the door opens and someone jumps out, I discover it's not necessary.

"Is she okay?" Uncle Damien asks in a rush, his eyes scanning the little bits of Brianna he can see.

"She will be. The others are all inside," I tell him, taking off again.

"I've got the basement ready for a new guest," he says with excitement in his tone.

Bradley fucking Whitlock doesn't know what's about to hit him.

Without another word, we take off in different directions.

I'm almost at my car when footsteps race up behind me.

"It's all under control. Get in. I'll take you both home."

I nod, ducking into the car with my girl still clutched to my chest.

In only minutes, Toby is in the driver's seat and he's got the pedal to the metal as we fly down the track to head back to the city.

"How's she doing?" he asks after long minutes of silence. His eyes meet mine in the mirror and he reads my answer loud and clear.

I have no idea.

He nods and pushes the car a little harder, trying to get us both home faster.

I swear I don't suck in my first proper breath since seeing her burst from that house until Toby drives into our underground garage.

The only two of us left behind come running the second they see us.

Both Jodie and Calli reach for the door when we pull to a stop, but to my surprise, neither of them fire a million questions at us. They're just... there. Silently supporting both of us.

"We're home, babe," I whisper, dropping a kiss to the top of Brianna's head before I gently slide out of the car.

I have no idea if she's awake, asleep, or unconscious. Every time I've spoken to her or tried to get a good look at her, she hasn't reacted to me. But that could just as easily be because she's shut down as it could be that she's totally exhausted.

"I'll call Dr. Rosi and wait down here to let him in," Toby tells me as he pulls Jodie into his arms and kisses her brow. "She's okay, Demon. Everything is going to be okay."

She nods and trails behind us as I walk Brianna toward the lift.

"I'll wait with Toby, give you both some space," she explains when the doors open and I step inside.

Calli, though, is unable to stay behind, and she apologetically slips into the lift with me.

After pressing the button for me, she steps up to my right, where Brianna's legs dangle over my arm, and snuggles into my side, wrapping her arm supportively around my waist.

She doesn't say anything. She doesn't need to. I feel her love and support all the way down to my toes.

She leads the way as we hit the top floor, presses her hand to the panel beside my door to unlock it, and holds it open for us.

"I won't interrupt, but if either of you need anything, I'll be right out here, okay?" she says softly.

"Could you get us some drinks?"

"Of course."

She disappears toward my kitchen as I head toward the bedroom, quietly closing the door behind us before walking toward my bed and sitting down.

"Hey, Siren," I whisper in case she's asleep and I startle her. "We're home, babe. It's just you and me now."

I rub my hand up and down her back, holding her against me, hoping that my warmth and support is helping in some way.

"Are you going to show me those hypnotising eyes of yours, beautiful?" I ask softly.

She remains still for a few seconds before she breaks her silence with a quiet, "I can't."

"There she is," I say softly. "My girl's there."

Shifting her position a little, I twist her so I'm able to cup her cheek.

"I've got you, babe. We're in my bedroom. Just you and me. There's nothing to be scared of now."

Brushing my thumb under her eye, I collect up the tears that continue to fall.

Her eyelashes flutter as she licks her dry lips.

"I didn't think you were coming," she confesses.

"Fuck, babe. I'm so fucking sorry it took us so long. I've been a fucking mess without you. I missed you so fucking much."

"Really?" she asks hesitantly.

"Babe," I sigh, unable to believe she could think anything else.

What the fuck did that motherfucker put her through for her to think I wouldn't come for her?

"I promise you. I will always come for you. I will always rescue you. I will always catch you."

A sob rips from her throat and I shift us again so I'm able to rest my brow against hers.

"Brianna, I love you. Nothing could stop me from ever getting to you. I need you to believe that."

It takes a moment, but those words finally seem to settle in her head, and her lids don't just flicker, they actually open.

The stunning blue of her irises stares up at me. They're darker, a little sadder, and a lot more exhausted than I'm used to, but they're hers, and the exact reminder I needed that she's right here in my arms.

"Fuck, Siren. Fuck, I missed you so fucking much."

Without thinking, I lean forward and press my lips to hers.

I need this connection more than I can compute. Unfortunately, she doesn't feel the same, and no sooner have our lips brushed than she pulls away from me.

My heart shatters, but I know it's not me, or us.

It's him.

He's up in her head.

"I'm going to clean you up. Bath or shower?"

"N-Nico, you don't have—"

"I do, Brianna. I need to give you everything and more right now. And there is nothing you can do that will talk me out of it."

"Bath," she whispers, tucking her face against my chest, hiding.

It breaks my heart that my strong little fighter is cowering from the world.

It won't last, though. Somehow, I'll figure out a way to put her back together again.

Just like she did to me.

We all break sometimes. I've learned that that's okay. What's important is the people around us who help put us back together.

"Hold on then, babe. It's bath time."

I lift her once more, somehow managing to shift her weight to allow me to open the door and slip down the hall into the master bathroom.

"You okay?" I ask after sitting her on the counter next to the basins. It reminds me of another time recently when I did the same thing. And I can only hope this night ends as happily. It might be wishful thinking, but I need something right now. It's that or let the crazy thoughts about what he might have done to her over the past week take over, and I refuse to do that. I will not jump to conclusions and rip myself apart wondering what-if.

"Yeah," she whispers, wrapping her arms protectively around herself. Making sure she's still covered in Toby's jacket to keep her warm, I reluctantly turn away from her and begin running the bath.

"I've even got fancy bubbles," I say with a laugh, holding the expensive bottle that somehow ended up in here. I certainly didn't fucking buy it.

The slightest of smiles kicks up at the corner of her lips, and I breathe a sigh of relief. It might be small, but it's everything.

Checking the temperature as the bubbles erupt before me, I turn back around and step in front of her, then peel Toby's jacket away.

She doesn't say a word, but she drops her head in shame as I take in the ruined shirt she's wearing beneath.

My teeth grind and my fists curl, but I refuse to let her see how her state affects me.

Her hair is wild, her face red and patchy from her tears, but it's the scratches, scrapes and bruises that hurt me the most.

Tucking my fingers under the fabric, I begin to push the shirt from her shoulders.

She visibly trembles before me and I pause.

"This okay?" I ask gently.

The second she nods in agreement, I quickly pull the ruined shirt away from her, needing it out of her sight.

But while that might help her, the sight of her body wrecks me.

She's covered in blood, bruises, cuts, and there's a big, blood-soaked bandage on her upper arm.

"I'm okay," she whispers.

"We're gonna kill that motherfucker so good, babe. I fucking promise you that. No one ever touches what's mine like this and gets away with it."

"Wash him away. I need—" She hiccups. "I need him gone."

"Whatever you need."

Scooping her up once more, I walk her the short distance to the tub and lower her legs in.

"Okay?"

She nods and I keep going, lowering her down until she vanishes in the bubbles.

I watch her for a few seconds before backing up.

Her head snaps up, her eyes wide and terrified.

"Where are you going?" she asks in a rush, her voice cracking.

"Nowhere, babe. I promise you."

Grabbing the shirt and Toby's jacket, I open the door and throw them out just as my sister rounds the corner carrying two mugs.

"What's that?" It's a pointless question, because the cream and marshmallow-topped mugs can really only mean one thing. "Thank you," I say, taking them from her.

"Anything."

With a quick smile, I duck back into the room and kick the door closed.

Brianna's eyes land on the mugs with longing.

"Here," I say, taking them over and placing them on the edge of the bath. "Calli made hot chocolate."

Without a word, she reaches for the mug, wraps her hands around it and brings it to her nose.

The sight of her is so welcome yet full of pain that I don't know what to do with myself as I stand in the middle of the room like a melon.

"Siren... c-can I—" I nod my head at the tub, praying she allows me to get in with her. I might only be a few feet away, but it's too much.

She nods, and the second I see the move, I start shedding my clothes.

I'm pretty sure I've never got naked faster, and for a manwhore like me, that's really saying something.

She watches my every move, but the usual heat that usually burns in her eyes when I get my cock out isn't there. I know I shouldn't be surprised, but it still makes worry saturate my muscles.

She shifts forward to give me some space, and I sink in behind her, immediately pulling her back so I can wrap her in both my arms and legs, and rest my chin on her shoulder.

"I meant what I said, Brianna. I'm in love with you, and I'll do whatever it takes to get you through this."

A sigh falls from her lips, and I try not to get too wrapped up in how contented it sounded.

"Drink up and relax. I've got you now. There's nothing to worry about."

13

BRIANNA

Warmth engulfs me from both inside and out as Nico practically wraps his entire body around me like a snake and the rich hot chocolate slides down my throat, warming my belly.

I sit in silence as my body continues to tremble.

I have no idea why. I'm no longer scared.

I haven't been since his voice; his words broke through the sheer terror buzzing through my system as I ran.

At first, I thought it was him. My skin burned with his touch, my need to fight stronger than ever.

But then I heard Nico. The deep rumble of his sexy voice tickled my ears, and I knew everything was going to be okay.

He found me and he came for me. At just the right time.

If he hadn't and it was Brad who'd got me...

A violent shudder rips down my spine at the thought of what could have happened next.

"I'm right here," Nico whispers, his arms around me tightening.

I nod, needing him to know just how grateful I am for that fact, but I'm struggling to process everything let alone find a way to tell him all the things I need to.

The second he notices I'm done with my drink, he plucks the mug from my hands and places it on the side, encouraging me to lie back with him.

"Relax, babe. You have all the time in the world to get your head around this."

My brows furrow. Can he read my mind?

Pressing a kiss to the top of my head, he breathes me in as his fingers begin drawing gentle, addictive patterns over my back until I have little choice but to relax into him.

"That's it, Siren. It's over. Just relax."

I let out a shuddering breath and try to focus on his words, on the fact he's right.

A million and one questions spin around my head. What happened to Brad? Is he still breathing? Where is he now? What about Mum? But none of them leave my lips. I'm too lost in Nico's drugging touches and the combined heat of his body and the water surrounding me.

I'm exhausted, my body begging for me to shut down and rest, but I refuse to shut my eyes. I'm terrified that if I do, all I'll be able to see is him. And I want to be here. I want to be with Nico where I know I'm safe.

I have no idea how long we lie there in silence as I soak up all the support he's offering, but eventually, voices begin rumbling on the other side of the door, making my muscles lock up.

Lifting my head, I risk a glance up at Nico.

"It's okay, babe. You don't have to see or talk to anyone you don't want. But Toby called the doctor. Will you let him check you over? For me?" he adds, his eyes silently begging me.

"Okay," I whisper; after all, I've got a few questions of my own I need to ask.

For the first time in a long time, my eyelids lower as shame washes through me. I allowed him to touch me, and he might have...

Nico's gentle caress doesn't falter.

"Whatever you're thinking, babe, it doesn't matter. No matter what happened in that house, it doesn't change anything. You're still my siren and you always will be."

Tears burn the backs of my eyes at his words.

I just wish they were true. But I can't help feeling like his siren got lost somewhere between my flat and the house he was keeping me locked in.

While I'd like to think he didn't take advantage of me after I passed out from the pain and exhaustion last night, there's still doubt in my mind.

When I was washing this morning, I didn't feel that ache that can be there after sex. And there certainly wasn't any evidence that I'd expect. But that isn't really a definite answer. And I need to know, or it's going to drive me to the brink of insanity.

Without another word, I sit up, making my intentions clear.

"Not yet," he growls, reaching for a bottle of shampoo that's sitting on the side. "Let me look after you."

My skin erupts in goosebumps as he starts lathering up my hair, massaging my scalp like a pro.

A wanton moan rips from my lips as his fingers hit all the right spots.

"That good, babe?"

All I can do is moan again and let him continue.

After putting some conditioner in, he starts working on my body, being super careful of all my cuts and bruises.

His attention lingers on my upper arm. It's still bleeding, the bandage utterly useless.

As gently as he can, he takes it off, but he doesn't say a word about what the injury is. He just looks after me in a way I wouldn't have thought he was capable of only a few months ago.

This man is brutal, dangerous, and unpredictable. But I've discovered he's also kind, caring, and one of the most thoughtful people I know. His gentle touch and soft murmurs of support make my eyes burn with tears.

None spill free, though. I'm pretty sure they've dried up.

Once he's happy that I'm clean, he drops a kiss on my shoulder and climbs out.

Spinning around, I watch as water runs down his sculpted back and over that glorious arse as he reaches for a towel.

The sight makes something stir inside me, and I almost scream in delight that maybe I'm not entirely broken.

Don't get me wrong, there's no way I'm about to jump him or do anything like that. But that tingle of excitement as I watch his muscles pull and flex gives me hope.

He tucks the fabric around his waist before turning toward me with another in his hand.

But I don't get a chance to look up, because my eyes lock on the slight tenting of the towel.

"Don't judge me," Nico teases. "You're hot, naked, and wet. Can't help myself."

"I'm a mess," I argue, ripping my eyes from his crotch and making my way up his body until I find his eyes.

He shrugs one shoulder, a sappy smile playing on his lips. "You're mine, and I want you. Always."

"Nico," I sigh, both hating and loving that I can only see

the truth reflected back at me. His eyes sparkle with honesty, the gold within them brighter than usual.

"Come on, Siren. You need to be curled up in my bed, not sitting in a tub of cold water."

Tucking his hands under my arms, he lifts me from the bath and then wraps me in the thick, fluffy towel. Thankfully, it's dark grey; otherwise, I'd be bleeding all over it. Not that I really think he cares. In fact, they're probably grey for a reason. He must turn up bleeding on a fairly regular occasion. That thought makes my chest ache in a whole new way.

"Stop, baby. You're safe here. Nothing or no one can touch you."

My mouth opens to argue, but no words come out.

After squeezing the excess water from my hair, he sweeps me into his arms once more and carries me back to his bedroom.

"I can walk," I confess quietly.

"I know. But you don't have to."

Once he's deposited me on his bed, he turns his back on me once more and begins rummaging through his drawers.

When he spins back around, he has a tank in his hands.

"The doc's going to want to get to that arm, Siren," he explains as he pulls the towel from around me and then lets his shirt fall over my body.

I nod and shuffle backwards on his bed until I'm resting against the headboard, watching him drop his towel and drag on a pair of sweats, going commando underneath.

Thank fuck any of the women who are probably going to be here tonight are either related to him or in serious relationships, I muse as I stare at the more-than-obvious outline of his semi.

"Glad you missed me too, babe," he teases.

"Shit. I'm sorry, I—"

"Babe," he sighs, coming over and crawling onto the bed. "You can stare at my dick all day long if you want. Anything to put that sparkle back into your eyes." He cups my cheek gently and rests his brow against mine. "You ready?"

I nod once, but it's enough.

He softly brushes his lips against mine, making me crave so much more from him, but he's gone before I've really registered the thought.

"Jojo," I say in a rush when he's at the door.

"You got it," he agrees before slipping out of the room and leaving me alone for the first time since he found me.

Pulling my thighs up to my chest, I rest my head on my knees as the low rumble of voices filters from the open door.

It's only two seconds before I hear her light footsteps as she runs for me.

I break once more when I see her fly through the doorway.

"Bri," she cries, launching herself onto the bed and pulling me into her arms.

"I'm sorry," I wail as I hold onto her just as tight.

"You have nothing to apologise for," she assures me firmly through her own sobs. "You're home now. It's over," she says, repeating the words that Nico has said over and over in the past few hours.

We're still clinging to each other when a soft knock comes from the door.

Pulling my head from the crook of Jodie's neck, I find an older man standing with a large black case hanging from his arm, a woman of similar age just behind him, and then Nico.

He smiles at me, his eyes telling me I'm safe and they're here to look after me.

"We'll be as fast as we can be, Brianna," the woman says softly as she steps ahead of the man. "I'm Elen, and this is my husband, Pearce. He's a doctor and I'm a nurse. Is it okay if we check you over?"

My eyes leave hers in favour of Nico's again.

"Yes," I whisper. "But they're not leaving."

"That's totally fine, sweetie. Nico has already told us about the cut on your arm. Shall we start there?"

I nod and they both move closer.

Jodie finally releases me, but I don't allow her to get far when I grab her hand, keeping her on the edge of the bed.

"We're right here, Bri. We're not going anywhere." She squeezes my hand in support, and I look over at where Nico is resting back against the wall with his hands in his pockets, watching with deep creases in his brow.

The husband and wife team work in perfect harmony. He stitches my wound up while she covers it in a bandage and works on cleaning up a few deeper cuts I've somehow sustained. Honestly, I have no idea if they came from running through the trees or if they've been there a while. Everything is quickly becoming a blur.

No one says anything about the reason they're patching up my arm. Jodie knows, I can see it in her eyes, and I can only imagine the medical professionals are aware of what's missing from that location. Nico though... we've never had that conversation.

I assured him before he took me bare that I had birth control covered, and in his need for me, he didn't stop to ask any more questions... and going into specifics wasn't exactly my top priority as he held his hard cock in his hand and promised me a whole world of pleasure.

He's not an idiot, though, and as his eyes burn into me from the other side of the room, I can almost hear the thoughts that are running rampant in his head.

The questions seem to be never-ending as they try to get a full picture of what I've been through. And with regret and pain gripping my chest, I answer them all honestly.

I can't look at anyone as I explain about him drugging me with something when he first abducted me from my flat, and how he kept that up sporadically during my time with him. I tell them about his rough treatment, how my head collided with the wall, all the things that I can think of other than the reason for the hole in my arm.

I know I shouldn't be putting that one off, but I don't want Nico to have to listen. If he learns what Brad may or may not have done to me, he might change his mind about everything he's said to me since he rescued me.

"Brianna, I'm sorry to have to ask this, but I'm sure you understand how important it is," Elen starts, making my body tense and Jodie's grip on my hand tighten. "Did he rape you?"

One single tear rolls down my cheek as a deep growl comes from Nico.

The atmosphere in the room turns dark, the air so thick it's hard to suck any of it in.

"I... um..."

"It's okay, Bri," Jodie assures me. "They just need to know so they can treat you properly. Right, Nico?" She looks up at him, and I can't help but follow her line of sight. However, I don't lift my eyes high enough to see his.

He's pushed from the wall, hovering in the middle of the room with anger coming off him in waves. I can practically see him vibrating with it.

Looking forward once more, I let my eyelids lower so I can give the answer I need to.

"I don't know." A sob rips from my throat as I remember the events before I passed out. "H-he..." I lower my head even more. "He tied me to the bed, stripped me, and I passed out there. I don't know if—"

The bed dips beside me, and I pray that it's Nico. That he's able to push past the anger over hearing those words and he's come to support me.

I realise just how hopeless that is the second his roar rips through the air. My head snaps up just in time to see him throw his fist into the wall.

"If you can't handle this, get out," Elen demands, showing a fierce side that she's kept under wraps thus far.

Nico hangs his head, his chest expanding with his deep, calming breath.

A massive part of me expects him to walk out and never look back.

And when he takes a step, I prepare myself for that scene playing out.

But then he moves, and it's not toward the door.

He comes closer, his dark, furious eyes locked on mine.

Elen is forced to hop out of the way so she's not trampled on as he crawls on to the bed on his knees.

His large, trembling hands frame my face as he stares down into my tear-filled eyes.

"I meant what I said, Brianna. Nothing, not a single fucking thing could make me walk away from you now. You're mine. I'm yours. Done fucking deal."

My tears free-fall over his fingers as he dips his head forward, sealing his promises with a kiss.

Jodie shamelessly sobs beside me, her own hand trembling in mine as Nico peppers my lips with kisses.

"I love you, Brianna," he whispers, although I doubt it's quiet enough for everyone else to miss it. "This changes nothing."

I'm barely able to nod my agreement, his grip on me is so tight.

"We can do a test to see if there is any DNA evidence. When did this possibly happen, Brianna?" Elen asks.

Nico releases my face so I can respond before dropping to my side and tucking me into his body.

"Um... l-last night, maybe. Time... it kinda didn't exist. I don't even know what day it is."

"It's Monday night."

"Monday," I murmur, trying to figure out what that means. "It's been over a week."

"Yeah, babe. Worst week of my life by a long shot."

Reaching out, I rest my hand on his abs, loving the way his muscles bunch in reaction to my touch.

"You probably don't need me to say this, and it's by far the firm medical answer you need, but there's no bruising to assume anything untoward has happened. Does your body feel like—"

"No," I answer quickly, cutting her off. "No soreness, no... evidence," I say with a wince.

"If you're okay with me taking an internal swab, we can pull in a few favours and get the results ASAP."

"Do it," I say, sucking in some strength and sliding my body down the bed.

"I'm going to leave you to it," Jodie says, pressing a kiss to my brow. "Nico has everything covered, but if you need me, I'll be right out there with Toby and Calli, okay?"

I nod, whispering an emotional, "Thank you" as she retreats.

"I'll be as fast and gentle as I can," Elen assures me after her husband also leaves the room to give me some privacy.

Tucking my face into Nico's side, I allow my legs to fall open as directed and let her do what she needs to do, silently sobbing the entire time.

Please have let him be so fucked in the head that he would have needed me awake to experience what he wanted to do to me.

14

———

NICO

Elen left soon after getting what she needed to put Brianna's mind to rest over what that motherfucker might have done to her.

The second we were left alone, I sank lower in the bed and gently pulled her onto my chest and wrapped her freshly bandaged arm around my body.

Her sobs continued for long minutes. Each one tears another strip off my heart. But other than holding her and proving that I meant every single word I said to her, I had no idea how to help.

I have never felt so utterly useless in my entire life.

But my unease and anger was nothing compared to what she was dealing with, so I focused on her and tried to be the rock she needed.

I had so many questions, so fucking many, but I kept them all locked down. The only things that matter are that she's here and okay. The wounds on her body will heal, and with time, she'll find a way to deal with the mental trauma of all of this as well.

I can only hope that talking will be therapeutic for her, because as hard as I know it'll be, I want to hear it all. I want to go through this with her. And that doesn't mean that she can fob me off with the CliffsNotes she gave Dr. Rosi and his wife.

Eventually, she cried herself to sleep. I couldn't find any peace, though, and I'm not sure I will until that motherfucker is dead, his body disposed of by wild animals like he never existed.

"Hey," Toby says, after I've convinced myself to slip from beneath Brianna to catch up with the guys.

"Hey."

My eyes scan my living room, taking everyone in. Jodie is fast asleep on Toby's lap, Calli in almost the exact same position, curled up on the opposite sofa with Daemon.

"She should be in a bed," I growl, feeling even more protective of her than usual.

"She refused to go anywhere."

"I have a guest room."

Daemon shrugs and shakes his head.

Stella and Emmie might be cuddled up with their men, but they're wide awake, watching me with cautious eyes as if I'm going to blow at any minute.

"How is she?" Stella asks quietly.

"Sleeping."

"Has she said much?" Emmie asks.

"No, not really. But it was enough to know that whatever you've done to that prick is nowhere near enough."

A ripple of anger and the need to spill more than just a little bit of that motherfucker's blood flows around the room.

"Where is he?"

"Hanging from a hook in the basement," Daemon says proudly. And to think I've allowed my sister to sleep with that.

"Good. Is he in pain?"

"Do you even know me at all?" Daemon murmurs.

My eyes drop to my sister on his lap and the protective hand that's resting on her belly.

"Sometimes I really wonder," I muse.

"He wasn't alone," Theo confesses.

My spine immediately straightens and my eyes lock on his.

"Who?"

"Her mother," Emmie states coldly.

"Oh fuck," I breathe, stumbling back and falling into an empty seat. "Did she know?"

"Says Brianna knows she was there, but the woman is a fucking crackpot," Seb deadpans. "Bri was better off without her, if you ask me."

"Still her mother, arsehole," Emmie snaps.

It's no secret that Emmie has had her own mummy issues. Hell, she still does, so it makes sense that she'd be the one to understand this better than the rest of us.

"What did she have to say?" I ask.

"Sorry, mostly," Theo says.

"She was in on this?"

"She said no," Daemon adds, "but like Seb said, she's a few marbles short of a full set."

"Christ," I mutter, dropping my head into my hands, scrubbing at my face. "We need the truth."

"When Brianna is ready. Those two aren't going anywhere."

Silence falls between us.

"Both of them were pretty fucked up," Alex says, speaking for the first time since I joined them. "They'd turned on each other, so if they were in on it together, something went very wrong."

I think for a minute. "Say she wasn't working with him. Why would he want them both?"

No one offers up any kind of answer to that question.

"You should all head home. It's late," I say, pushing to my feet and heading to my kitchen for a drink.

"We'll check in in the morning, yeah?" Seb says as he pulls Stella to her feet.

"We'll be here."

As he walks past, he claps me on the shoulder. "She'll be okay," he assures me. "She's stronger than that wankstain."

"I know," I say confidently.

They disappear, quickly followed by Alex, Ant, and then Daemon, carrying my exhausted sister in his arms.

With a quick nod, he disappears down the hallway, leaving just Toby, a still-asleep Jodie, and Theo and Emmie.

"You can take the guest room if you want," I offer Toby, aware that Jodie won't be happy to leave Brianna.

"Thanks, man."

He scoops her up much like Daemon did Calli, and they head off.

It's not until they've gone that I look up, locking eyes with my cousin.

"The dude is fucked up, man," he confesses.

"And they're right, her mum is... fuck, I don't even know," Emmie sighs. "But my gut tells me that she wasn't his accomplice in this. All she did was cry for Brianna and beg for her to be looked after. I think she cares... in her own screwed-up way."

"You really have no idea why he did this? Why he wanted her so badly?"

Something dark flickers through Theo's eyes, making my stomach knot up painfully.

"He kept chanting things about her being his. About them taking over the city together."

"The city?" I ask. "He wanted to overthrow us? Why would he think the two of them have the power? He's... a Rivera associate, that's all, right?"

"Well," Theo starts, leaning forward and resting his elbows on his knees, "I ran his DNA, found out who Bradley Whitlock really is."

Nerves explode in my stomach as I find myself walking closer as if he's about to whisper the answer.

"His great-grandfather was Rivera. He was one of the first to come over here. But his grandfather fucked up. He double-crossed them and their entire family was cast out."

I shake my head. "What does this have to do with Brianna?"

"That I don't know. Not yet, at least. I don't doubt that we'll get it from the horse's mouth sometime soon."

"Or Brianna might already know," Emmie says, twisting her fingers with Theo's, a move that instantly relaxes him.

"There's every chance she's holding everything we need."

"I'm not going to push her," I bark defensively.

"We're not suggesting you do."

Silence falls as the weight of all this presses down on us. It's soon shattered, though, when a blood-curdling scream rips through my flat.

I'm on my feet and running toward my bedroom before I've registered that my legs are moving.

Throwing the door open, I practically fly to the bed, wrapping my arms around my girl and holding her tight against me as she trembles and cries.

"It's okay, babe. I'm here. I'm right here."

Her breathing is erratic, a quiet whimper falling from her lips.

"You left me."

Those three words fucking wreck me; they rip my heart right in two and leave me bleeding out on the floor.

"Never, Siren. I'd never do that. I was in the living room debriefing with Theo. I fucking swear, Bri, I'm not leaving you. Not ever."

She sniffles, her panic reducing with every word I say.

"You promise?"

"I promise." Pulling her into my body, I lay her back down. She immediately twists her legs with mine and holds me tight. "I love you, Brianna," I say, amazed by how easily the words roll off my tongue.

It's something I never thought I'd say to a woman, but it turns out, confessing how I really feel about her is one of the easiest things I've ever done in my life.

I guess that means it's right... right?

"I love you too, Nico," she says so quietly that I wonder if I imagined it when her breathing gets shallower, and she slips back into a peaceful sleep.

Over the next twenty-four hours, Brianna alternated between sleeping and waking up screaming.

It was fucking terrifying, and every time that painful,

terrified shriek hit my ears, I swear I actually died a little bit.

I never left the room after she freaked out that first time. I couldn't. The farthest I went was the door to talk to the others when they had something to say that couldn't wait, or the toilet, but I figured that was technically the same room, and I kept my eyes on her the whole time, something she probably won't appreciate when she finally makes use of this room herself and realises I missed the target more often than not in my concern for her.

Fuck it, a little piss never hurt anyone.

Those fucking nightmares she's having, though, sound all kinds of brutal.

And if I hadn't told myself that I wouldn't step foot out of this room again, I'd be in the basement torturing the motherfucker who did this to her within an inch of his life.

A soft knock comes on the bedroom door, and I swing my legs off the edge and pad over.

"Hey," Jodie says, holding out a plate of food for me. "How's she doing?"

Standing aside, I allow her to peer in and see her best friend still curled up in my bed.

"Sleeping. She hasn't had a nightmare for a few hours either," I say, hoping they might have ended. I know it's probably pointless, but if we don't have hope, what do we have?

Jodie lets out a pained sigh. She wants to magically fix all of this just like I do, but she's feeling as equally useless as I am.

"You need to eat this," she says, poking me in the chest with the plate I haven't taken from her.

"Yes, Boss," I tease.

"I'm serious. She needs you fighting fit."

"You too. Did you sleep at all last night?" I ask, unable to miss the dark shadows under her eyes.

"A bit. It just brings it all back, you know?"

I give her a sympathetic smile. As much as I want to be able to fully understand what both Jodie and Brianna have been through, it's really fucking hard to comprehend being at someone's mercy like that.

I startle when a whimper comes from behind me before the sheets rustle with movement.

"Get back to her," Jodie instructs, practically shoving me and the plate back into the room.

The door has barely clicked closed when the most incredible sound hits my ears.

"Nico?"

"Right here, babe," I say softly as I lower the plate to the bedside table and climb back into bed.

Resting on my side just a foot away from her, I search her pale face, praying she'll wake up enough to open her eyes.

I can't even comprehend how much I miss my girl.

Lifting my hand, I tuck a lock of her wild curls behind her ear before brushing my knuckles over her cheek.

Her eyelids flutter and my heart jumps into my throat.

Not a second later, I'm gifted with the sight of her blue eyes that I love so much.

Okay, so they're a little bloodshot, and despite the hours of sleep she's had, they show the evidence of her exhaustion from what she's been through. But still, they're hers. She's here. Lying right in front of me.

"Hey," I say, a ridiculously goofy smile pulling at my lips.

"Hey." In a rare show of vulnerability, her cheeks actually redden. It's so fucking cute I can barely stand it.

"How are you feeling?"

"Would you believe me if I said tired?" she asks lightly.

"Yeah, babe. I would."

She sucks in a breath, and I can't help but wonder if she's remembering her fitful, nightmare-filled sleep.

But as much as I might want to ask, I don't, in case by some luck that isn't already what she's thinking about.

15

BRIANNA

He stares at me as if I'm something special. Something precious.

Secretly, it's what I've been hoping for for so long that I should be happy. But all I feel is pain.

I'm no longer the girl he thinks I am.

I'm broken. Tarnished. Ruined. And I'm not sure I'm ever going to be the same.

I wanted to be strong. I didn't want to let Brad get inside my head, but the second his face appeared in my sleep, haunting me despite escaping physically, I knew he'd managed it.

Without my permission, he managed to worm his way under my skin, leaving me questioning everything.

"Please don't look at me like that," I say, ripping my gaze away from his.

The love, the concern in his dark gaze is just too much.

"I'm not looking at you like anything," he argues, tucking his fingers beneath my chin and giving me little choice but to look back at him.

"Did the doctor call?" I have no idea how long I've been asleep, but something tells me it's been a while.

A little bit of hope trickles through my veins that I might at least be free of one nightmare. If I can have it confirmed that he didn't do the worst then I might... might be able to somehow figure out a way through this.

But then that shrivels and dies when Nico subtly shakes his head.

"There was a problem at the lab. But they said it could be any minute."

"Nico, I—"

"Don't do that, Brianna," he warns when I try to sever our connection once more. "Don't hide from me."

"B-but—"

"It doesn't matter. I've already told you, nothing matters. I'll do anything, fucking anything to help you through this, Siren, but I refuse to allow you to think that he's changed anything between us."

"I'm sorry." The words tumble from my lips without permission from my brain.

"What are you talking about? You have nothing to apologise for. The only one who should be is me. It took me too long to find you. I was so focused on it being the Italians that I didn't even consider that–"

"That's what he wanted. What he planned," I confess. "He was biding his time, watching, waiting for the perfect moment."

Nico's entire body tenses at my words, his grip on me tightening.

"There was nothing more you could have done."

"I never should have left you in your flat. I knew it was wrong. It went against all of my instincts."

"You couldn't have known," I whisper, aware that it's

entirely my fault I was there. If I weren't so stubbornly independent, then I would have picked up what I needed and agreed to spend the rest of the night, the rest of my life, here, safe in Nico's arms.

Fuck Brad and his twisted games. All of this is my fault.

"No," Nico states as if he can read my mind. "None of this is on you."

He searches my eyes, allowing me to see everything he's holding back, all the questions dancing on the tip of his tongue.

"Brianna, why did—"

The vibration of his phone on the bedside table stops whatever was about to fall from his lips.

With a sigh, he twists around to grab it.

"Doc," he says before swiping the screen and offering it to me.

My heart jumps into my throat as I think about the answer he's about to give me and I panic.

Pushing his arm away, I shake my head violently, much to his confusion.

"Hello?" Elen says down the line. "Nico?"

He searches my eyes as he lifts his phone to his ear.

"Hi, Elen. I'm here. We're here," he corrects.

She speaks, the softness of her voice floating through the air, but I can't make out the words.

My hands tremble as I try to read Nico's expression to discover my fate.

Did that arsehole take advantage of me in order to get what he was so desperate for while I was unconscious, or was there a teeny tiny part of him that wasn't a total monster?

Nico nods. "Okay. Yeah. Makes total sense."

Elen speaks again, and Nico continues listening, his face completely emotionless.

He's all business right now. I understand why; it's easier to deal with all the hard shit if you pull your impenetrable mask on. But the longer this goes on, the more I'm regretting pussying out of accepting this call myself.

"Okay, yeah, we will. Thank you so much. We really appreciate it."

Silence hangs between us as Nico cuts the call and drops his phone on the bed between us.

His eyes find mine, searching deep for something that I'm pretty sure is no longer there.

"Nico?" I whimper, needing the answer but terrified the truth will only break me more.

"The only DNA they found alongside yours was mine, babe."

All the air rushes out of my lungs as a weird, relieved laugh tumbles from my lips.

"J-just you?"

His brows pinch. "No. Not just me. Me and you. Just like it's meant to be."

"Nico," I sob, my emotions flipping so fast I have no idea what to focus on.

"Everything is going to be okay, Brianna. You're exactly where you're meant to be, and we'll figure this shit out together."

Wrapping his hand around the back of my neck, his forehead finds mine as he looks deep into my eyes.

Everything I've ever felt for him, the hate, the love and everything in between collides, making my heart feel like it's about to explode.

"I love you," I whisper.

"Babe, I love you more than I thought possible. Now,

tell me what you need. I don't want to fuck this up, but right now, I need to kiss you more than I need to breathe."

I swallow nervously, aware of just how minging my breath is.

"I need... I need to brush my teeth, I need a coffee and a shower. And..." I hesitate, wondering if he'll think I'm insane for what I want just as much as those things.

"And?"

"And I want... you." I stare up at him through my lashes, utterly terrified that he'll turn me down even with the test result Elen just delivered.

"Babe. You've got me, always. You want any part of me, all you've got to do is say the word."

Like the doting boyfriend I was convinced he wasn't able to be, he helps me to the bathroom on unsteady legs.

I can barely remember the last time I walked on them... no... ran.

A tremor rips through my body as the memory of running from the devil comes back to me.

I want to try and hide it, to appear strong and in control, but I fail.

"It's okay, I've got you." Nico's grip on me tightens as we turn to slip through the doorway. "Toilet?" he asks.

I nod, embarrassment heating my cheeks.

This isn't how I wanted the beginning of us to go. Him helping me to pee.

"I'll be okay," I whisper when my arse hits the seat.

He studies me as I fight not to just let go and pee right in front of him. But he doesn't fucking move.

"Babe?" he questions, his eyes bouncing between mine.

"I'm okay," I say even quieter. "Can you make the coffee?"

I love having him close. I love how supportive he's been in the few lucid moments I've had since he found me. But this is pushing things a little too far for me.

He doesn't look convinced, but after forcing a smile onto my lips, he takes a step back.

"Call me if—"

"I'm okay." I figure that eventually, if I say those words enough, then they'll become true... right?

He nods and takes off, although hesitantly.

The second his footsteps fade, I relax, allowing my body to do its thing.

The relief is real, but it only takes me back there once again. To a less-than-pleasant memory of what he forced me to do.

Battling with the tears that threaten to spill, I finish up and test out my legs.

They're still wobbly as fuck, but I manage to make it over to the basin to wash my hands and brush my teeth.

I keep my head lowered the whole time, terrified of what I'll find staring back at me if I were to look up.

I have good memories of standing right here as Nico railed me from behind. Memories I don't want him to steal as well.

But after lowering my toothbrush, I know I can't put it off any longer.

With the sound of Nico crashing around out in the kitchen—something I suspect he's doing on purpose so I can hear him—I force my head up.

My breath catches, my initial reaction to my reflection is the shock I was terrified of.

I'm pale with dark bruises under my eyes despite the

hours of sleep I've had. My hair is wild, but it's my neck and arms that really catch my attention. The dark bruising is unmistakable.

The sight makes a fire burn so hot in my belly, I wonder how I haven't been engulfed by the flames.

Instead of pitying myself, losing myself in the nightmare I've endured, staring at the evidence of it has a very different effect.

Somehow, it's given me strength. Because while I might be standing here looking like a car crash, I'm not actually the loser.

I got out. I beat him.

Yes, okay, Nico found me just at the right time, but I did it. I escaped that house. And I'd like to think that if I were forced to keep running, I still would have managed it.

Looking up, I stare right into my eyes. And yes, while I might see a broken, weak woman staring back at me, that's not all I find. I see that fire burning within, my need to show my strength, to prove to everyone around me that I'm better than this, better than him.

Wrapping my fingers around the bottom of Nico's tank, I drag the fabric over my head, allowing my eyes to wander over all my injuries.

My chest heaves as I take in each one. I'm like a fucking dot-to-dot of bruises.

Suddenly, those scars on my shoulder seem less ugly.

He hated them, and in some weird kind way, his bullshit opinion on my body has helped me embrace them.

My skin might not be flawless like it once was, but it's me.

Those marks tell my story; they show the world that I won't bow down when times get hard, no matter what is thrown at me.

I'm still lost in my own thoughts, staring at myself in the mirror, when Nico's shadow darkens the doorway.

My cheeks heat as his eyes land on my face, but I don't move for a beat.

I need just one more moment to fully own this shit.

Then, after sucking in a deep breath, I turn to him.

"Siren," he breathes, his eyes holding mine steady, his brow creased with his concern.

"I'm okay," I say, my voice stronger than it has been in a while.

"Yeah?" he asks, one side of his mouth kicking up in the beginning of a smile that I'm sure will make my knees weak.

"Yeah. I'm Brianna A-Andrews," I stutter when the words he spat at me before I found my escape come back to me. "I'm stronger than that psycho."

His smile grows as he hears the conviction in my tone.

"Hell yeah, you are."

Finally, his eyes drop from mine in favour of checking out my body.

If he sees the bruises and cuts, then they don't faze him at all. Instead, his eyes linger on my breasts, trace the lines of my waist, then over my hips. He takes in every inch of my legs before he finally focuses on my now very unshaven pussy before he eventually gets back up my eyes.

"Hey," I say, almost shyly as the tenting of his sweats becomes more and more obvious.

"Fucking hell, I missed you, Siren."

He takes a step closer, two steaming mugs of coffee in his hands. Add that to him being shirtless and obviously turned on... Well, it's a sight for sore eyes, that's for sure.

"And I've really missed..." I start, taking a step closer with every word. "Decent coffee."

He barks out a laugh as I pluck one of the mugs from his fingers and breathe in the scent of the rich beans.

"Fuck yes," I moan like a whore before taking my first burning sip.

A growl rumbles deep in his throat as he watches me with hungry eyes.

The sight of that heat helps to push those demons a little further away.

I'm not naïve enough to think that'll last. But right now, I'll take the reprieve from the images of the past week that have been a constant in my head.

I'm more than ready to focus on something else.

I drink half of my coffee, the scorching liquid damn near burning a layer of skin off my tongue, before I place it on the counter and step into the shower.

Nico's eyes don't leave me as I blindly reach behind me for the dial.

My shriek of shock fills the air when the cold water hits me, but it quickly warms, helping my muscles to relax.

"Are you just going to stand there gawping or are you going to get naked and join me?" I taunt, lifting a brow.

It takes him a second to translate my question, and it's just enough time for a couple of the fears that have been instilled in me over the past week to raise their ugly heads.

But then, he practically throws his coffee onto the side and attempts to shed his sweats so fast that he ends up getting one leg stuck around his ankle and almost joins me head first.

"You're a fucking idiot," I laugh as he fights to fix the situation.

"Babe," he says, finally stepping up to me, allowing the water to rain down over his body. "I'll be anything you want if it makes you laugh like that."

"You already are. You're mine," I state before wrapping my hand around the back of his neck, dragging his face closer and taking exactly what I need to ensure those fears and demons stay well back.

When we're together, nothing can touch us.

And that's exactly what I need right now.

One of his hands lands on my hip, while the other tangles in my wet hair as he kisses me back with the same ferocity I do him.

Our tongues tangle, exploring each other's mouths as if it's the first time, and our teeth clash with our need for more, our desire to get closer, to consume each other.

Hiking my leg up around his waist, a low groan rumbles in his throat as his hand slides down to my arse and his hard length brushes exactly where I want it.

"Siren," he warns into our kiss. "I don't want to hurt you."

I pull back and look him dead in the eyes as my chest heaves and my panting breaths dance over his face.

"The only thing that could hurt me right now is if you reject me. Please, Nico, I need—"

"Whoa," he says, halting my words as he slides his hand up my chest before cupping my jaw. "When did I ever give you the impression I'd reject you?" he asks, concern and possibly a little hurt darkening his eyes.

"I-I," I stutter, hating that the second I close my eyes, *he's* there.

"No. Open your eyes," Nico demands almost harshly. "Don't do that. Don't go there. This is me and you. He is not a part of this. He is nothing. Worthless. Gone."

I nod, trying to follow his orders, focusing on his eyes and his mouth.

"Fuck me, Nico. Remind me who I belong to, who owns my pussy."

"Fuck," he barks. "You ask so nicely, babe."

Then, his lips are back on mine, ensuring that all my thoughts are stolen by him, that every sensation zapping around my body is because of him.

"Nico," I beg, shamelessly grinding myself against him in order to achieve what I crave.

"I'm not going to fuck you, Siren. Not in here," he confesses after kissing along my jaw toward my ear.

"B-but—" I stutter, my heart sinking into my feet.

One second he's there, and then the next, he's gone.

His knees hit the shower tray with a thud, and his eyes crawl up my body.

"But I will get things started."

With his giant hand wrapped around my right thigh, he lifts the other and throws it over his shoulder.

"Hold on, babe. I can't promise this will be slow or gentle."

"NI-CO," I cry as he leans forward and latches onto my clit.

16

———

NICO

Should I be doing this?

No, probably not.

Am I strong enough to deny my girl of anything, especially when she asks me so nicely?

Nope. Not a fucking chance.

I moan in delight as her sweet taste coats my tongue. There were so many times in the past week when I thought I'd never get to experience this again. And now she's here, I fully intend to show her just how much I fucking missed her.

Her entire body trembles as I lap at her.

Her back arches from the tiled wall behind her, and she has her head thrown back in pleasure as I eat her as if she's the only thing I need to survive.

"Nico," she whimpers as the one leg that's holding her up starts to buckle.

I'm not worried; I can more than take her weight if she needs me to.

There's no fucking way I'll let her fall.

Not now. Not ever.

"Look at me," I demand, barely moving away from her pussy.

Instantly, she pulls her head from the wall and looks down at me.

"Watch. Watch as I eat you, Siren."

She whimpers as I lick up the length of her.

"And watch as I make you come all over my face."

Lifting my hand, I slide two fingers deep inside her, finding her G-spot with ease.

Her fingers twist painfully in my hair as I bring her closer and closer to the edge.

"That's it, Siren. Come for me," I command.

And not four seconds later does she do exactly what she's told.

She screams through her release; her eyes are desperate to close, but she follows orders and keeps them locked on mine.

My cock aches, bobbing between my thighs, desperate to get in on the action.

Soon, dude. Really fucking soon.

Placing her foot back on the floor, I slam my lips against hers, reach for the dial to stop the water, and sweep her into my arms.

"I hope you're done in here," I say into our kiss.

"So done. I'm all clean."

"Good. Now I have every intention of dirtying you up again."

Leaving puddles behind us, I march out of the bathroom and lay her out on my bed.

I stand back, taking in every inch of her as water runs over her curves.

"Nico."

"Do you have any idea how fucking beautiful you are?"

"Please," she begs. "I need—"

"I know, babe. And I'm right here. Use me."

I fall on top of her, catching my weight on my arms before I hurt her more than I'm sure she already is.

I've tried to give her the painkillers Dr. Rosi left, but with her sleeping almost every hour since he left, it's not exactly been easy. When she has been lucid enough, she's refused to take them, telling me that they'll make her drowsy and that she'd prefer the pain over not feeling.

I mean, I fucking get it. I've been there, and I agree. But it hurts to know she's suffering.

Spreading her legs with mine, I wrap my fingers around my shaft and tease her with the head, circling her swollen clit and dipping it lower, just pushing the tip inside, driving her crazy.

"Argh, I hate you," she cries when I pull back again, not giving her what she needs.

"No you don't," I argue. "Pretty sure you never did either."

"Fuck you, Nico Cirillo. Fuck YOU," she screams when I finally sink inside her tight body.

"Tell me what you need. Slow and gentle or rough and fast?"

"Rough and fast," she says without missing a beat. "I need you to fuck him and the past week right out of my head."

Is this the best form of therapy for what she's been through?

Possibly not. But honestly, I can't think of a better option right now.

And like I said earlier. If my siren wants something, then I'm going to damn well give it to her.

"YES," she screams when I pull out almost all the way

before slamming back inside her. "Yes, yes, yes," she chants as I fuck her so hard she'd shoot up the bed if I weren't holding her hips in a vice grip.

Sweat mingles with the water droplets still clinging to my skin as I take her as hard as I dare.

The bruises and healing cuts littering her body are a constant reminder of what she's been through, and I'd never forgive myself if I made any of them worse.

With every thrust, cold water drops from my hair, splashing on her stomach, making her flinch and pushing her closer to the release that's just in touching distance.

"Your cunt's getting tighter, babe. Are you about to come all over my dick?"

"Yes, please. Please."

"You beg so good, Siren. Such a good little whore for me."

"Nico," she cries, grabbing both my forearms and sinking her nails into my skin as she crashes over the edge.

"FUCK," I roar as the bite of pain along with her insane pussy makes me fall with her.

The second I come back to myself, I feel like the shittiest person in the world.

Brianna is laid out before me with my dick still inside her, sobbing into her hands.

"Fuck, babe. I'm sorry. I shouldn't have—"

Opening her arms, she gestures for me to pull her into my body, and I do without any hesitation.

Once again, she sobs until she passes out. Leaving me feeling like a massive fuck-up.

I thought I was helping giving her what she asked for, but I can't help feeling like I just fucked everything up.

Jesus. This whole boyfriend thing is a fucking minefield.

Assuming I'm actually her boyfriend, of course. We might have made the promises and even said the L word, but we haven't exactly named this thing between us.

Boyfriend.

I let that word roll around my head as Brianna sleeps against my chest.

Despite avoiding being one like the plague for the previous nineteen years of my life, for some reason, the commitment of being her boyfriend doesn't feel like enough.

Although, I'm not sure anything will be enough when it comes to my siren.

"I'm sorry I freaked out." Her soft voice startles me awake.

"It's okay. I shouldn't have—"

"No, you should. I... I needed that. I needed to remember who I am and who I belong to. I needed to hear you say those words to help push him out."

She doesn't lift her head from my chest, or move at all as she confesses this to me.

"He called me his. Said I was his whore. But I'm not." My grip on her waist tightens as I fight the need to say anything and just let her talk. "I'm not his anything. I'm yours."

Fuck yes, you are, I want to scream.

"I don't know how I didn't see it before. But there is something very, very wrong with that man. Like, mentally. He's on this weird power trip. You should have seen the way he controlled my mother with just one look. It was fucking bizarre."

I don't react to her admission about her mother being

there, and I can only assume that she's figured I already know, so I keep my mouth shut.

"But she had these moments. Just a few minutes when she seemed to see clearly and she'd try and help. I hate to admit it, but she's the reason I got away. The reason he never..."

She trails off, letting her unspoken words hang in the air around us.

I hate to be grateful to that bitch. All I knew about her up until this moment is that she was the world's shittiest mother. I want to say it's too little too late, but if what Brianna is saying is true, then I owe her everything.

"I smashed a glass over his head. I tried to run, but he came to faster than I expected, and he had me pinned against the floor.

"He was going to... to rape me, but she... she stabbed him with something. A shard of glass, I guess, and dragged him off me.

"Without looking back, I just turned and ran. Does that make me the most selfish person in the world, leaving her there like that?"

"No, babe. It makes you human. You don't owe her anything," I say, finally breaking my silence.

She nods against my chest as wetness pools against my skin.

"It was weird seeing her again," she admits quietly. "On one hand, it was like no time had passed at all. And on the other, everything was different."

"Was she... clean?"

"I..." She sucks in a deep breath. "She was on something, but I have no idea if that was by choice or force."

"Jesus," I mutter, trailing my fingertips up and down her arm, tracing the edge of her bandage every time I pass it.

"She didn't look healthy, but I've seen her worse." She pauses, considering her next question, and when it comes, I'm not surprised by it. "What happened to her?"

"We've got her safe. We're hoping she might be able to provide some answers for us all."

"And if I want to see her?"

"Then all you have to do is ask."

She nods but gives me no indication as to whether she might want to or not. Honestly, it really could go either way.

"Nico?" she suddenly asks, making my heart skip a beat.

"Yeah, babe."

"Do you know who my father is?"

"No, Siren. I don't. Do you?"

She falls silent again.

I wait her out, although it damn near kills me to do so when I know she's got so many things to say.

"Brad seems to think he knows. That's what this was all about."

"Theo said..." I start, questioning whether I should draw her into a conversation about this. I don't want to push her to talk if she's not ready. "He... Brad said after they collected him was that he needed you to take over the city. Do you know what he meant by that?"

She lets out a heavy sigh. "He told me... he told me that I wasn't just an accident, that my mother was groomed at a young age with the intention of providing someone with a kid that they'd be able to..."

My heart pounds as I come up with my own conclusion to that sentence.

"To sell," she whispers so quietly I have to strain to hear her. "He said I was conceived to be a whore."

My teeth grind, and I can barely hold myself back from gripping her so hard I know it'll hurt.

"He said that I was fake, that my name is made up to hide my identity. To keep me safe."

"Okay," I murmur. "But you thought your mum ran from your grandparents?"

"Yeah. That's what I've always been told. But I think the reality is worse than that. I assumed Andrews was my father's name and my mother was so far gone she didn't see how fucked up that was. But the way Brad was talking, he... I dunno, but it's bad."

"Did he give you a name or anything?" I ask, my unease over this conversation growing by the second.

"He just said something along the lines of, I couldn't be a Walker like Jodie, and that I really couldn't be a Harris."

She shrugs like it's nothing but bullshit, but the second that second surname rolls off her tongue, I freeze up.

"What?" she asks, finally. "Do you know who that is?"

"I have an idea, yeah."

"Is it bad?"

17

—————

BRIANNA

His reaction, the way his entire body tenses, finally makes me move.

Pushing up so I'm sitting beside him, I stare down at his wrinkled brow.

"Nico?"

"I'm sure it's not what I'm thinking," he says, forcing himself to relax. "There are millions of Harrises in the world. It could be any of them."

"It's not though, is it? Tell me what you're thinking," I beg.

"Siren, I—"

A door slamming out in my flat stops my words before the sound of deep male chatter rumbles through the air.

"I really need to talk to Theo. I know you want answers, but I don't want to fill your head with stuff that might not be true."

My lips part to argue, but I let the words float away.

"Trust me?" he asks, pushing to sit up in front of me.

His warm hand cups my face as he silently begs me to give him a little time.

"Always," I say. And I'm so fucking glad I do, because his entire expression softens.

"Fuck. I love you," he confesses, his lips finding mine for a searing kiss.

His other hand slides down my arm, coming to a stop on the bandage on my upper arm once more.

He still hasn't said a word about it. I'm not sure what to think.

Does he know? But if he does, surely, he wouldn't have fucked me bare earlier.

Or would he?

My head spins as he pulls back from our kiss and rests his brow against mine.

"I promise, I won't keep anything from you. But I need facts before I start gossiping."

"Okay," I breathe.

"Are you going to be okay?"

"Is Jodie here?" I ask, desperate for some time with my girl.

"Not sure. I can go find out."

With one more chaste kiss to my lips, he climbs out of bed and pulls on a clean pair of sweats before throwing me a fresh shirt and slipping out of the room.

The second he's gone, reality comes crashing down around me.

It's easy to push it all aside when he's here, touching me, distracting me.

But without him. I'm left cold, the strength of my memories enough to engulf me in the darkness again.

Being with him earlier... It was everything I needed.

Feeling his body against—inside—mine. It was everything.

I needed to remember who I was. I needed that physical

reminder that I was okay, that the only person with the power is me.

I knew what I wanted and I took it. Something that twisted fuck tried to steal from me.

Should I have been more sensible and demanded he put a condom on, or at least pull out, yeah, I really fucking should. But it's too late now.

After pulling Nico's shirt on, I climb from the bed with his scent filling my nose. It helps to keep me grounded and the dark thoughts at bay as I shuffle toward the bathroom.

Every muscle in my body aches. I have no idea if that's from my ordeal or just being laid in bed for so freaking long.

Having sex with Nico sure didn't help, but there wasn't a lot that would have stopped me from seeing that little idea through.

And just in case I needed another reminder of the fact he came inside me, his cum begins to run down my thighs.

Great.

I'm still in the bathroom, trying to get my head on straight, when there's a soft knock on the bedroom door before my best friend's voice fills the air.

"Bri?"

Sucking in some strength, I pull the bathroom door open and step out on slightly steadier legs.

"Oh my God," I breathe when I find her standing there with a Bettie's box in her hand.

"I thought you might be hungry." There's a naughty glint in her eyes that makes me smile.

"Should have known you two would have been out there listening, you kinky fucks," I tease.

"Babe, we weren't trying to listen." Lowering the box of pastries to the bed, she rushes out of the room before returning with two massive coffees. "Whoa, they're big."

"You can take it." She winks, and I can't help but laugh.

It feels so fucking good.

After fixing the mess we made of Nico's bed, the two of us climb on and sit cross-legged opposite each other with the box of pastries between us.

My mouth waters as I stare down at Bettie's light and fluffy treats.

"Go on. You get first dibs."

Flipping open the box, I reach for a vanilla crème crown.

The second I bite into it and the sweetness hits my tongue, I moan like a whore.

"Best thing I've had in my mouth for a while," I mumble around the mouthful, savouring every single taste.

"Better not confess that to Nico."

I laugh, swallowing the last bite.

"Only one of us had breakfast this morning, and I'm fucking starving."

"Yes, girl. Get that man bowing down and worshipping at your altar."

"Amen," I praise before stuffing more pastry into my mouth. "So, tell me something other than the depressing stuff from the last week."

"Uhh..." She thinks for a minute, making me realise just how hard the last few days have been on everyone. "Nico turned up to his first exam."

All the air rushes out of my lungs.

Fuck. I hadn't even considered...

"Oh no, do not give me that look," she warns, able to see the guilt that's written across my face.

"He was already struggling. He's going to fail because of me."

"No, he's not."

"How can you—"

"Have some faith, Brianna. He had a kick-arse teacher," she teases.

"Hardly. The only thing he was studying during our sessions was my pussy."

"As it should be."

"I'm serious. I'll never forgive myself if—"

"It wasn't your fault. You didn't call the bellend over and ask to be his fucking prisoner."

"The bellend?" I ask, choosing to ignore the rest of her comment.

"Nico nicknamed him a while ago, apparently. Suits him, don't you think?"

"No," I argue. "It's not strong enough. The things he did, Jojo. The things he said," I start, shaking my head as I continue to struggle to blend the Brad I knew before with the psychopath I was forced to endure over the past week.

"Do you want to talk about it?" Jodie offers.

I hang my head, not even sure where I would really start. But after a few seconds, my lips part and words just start spilling out. And before long, I've told my best friend almost everything about what I went through.

She listens to it all and doesn't once let go of my hand.

I appreciate the fuck out of it.

"So Nico thinks he knows who your dad actually is?" she asks when I finally get to what happened before she arrived.

"Seems that way. And he wasn't happy about it."

"Can it really be that bad? I mean, look at us. We're practically in the fucking mafia, babe."

"Yeah, it could be worse."

"That guy out there isn't going to let you out of his sight

for the rest of your life. And if this man is a threat in any kind of way, then he'll be six feet under before you know it."

"After all these years, I don't think I want a father," I confess. "I mean, I did pretty good without parents, right?" She nods eagerly. "Why would I need any now?"

"You don't. But you want answers, don't you?"

Do I? If the man who gave me half my DNA turns out to be anything like the man I just escaped from, then I think I'd rather not know.

"You might have family out there. Siblings."

"You're romanticising it," I mutter.

"Maybe. But this doesn't need to be a bad thing."

"I don't need family. I've got all I could need here."

I reach for her other hand and squeeze tightly.

"Nothing wrong with having more people on your team."

"I'm more concerned about having more against me. This could open a massive bag of worms. If what Brad said is true, then Mum ran with me. She was actively trying to hide me. I'm not sure anyone I'm related to is worthy of knowing."

"Yeah, you've got a point."

Silence falls between us as my mind spins with all the unknowns.

All I do know is that I trust Nico. And if he thinks this needs looking into before telling me what he suspects, then I'm going to let him.

"Jojo?" I say after a long silence. "I need a favour."

"Name it. I got you."

After we've eaten the entire box of pastries between us, I put a brave face on and follow Jodie out of Nico's bedroom.

As much as I want to continue hiding, I know I can't.

I refuse to allow that dick to take more from me than he already has.

He's locked up and can no longer hurt me. I have no reason to hide or cower.

While his days might be numbered, I've got a whole life to lead.

But before Jodie and I enter the main living area, Nico's voice makes my steps falter. Reaching out, I grab her hand, forcing her to stop.

"I thought you looked into her. You said you had no idea who her father was," he snaps.

"I did a background check and ran her DNA against our database to find out if she was Cirillo. I didn't run her fully. That would have been an invasion of privacy," Theo points out, making my brows lift.

Really, I'm not all that shocked they looked into me. Although, it does piss me off that they'd gone to those lengths and Nico still claimed to not trust me.

I know now that that was more of a him issue than it was a me issue. But still.

"Did you know about this?" I whisper to Jodie.

"Not in so many words."

"Bit fucking late to worry about that. You need to run it; we need to know if that prick is telling the truth."

"Surely not," Toby says. "It has to be some other Harris."

"Let's hope, huh?"

Not willing to miss out on wherever this conversation is leading, I march forward.

"Did you actually want some DNA from me this time?

Or are you going to steal it, like I assume you did the first time?"

Three guilty faces all turn toward me as I grace them with my presence.

"Babe, please don't be pissed. We need to—"

"I get it," I say, stepping into Nico's open arms. "I'd just rather know about it. What else do you know about me that you're keeping hidden?" I accuse, narrowing my eyes at Theo.

"Nothing. I swear," he says, holding his hands up in defence.

Silence falls around us.

"It's good to see you up and about, Bri," Toby says, wrapping his arms around Jodie.

I have so many things I want to ask them.

Is Brad in enough pain? What's happening with Mum? Who the hell are the Harrises? But all of those questions remain stuck on the end of my tongue.

The silence is soon shattered, though, when both Nico and Theo's phones ping simultaneously.

They glance at each other before pulling their phones from their pockets and staring down at them.

Unable to look anywhere else, I glance down at his screen.

Jocelyn: Kállos. Right now.

"That's your mum's spa, isn't it?" I ask

"Yeah, it is. Are you going to be okay if we—"

"Yes, go," I encourage. If Jocelyn needs him for something, then he needs to go.

His phone lights up again as Theo replies to say that they're on their way.

"Toby will stay."

"It's okay," I assure him. "Go."

"I'll get Daemon to come up, then. The others are in exams."

"Nico, it's okay. We're okay."

Releasing him, I rest my back against the counter, letting him go and do what he needs to do.

But despite the woman who's been more of a mother than the one who actually gave birth to him needing him, he still looks utterly torn.

He sucks in a deep breath, threading his fingers through his hair and pulling until it has to hurt.

"Fuck. I promised I wouldn't leave you," he says quietly.

"Nico," I say, stepping up to him and running my hands up his bare chest. "You need to go. Jocelyn needs you. I'll be right here with Jodie."

"Yeah, okay. Shit. Yeah."

Finally, he takes a step back and then disappears down the hall.

"What do you think she wants?" Jodie muses.

"With any luck, Cassandra has had a tragic accident," Toby mutters as Theo gets ready to leave.

"We're due some luck," he adds.

Nico is back in no more than three minutes and wearing a black hoodie and trainers.

"Here, take this," he says, thrusting a gun into my hands.

"What?" I shriek. "I don't need this. What the hell?"

"Please, babe. It'll make me feel better."

"We're in one of the most fiercely protected buildings in the city," Jodie says, repeating a fact we were told numerous times since the Italian attack.

"Okay," I say, sensing that he won't leave without my agreement.

"Daemon and the others have access, but do not answer the door to anyone."

"We mean it this time," Toby warns.

"Hey, we didn't open the door the last time. That was all Stella," Jodie argues.

"We'll be fine," I say, wrapping my free hand around the back of his neck and lifting up on my toes so I can kiss him.

"Be good," he warns against my lips.

"As if I'd be anything else."

"Love you, Siren."

"Love you too. Now go, Jocelyn needs you."

"We're going," Theo announces, wrapping his hand around Nico's upper arm and physically dragging him away from me.

It would be funny if the pained expression on Nico's face didn't exist.

'I love you,' I mouth just before he disappears around the corner.

"Well," Jodie sings happily. "If there was any doubt before that you own that guy's balls, then he's just confirmed he's handed them over to you with a bow on."

18

———

NICO

By the time I pull up outside Mum's spa, I'm white-knuckling the steering wheel and my heart is racing.

I didn't want to leave Brianna, but I want to leave her in favour of my mother even less. She doesn't deserve any of my time or attention, but my girl does.

But, if Jocelyn thinks we need to be here, then... here we are.

Theo and Toby have talked most of the way here, trying to figure out what's going on. I've ignored them.

I'm not interested in gossip. I want to get this over with and get back to my girl where I should be.

"Come on," I bark the second I pull up at the curb outside and kill the engine.

I can't see Mum's car, or anyone else's I recognise as I scan the busy street.

I'm at the entrance, taking in the closed state of the place long before two car doors close behind me.

"It's shut," Toby announces.

"Well done, Sherlock," I mutter, pressing my hand to the scanner to grant us entry.

There's a part of me that thinks it'll decline me, that Mum has kicked me this far out of her life, but I'm wrong, and the little light quickly flashes green.

Silence greets us as we step inside. There's no perfectly presented woman giving us her best fake smile and then pushing her tits up and pouting her lips as she discovers who's just walked in.

There's just nothing.

"I guess we're heading up," I say, marching toward the lift.

We might own this building, but Mum only has the entrance and the two floors a little higher up. The rest is for other things with separate access.

As we climb higher, my irritation levels grow.

I trust Jocelyn, but my faith is already waning on my need to be here.

Although, that all changes when the doors open to the main spa entrance and we spill out toward the woman in question.

Her eyes find mine. Soft, gentle eyes that have always filled me with comfort. But right now, they're hard set, determined in a way I'm not sure I've ever seen before, and it makes something uncomfortable stir in my stomach.

"I'm sorry," she says, taking a step toward us. "But you need to see this."

My brows pinch as I stare at her.

"Come on," she encourages before spinning on her heels and marching through a set of double doors that lead to the main spa and the offices.

"Well, go on then," Theo barks when I don't make a move to follow.

The place is deathly quiet aside from our footsteps as we trail Jocelyn.

Eventually, she turns and pushes the security door open. We slip inside behind her, finding the computer screens illuminated and the footage from one of the rooms paused on one.

"What's going on?" Theo asks.

"After you were at the house last week," Jocelyn starts, keeping her eyes trained on me, "I started getting suspicious. While that was the first time I'd ever seen him come to the house alone, it made me think of a few things that weren't quite right. So I started following her."

"Who?" Toby asks, while I'm rendered speechless.

"Cassandra."

"Who was at the house?" Theo asks.

"Christos," I mutter, thinking back to that night.

As I stood there in front of both of them, I smelled a rat, but then with everything that happened, I easily pushed it aside.

"Everything seemed okay, and I didn't want to bother you with it while you were trying to find Brianna, but then—"

"They're fucking, aren't they?" I snap, making Jocelyn's cheeks redden.

"Yes. But that isn't the worst of it."

She gestures toward the screen, and I mindlessly take a step closer.

Jocelyn leans forward and presses play.

We only have to wait two seconds before the door to the treatment room opens and two recognisable figures walk in.

I'm expecting them to say something, but there are no words. Instead, they stare at each other until the door is closed behind them, and then they both pounce.

"Jesus, J. Did I really need to see this?" I ask, desperately trying to look away but failing.

"Yes," she confirms.

"I missed you," Mum purrs, making quick work of unbuttoning Christos's shirt. "Where have you been? What's going on?"

"Cassie," he groans as she pulls his shirt free from his trousers and runs her hand down to his waistband.

Bile swims in the depth of my stomach.

Everything in me screams to stop watching. Listening will be more than enough. But I can't seem to rip my eyes away from the car crash playing out before me.

"Oh fuck," Theo grunts, sounding almost as horrified as I feel as my fucking mother drops to her knees in front of Jerome's father. His married father.

Thankfully, the camera angle stops this from turning into a full-on porno, but there's no mistaking what's going on.

"B-been busy out looking for Nico's girl," Christos manages to grit out as Mum... well...

My eyes almost pop out of my head when Mum scoffs, "Idiot."

I have no idea if she's talking about me or Brianna, but I see red.

"Where the fuck is she?" I growl, my body trembling with the need to wrap my hands around her throat and never let go.

Brianna is more of a woman than she's ever been.

She's more loving, caring, compassionate—

"Keep it together, man," Toby says, wrapping his hand around my shoulder.

"Are you fucking watching and listening to the same shit I am?" I bark, barely able to continue with this bullshit.

"Where are they?" I seethe. "Are they still here?"

"No, they left."

"Fucking good job, too," Theo snaps before his palms land on my chest, shoving me back a few steps.

I bare my teeth, ready to go at him over this.

"Calm the fuck down. Jocelyn hasn't called you here to hurt you. She's not your fucking mother," he hisses.

It's not until we've glared at each other for a few seconds that I realise the small room around us is silent apart from our heaving breaths.

"It's them, isn't it? They're our leak," I state. I don't even know why I'm asking the question; it's fucking obvious.

Ripping my eyes from Theo's, I find Jocelyn standing awkwardly in front of the screen where my mother is frozen mid-blow job.

Fucking whore.

My fists curl at my sides before I barge around Theo and hit play. We're here, might as well get the whole experience.

"They've got her," Christos pants. "Their attention is about to turn back to the Italians."

"Not for long," Mum confesses, making my blood run cold.

Christos's grip on her hair tightens as she continues what she's doing, and in an embarrassingly short time, he finds the end, roaring out my fucking mother's name loud enough to wake the dead.

"I'm going to be sick," I mutter.

"Wait," Jocelyn says.

"Ricardo has a meeting with a supplier tonight. This is going to end. And we're going to get everything we've been waiting for."

Unease flickers through Christos's post-orgasm face, but Mum catches it before it can take hold.

"It's what we've always dreamed of, baby. No more being no one. Over there, we'll be someone."

"What a load of horse shit," Theo barks, kicking something behind me.

"Where are they now?"

"Christos has gone home. Your mother..." Jocelyn swallows nervously.

"Where is she, J?" I ask, trying to keep my anger at bay. None of this is her fault, and as fucking mortified as I might be after watching that, I'm glad she showed me and didn't just try and describe it.

Pulling her phone from her pocket, she wakes it up, briefly glances at the screen and then passes it over.

Theo and Toby crowd around behind me.

"That's an Italian hotel," Toby points out.

"She's with Ricardo," I surmise. "You tracked her?"

"Both of them."

Silence falls around us as everything we've just witnessed settles in our heads.

"She's playing him, isn't she?" Theo muses.

"I assume so, yes," Jocelyn agrees. "He's your leak. She's been sucking the intel out of him."

"Literally," Toby deadpans.

"So fucking gross," I mutter.

"And she's been taking it straight back."

"Okay, so say she is with Ricardo and we have his location. What do we do now? Hit it, or wait for this supplier meeting tonight?"

"Both," Theo says, pulling his phone from his pocket. "Where are you?" he barks the second the call connects.

There's a deep rumbling on the other end that I can

only assume belongs to Uncle Damien before Theo instructs, "Call a meeting. Now," and hangs up as if he's not talking to one of the most notorious gang leaders in the city. "Jocelyn, is there any more we need to know?"

"Screw that, she's coming with us. I've got a million questions."

"There's more of this footage. Nothing else as good as this, though. I'm sorry I had to drag you here, I just didn't know how to get this to you."

"You're amazing, J," I assure her as both Theo and Toby descend on the computer.

"We'll just pull this off and head in. "We're getting this motherfucker tonight."

"What about Cassandra and Christos?" Jocelyn asks.

"Don't worry, we'll ensure all the rubbish is collected and disposed of efficiently."

Jocelyn's eyes shoot to mine at Theo's words, but if she thinks she's going to find any argument in my angry depths over this, then she's going to be disappointed.

As far as I'm concerned, my mother is already long dead.

All of this has been her fault. Right now, I don't even care about her reasons for what she's done. I just want her gone and to be able to put all this behind us.

I'm never going to get my dad back, and while that still rips me apart, I can't deny it's getting easier to deal with. Or that might just be Brianna's influence.

Letting the guys do their IT geek thing, I take a step closer to her.

"You're something else, J," I confess, pulling her in for a hug. "Where did you get the tracking devices from?"

"I spoke to Damien, told him our concerns, and he tasked me to find the evidence we needed."

"He trusted you with that?" I don't mean for it to come out sounding quite as condescending as it does. "Shit, I didn't mean—"

"It's okay. Nico," she says with a sigh, her eyes finally drifting from mine.

"What is it?"

"All I've done since I started working for your parents is protect both you and Calli in any way I could."

"What aren't you saying, J?"

"Damien... he..."

"Spit it out, J," Theo adds with a laugh without taking his eyes from the screen.

"He never trusted your mother. Me, and your previous housekeepers and nannies were all hired by the Family—by Damien—and tasked to keep a very close eye on what was going on in your house."

"Seriously?"

Jocelyn shrugs. "Just doing my job."

"I can't believe—"

"You have no fucking idea how much we appreciate it, J," Toby says, getting up and wrapping an arm around her shoulder.

"Let's go set this plan into action."

With the security footage safe, and Jocelyn huddled protectively between the three of us, we make our way outside and to my car.

"I can drive," Jocelyn argues. "My car is in the next street—"

"No," I bark. "We'll get someone to pick it up."

Jocelyn's eyes widen at the harshness of my demand, but fuck letting her go off alone right now.

Throwing my arm around her shoulder, I tuck her small body into my side.

"You don't work for my parents anymore, J. You work for me, and I fully intend to treat you like the queen you are."

"Nico," she giggles.

"In you get, your highness," I say, pulling the back door of my car open for her.

"You're an idiot," she whispers happily as she climbs in.

"Boss, you're driving." I throw my keys at Theo and slide in beside Jocelyn.

I should be pissed, fucking livid at how this has turned out. But I'm weirdly calm.

"I hope you know that I never in my entire life wanted to watch my mother give anyone a blow job."

"All the shit you've seen and done and that is the thing that's going to scar you for life?" Toby jokes from the passenger seat.

"How the fuck would you feel if you just watched your mum on her knees for Galen," I tease back.

"Nico, do we have to?" Jocelyn begs.

"Sorry, J. But you have to confess to starting this. The audio of that footage would have been more than adequate."

Sitting back, I catch Theo's eyes in my rear-view mirror. "You okay?"

Sure, there's plenty of anger bubbling up inside right now. But mostly, I kinda feel like the final few pieces of my broken jigsaw puzzle have just been slotted into place.

Something has been off with Mum for ages. Long before we lost Dad. We were all too distracted to notice.

I'm sure we can all look back and see signs that we missed. But honestly, what's the fucking point?

It's done. Dad is gone, and no number of what-ifs or should-haves is going to bring him back. I've got Brianna where she should be, and as long as we deliver on the promise we made Luciana Rivera by wiping out Ricardo and his twisted bunch of supporters, then we might just be able to move forward from all this.

We've had enemies hanging over us all fucking year, and I don't know about anyone else, but I am fucking done.

Done.

"Yeah, man. I'm good. We're finishing this tonight, then I'm going home to my fucking girl."

"You know," Jocelyn says, "there's going to be an empty house up for grabs. History states it's the underboss's house."

Images that I never ever thought would fill my head immediately emerge. Brianna and I cooking together in that massive kitchen, chilling out in the family room with our feet up on the sofa like Calli and I were never allowed to do. I think about us in the master bedroom that looks out over the land beyond while fucking her over the balcony before my thoughts take an even more serious turn.

Would our kids have her blue eyes and curly hair, or my darker features?

"Are you okay? All the blood just drained from your face," Toby asks, twisting around in his seat with a smug-as-fuck grin on his face.

"Fuck you," I hiss before turning to Jocelyn. "We'll see. I might decide to burn it to the ground yet."

"That's your legacy; you wouldn't dream of it."

Fuck's sake. Why is she always right?

Our phones all ding a few minutes later when Uncle Damien calls the troops in. If he's spoken to Jocelyn, then I can only assume he has an idea of what's going on.

"Why didn't you say anything sooner?" I say quietly.

"You needed to focus on Brianna. Anyway, I can more than handle your mother."

"You know, I think we may have underestimated you."

She chuckles to herself. "My darling husband taught me a few things over the years."

"He was a soldier, wasn't he?"

"One of the best." She smiles softly as she remembers. "You know, you remind me a lot of him. He had your passion. Your wit."

"Ah, so he was funny too."

"She said wit, Nico. Nothing about you actually being funny," Toby adds.

"How is she?" Jocelyn asks when our banter comes to a stop once more.

"I think... I think she's going to be okay. I'm going to talk to Jade though, see if she'll speak with her."

"You're right, you do underestimate me."

"You've already done it," I guess.

"Sure have. You just need to ring her."

"Why weren't you our mother, J?" I ask, and not for the first time.

"What? Ruin my figure and the ability to control my bladder for you? Pfft. You're not that special, Mr. Cirillo."

"Now who's the funny one."

Theo drives us to the underground car park beneath The Empire, and not two seconds after we step out of the car do Seb and Alex pull in next to us.

"How was the exam?" Toby asks when they join us.

"It was an exam," Seb mutters. "What's going on?"

"Auntie Cassandra has been getting on her knees for the wrong man," Theo states before marching forward, leaving Seb and Alex speechless.

19

BRIANNA

As promised, Daemon turned up for babysitting duties only minutes after Nico, Theo and Toby left.

It wasn't necessary, but I also wasn't going to argue.

I might have encouraged Nico to go and find out what Jocelyn wanted, but I can't lie; I wasn't all that happy about watching him walk out the front door.

I'm not sure what I really expected of Daemon. I guess, at least a question or two about what I'd been through. Since he's got with Calli, he's been much more laid-back and approachable. But we soon discovered that he wasn't up for much chit-chat when he fell onto the sofa and pulled his phone out. He really was there just for security.

Jodie and I soon fell into our own world, forgetting that he was even there until he popped his head up about an hour later to let us know that Calli was out of her exam and heading home.

The second she's inside Nico's flat, she's practically running toward me.

"Bri," she cries before her small body collides with mine.

Her arms wrap around me tightly, refusing to release me in case I up and vanish again.

"Please, never do that to me or Nico again," she whispers in my ear.

"I'll really try," I say with a laugh.

"I'm serious, Bri. I've never seen Nico like he was last week. He was a fucking mess."

"He's always a mess."

"Not like that. It was... it was different. He loves you so fucking hard, Bri. I really hope he's told you that."

I can't help but smile at her. "He has."

All the air comes rushing out of her lungs as her eyes widen in shock.

"He has?" she asks in disbelief.

"Yeah. He's been amazing."

"Uh... I hate to break up this little... whatever," Daemon says, pushing to the edge of the sofa, his eyes locking on Calli.

"Shit, sorry, devil boy," Calli says with a wince before hopping over and giving him some love.

"That wasn't what I meant, but I'm not complaining," he teases when she finally lets him up for air.

"What's wrong?" Calli asks, able to read into Daemon's black expression.

"They've found the leak and Ricardo."

My heart jumps into my throat, fear and excitement exploding in my stomach.

"Seriously? This is going to be over?"

"Yeah."

"What?" Calli asks, narrowing her eyes at her boyfriend.

"Uh..."

"Just spit it out," Calli snaps. "Nothing can be worse than what we've all lived through in the past few weeks."

"It's your mum, Angel."

"What is?" she asks, not following. Although Jodie seems to be, if the look she just shot me says anything.

"The leak."

"No," she breathes, hopping up from Daemon's lap in shock. "She wouldn't. She... she killed Dad?"

"I'm sorry, Angel."

Calli drops her head into her hands as she tries to process this new information.

"She's been hooking up with Christos. She—"

"Who?" I ask, unfamiliar with that name.

"Jerome's dad."

"Oh. And he's married, right?"

"Angel," Daemon breathes, stepping up to Calli when her shoulders begin to shake. "W-wha—"

My eyes narrow on the pair of them, but I quickly discover why Daemon is so confused, because Calli isn't crying. She's laughing. Hysterically.

"Baby, what's going on?" he asks, dipping lower to look into her eyes.

She shakes her head, wiping the tears from her eyes.

"Y-you should go," she tells him. "They're going to need you."

He shakes his head. "They instructed me to stay put for now. Are you okay? What's so funny?"

"All of this," Calli says, throwing her arms out. "All of this. Because of her. Why didn't we see it earlier? Who even is she, Daemon? Who is the woman who brought me into the world? And what made her turn on those she was meant to love?"

"I have no idea, Angel. Hopefully, we'll get a chance to find out." Dark intent flickers through his eyes, and I can't help but wonder if Calli will allow him to do what he does best where her mother is concerned.

I might have no issue with him going full-on devil with Brad. But I might have to at least think twice about him doing the same to my mother, even if she is a useless piece of shit.

"Do what you've got to do. The world is a better place without her," Calli says coldly, making Daemon's brows shoot up.

Out of his depth, he glances up at me.

All I can do is shake my head. If this is how Calli feels right now, then there's no point in convincing her otherwise.

Silence falls around us as the weight of Daemon's words continues to settle over us.

"Are you going to be okay if I pop out quickly?" Jodie asks.

"No, you need to stay put," Daemon says, and I almost agree, until Jodie's eyes catch mine and I understand what she's going for.

"Have you still got security?" I ask.

"Yep. More, in fact. There's an entire team in and around this building right now. I'll take two with me."

"Jodie," Daemon growls.

"Calli, do what you need to do to distract him for a few, yeah? I'll even take this," she says, picking up Nico's gun and tucking it into the back of her jeans like a bad-arse.

Taking one for the team, not that she needs all that much convincing, Calli shoves Daemon down on the sofa and quickly straddles his lap.

Jodie and I both laugh as he quickly forgets his own

name let alone what we're doing when Calli steals his lips in a filthy kiss.

"I won't be long," Jodie says as I follow her toward the front door. "Straight there and straight back."

"Thank you."

"Anything, you know that."

She pulls me in for a quick hug before slipping out of the flat with the promise of being back with what I need.

My heart is in my throat as I watch her go, but I need this.

When I get back into the living room, Calli is dry-humping Daemon on the sofa.

I shamelessly watch them for a few minutes, my blood heating with every moan and groan that falls from either of them.

"You two sure know how to give Seb and Stella a run for their money," I mutter, convinced they won't hear a word I say.

"Not every day I get to tarnish Nico's sofa," Calli says with a laugh as she kisses down Daemon's neck.

"Cal, did you mean what you said about your Mum?" I ask, aware that I'm throwing a bucket of ice-cold water on their little make-out session.

"Yeah," she agrees without missing a beat. "I made peace with the fact she's no longer going to be a part of my life a while ago. I've got more important things to focus on now."

I nod.

"Why?"

"Do you have questions about it all?"

"Yes and no." She twists around so she's sitting across Daemon's lap and focusing on me instead of straddling him. Much to his irritation.

My eyes drop to her stomach as she presses her hand protectively against it.

"I'm not sure I'll ever be able to understand anyone who allowed others to hurt their children, or the man they love."

I nod, understanding exactly what she's saying.

"Daemon, would you be able to do something for me?" I ask.

"S-sure," he grunts, his voice raspy with desire.

I pause, questioning what I'm about to ask of him.

My hands tremble, but unlike Calli, I need answers, even if I don't like them.

"My mother is in the basement, right?"

He nods slowly and reluctantly.

"Could you take me down to her?"

"Bri," he warns. "I'm under strict instructions."

"Please. I need..." I trail off. Honestly, I have no idea what I need. But I kinda hope that looking her in the eye and trying to get some answers might be it.

"Fine. But you can explain it to Nico if they get back here and he loses his shit that you've gone."

"I'll leave a note," I reassure him. "And we won't be long. I might even pussy out before we get there."

"You sure you want to do this?" Calli asks.

"Yes," I state, pushing to my feet before I change my mind.

Before Jodie gets back and hands me the pill I've sent her out for, I need to look the woman who gave birth to me in the eye and get some answers.

"Well, this place is just about as creepy as I was expecting," I mutter as I follow Daemon and Calli down to the level below the basement gym.

If you didn't know the entrance existed, you'd never find it. There's no way I would have if I had tried to do this alone.

The air changes as we descend a set of stairs. It turns cold, and a scent familiar to a sterile hospital fills my nose.

"Welcome to my favourite place in the world," Daemon says with a devilish grin playing on his lips.

"Huh, weird, because I thought that was Calli's pussy."

The girl in question gasps in shock, while Daemon's smirk gets wider.

"Oh, how life changes," he muses, pulling his girl into his side and kissing the top of her head. "I could spend the rest of my days inside you, Angel, and die one very happy man."

"Well, that's just..."

"Love," I sigh teasingly.

Calli's lips part to argue, but one look at me and she seems to forget what she was about to say.

"You're in love with my brother and he's all kinds of vulgar, so there's really no point in commenting, is there?"

"Jesus Christ," I mutter under my breath. "I'm in love. With your brother."

"Honestly, it was about time you figured it out," Daemon helpfully supplies.

"Wow, romance advice from the devil himself. What is the world coming to?" I tease.

It's easier to focus on our meaningless banter than it is to think about what we're really doing, and where we're going.

But with each step I take, that avoidance is getting harder and harder to achieve.

I did this. I demanded he bring me down here.

While we were in the safety of Nico's fancy penthouse, it seemed like a good idea.

But as we pass door after door, I'm starting to wonder if my life would have been just fine without exploring their little torture chamber in the basement.

My eyes linger on each dark grey door, as if I'll be able to see behind them if I look hard enough.

"Are there people in every one of these?" I ask, although I'm not entirely sure I'm prepared for the answer.

"No. Things are pretty quiet right now, which, given the circumstances, is surprising. I was getting a little bored, so I'm glad you brought me some new pets."

Panic floods my veins and my mouth runs away with me before I've even realised what I'm thinking.

"Tell me you're not hurting my mother." I spin around, giving Daemon little choice but to stop.

"I thought you hated her," he states, his eyes cold and his expression unreadable.

His words spin around in my head.

"I-I do. She was a shitty mother. But that doesn't mean I want you... doing what you do."

"Well, that's good then. She's one of my most comfortable guests down here."

"And... Brad?" I whisper.

"Oh." An evil smile tugs at the corners of Daemon's lips. "He's getting my very, very best treatment."

"Good."

"If you listen really hard, you can probably hear him crying out for his own mother."

A shudder rips through me as images from my past with a man I thought was a decent person play out like a movie.

As far as I was concerned, his biggest fault was that he was dull as fuck.

Who'd have thought that he'd turn out to be one of the most interesting people I've ever met?

Unable to deal with him and everything he's done to me, I force any thoughts of him aside.

"Where is she?" I ask.

"Just behind that door," Daemon says, pointing behind me.

Stepping out from his side, Calli closes the space between us and takes my hand.

"You don't have to do this. She's not going anywhere. There's time."

"No. I need..." I trail off, because honestly, I have no fucking clue what I need.

Releasing her, I step closer to the door but quickly stop when I realise I can't do anything more.

"It's okay. I permitted your handprint access to her cell," Daemon informs me. "You can come down here at any time. And if you decide to let her go, that's your decision too."

My lips open and close like a fish.

I'm not sure I like that amount of power on my shoulders.

"And if I don't want to let her go?"

"Then she stays. You want her dead, just say the word."

Unable to say anything in response to that, I just nod and turn my back on both of them.

Lifting my hand, I hold it just an inch away from the scanner.

Do I even want to do this? Look this woman in the eyes after everything she's done to ruin my life?

But did she?

If what Brad told me was true and she ran with me, changed my identity, was she protecting me all along?

Fucking hell, my head is a mess.

Forcing myself to do something before I overthink everything, I press my hand against the black panel. My stomach knots the second the red light flashes green and a series of locks disengage.

"We'll be right out here," Calli says softly as I reach for the handle and push the door open.

The cell is pretty much what I expected. Small, sterile, bare. Hell.

The walls are cold and grey. There's a bed in one corner and toilet and sink in the other, and very little else. Although, it's easy to see the evidence of Mum's more comfortable stay.

"Brianna," she breathes as I step inside.

Flipping the thick duvet from her body, she pushes from the pillow she was resting her head on.

"Oh my God," she sobs. "You're okay. Th-they told me th-th-that you were b-but—"

Slowly, she pushes to her feet and takes a step toward me.

But I'm frozen. Completely fucking frozen.

"I know that nothing I can say can fix anything, but I'm sorry, Brianna. I truly am. For everything."

"You're sober," I state, the only thing I can focus on at this moment.

"Yeah. I had been for a while. Life was good. I was getting back on track. I had a job. A boyfriend. I was stronger than I'd ever been. And then *he* stumbled into my life."

I stand there staring at her, unable to decide if I can believe a word that comes out of her mouth.

"Please, Brianna. I know this is hard. Trust me, I do. But let me try and explain."

I hold her tired eyes for a few seconds before looking back. I find Calli and Daemon right there.

"They can listen too. It's time everyone knew what really happened."

Sensing that I'm on the edge, Calli steps into the room and takes my hand in hers.

"Maybe we should wait for Jodie or Nico for this," she whispers in my ear.

I suck in a deep breath, trying to find some courage to hear my mother out after all these years.

"No, it's okay."

I squeeze her fingers, silently letting her know that she's not going anywhere as two chairs appear behind us.

I lower myself down almost in a daze before Daemon takes up his place as a bodyguard at the door once more.

"I just need to know one thing," I say, holding her eyes and praying I'm about to finally get the truth. "Who is my father?"

20

NICO

Theo reaches out, taking his phone back from the boss's desk after letting everyone hear the audio from the video Jocelyn had captured.

"Well," Uncle Damien says, resting back in his chair and cracking his knuckles. "I'd like to say I'm surprised but—"

"Why didn't you look into her before?" Galen snaps from beside him.

"I have."

"Jocelyn said you've had all our housekeepers watching her over the years."

"Yes. Before you were even born, I was suspicious. But I never found anything to back up my gut feeling, so I was forced to ignore it. Your father loved her beyond belief, and without anything to prove my suspicions correct, there was nothing I could do."

"You think she's always been trying to bring us down?" I ask, my brows knitting together.

"Honestly, no. Over the past year, even your father admitted to me that something was different with her."

"This is all well and good, but what are we going to do about it?" Stefanos snaps, clearly pissed off.

I get it. He's been working on this for months, and he's just been outsmarted by our sweet and loyal housekeeper. Must sting.

I wanted Jocelyn to come to this meeting with us. She deserves the praise for this. But the second we emerged on the top floor of this building, she point-blank refused. So instead of being in here, planning the demise of our traitors, she's outside in the security office having coffee and cake with our soldiers who are on shift.

"That's up to Nico," Uncle Damien responds, making my head spin.

"Me?" I blurt.

"For your dad. For our future."

I sit there speechless for a few seconds, but the moment Theo reaches out and claps me on the shoulder, I jump into action, planning out a three-pronged attack on the Italians tonight. One which, thankfully, everyone in the room agrees with.

"Right, you heard him. Galen, Stefanos, you have soldiers to organise. Get out of here."

The men standing behind Uncle Damien share a look, but they're not brave enough to say anything and quickly leave the room, following orders.

"They looked pleased," Alex quips the second the door closes, making Seb snort in amusement.

"We're building our future," Uncle Damien states. "And the six of you are it. I remember the day your father first took charge over your grandfather," he says, his eyes focused on Alex. "Your grandfather was formidable, but I'd never seen him quite that angry before."

I glance over just in time to see Alex swallow almost nervously.

"Obviously, your father did a fantastic job thanks to all the training your grandfather had put him through. But power shifting is never easy for those who will eventually begin to step down."

Uncle Damien's eyes find Theo's for a few seconds before they return to me once more.

"I have every confidence in the six of you. Our Family is going to be in safe hands when your time comes. But until then, you've all got jobs to do.

"Nico has given his orders. Get moving, soldiers."

"Boss," I state, nodding once and pushing from my chair.

I wait for Theo to stand and then fall into step behind the others as they move toward the door.

"Nico, wait," Uncle Damien calls before I leave the room.

Looking back over my shoulder, I hold his stare.

"I'm proud of you, son. Your father would be too."

I try to fight the huge ball of emotion that crawls up my throat.

He's right, I'm sure Dad would be proud. But at what cost? We're about to wipe the woman he spent his entire life loving from the face of the Earth for trying to destroy us.

Maybe that's why that night ended the way it did. He would never have been able to do what needs to be done in light of all this.

He loved her too much.

And honestly, I can't really fault him for that. Despite appearances, he had a huge heart and was as soft as a teddy bear.

It's something I'd never want to change about him. I just hope I can embrace some of it, keep his legacy going.

"Thank you, Boss. For everything."

I step out of the room, letting the door close behind me and cutting off anything he might have to say to that.

Theo, Toby, Seb, and Alex are right there waiting for me.

"He's right, man. He'd be so fucking proud of you," Theo says.

"We're proud of you," Alex adds, launching himself on me and wrapping both his arms and legs around me.

"Get off me, you fucking moron."

"You love it really," he teases as I manage to shove him off me.

"If I ever decide to bat for the other team, I'll let you know," I say, watching as his eyes almost pop out of his head. His lips part to say something, but I cut him off. "But right now, I need my girl, and then we've got a war to win."

"Hell yeah. Get laid then go shed some Italian blood. Sounds like the perfect fucking night to me," Seb announces like the pest he is just as Jocelyn joins us.

"Shut the fuck up, man," Toby barks, smacking him around the head, making J smile.

She's more than aware of what we're like.

The guys are still ribbing each other as we step into the lift, but my phone buzzing in my pocket distracts me from their banter.

Daemon: We're in the basement. Bri wanted to see her mum.

"The fuck," I bark, turning everyone's eyes on me.

"What's wrong?"

"Nothing," I mumble. "Bri's gone to see Jennifer."

"Didn't we tell them not to fucking leave the flat?" Toby hisses.

"Because your girls always do what they're told," Alex quips.

"You can wipe that smug look off your face, Deimos. One day soon, some pain-in-the-arse woman is going to sideswipe you straight off your feet," Seb barks.

"Fucking like to see her try."

"Oh, bro. We can't fucking wait," Toby joins in.

"How about we just fucking focus on what we're doing instead of being worried about Alex's underused dick," Theo hisses, focusing on the last single guy in our group. "You got hold of Ant yet? We need Enzo and Matteo in on this and waiting at the other side."

"He's not responding," Alex grumbles, looking down at his phone.

"Well, make him," Theo snaps. "I don't care what it takes. We're not fucking anything about tonight up."

"Fucking hell, who made you the boss? I thought this was Nico's plan," Seb says, poking the already angry bear beside me.

"It is," Theo seethes. "And we're going to make sure it runs like fucking clockwork, because he deserves this."

The car ride home is quiet, all of us lost in our own heads over what we've discovered today.

I wanted to take Jocelyn back to the house, but my need to get to Bri is stronger, so I trusted Seb and Alex to deliver her back safely with the promise of catching up with her tomorrow once all of this is over.

The second the car pulls to a stop, I'm out of there and

running toward the hidden entrance to the deepest floor of our building.

I want to be pissed with Daemon for letting her do this without me, but I know better than that.

If Bri decided now was the time for this little heart-to-heart, then there wouldn't have been much that would have stopped her.

As I descend the stairs, soft voices begin to float up to me, making my heart jump into my throat.

I might be relieved that there's no shouting, but that doesn't mean whatever's being said isn't hurting my girl.

Daemon's eyes track me cautiously as I round the bottom of the stairs, and it's not until I nod in greeting that he relaxes slightly.

"I tried to stop her," he says quietly.

"It's good, man. Thanks for the heads-up."

He steps aside, allowing me to see into the room we've put Jennifer in.

I wasn't a part of the decision of what to do with her; I was too busy with Bri when the guys brought her back here. Jodie was the one to demand she gets locked up the same as the other arsehole she came with.

They might have made her stay in a cell a little more comfortable. As far as I know, they haven't hung her from the ceiling like they have the bellend, but it's hardly five-star luxury.

"I didn't have a choice," Jennifer says as I slip into the room.

Calli notices me join them, but Bri is too focused on the woman sitting on the edge of the bed.

"There's always a choice," Bri seethes.

"No. The only choice I had was to keep you safe. If I stayed at home, I would have either been made to abort you, or..." She trails off, tears barely clinging onto her lashes.

"Or what?" Bri snaps, hopping to her feet in frustration. "You promised to tell me everything, yet you're successfully avoiding answering the only question I've asked."

Stepping up behind her, I wrap my arms around her waist and rest my chin on her shoulder.

She startles at first but soon realises it's me.

"It's okay, Siren. I've got you."

I press a kiss to the side of her neck, feeling her thundering pulse beneath her warm skin.

"I know, I'm sorry, I—"

"The truth, Jennifer," I growl. "No matter how hard it is, my girl can handle it."

Jennifer's eyes soften at my words.

"I know she can," she states firmly. "My daughter is a better woman than I've ever been."

"And she deserves the truth."

Jennifer nods. "What Brad told you was true. I met a man when I was thirteen. I was wild, desperate for a way to break free from my boring life. Joanne was out running around town with her bad boy, and I wanted in on the action.

"When he started paying me attention, I forgot all about the age difference, how wrong it was. It didn't feel wrong. He made me feel good, wanted, and desired.

"Obviously, I know now that he wanted it that way. Played on my insecurities. But back then, I fell head over heels in love with him.

"In only weeks, I was so gone for him that I'd have jumped in front of a bus if he told me too. So when things started getting... more serious, I didn't think twice. We were only together a handful of times, but it was enough.

"I might have been naïve, but I wasn't stupid. I knew what I was risking, but I couldn't find it in me to stop it. I figured he was a man who knew what he wanted, and that was me. Me and a future.

"As soon as I missed my period, I knew. Despite being so young, I was excited. I thought it was a new beginning for me. I could get away from my parents and embark on a new life with someone who loved me."

She hangs her head.

"The next few months were... well, I want to say the worst of my life, but things got even worse in the years that followed, as I'm sure Brianna has told you."

"Was he really going to sell me?" Brianna suddenly asks.

Jennifer swallows nervously.

"I waited a long time before I told my parents, to their utter horror. Their first reaction was that I should abort the pregnancy, despite how far gone I already was. I was too young and stupid. But there was no way that was happening. And I wasn't even considering any other option, so I packed a bag and left.

"I had every intention of going to the place he stayed when he was in town and begging for him to look after me. After us.

"But when I reached his place, I found someone else waiting for me. This man was younger and had kind eyes and a gentle smile.

"I was in such a mess that I had no choice but to agree when he promised to take me somewhere safe. I just had no idea that that safe place would be away from *him*.

"This guy told me all this crazy stuff about the man I'd allowed to get me pregnant. He told me all these stories that sounded more like something that should be on the news than a part of my life.

"He told me about this child-trafficking ring that several gangs were involved in both in England and in America.

"I didn't believe it. I point-blank refused. But before long, everything started making sense, and the fear he instilled in me that my unborn child was at risk became so terrifying that I had no choice but to believe him.

"He did everything he could to help me. New identities, a place to live, money. And in return, I did everything he asked of me. I stayed hidden and talked to no one.

"I did everything I should. I looked after you the best I could. He moved us from place to place, never leaving any kind of trail behind.

"Every now and then, he would show me evidence of these gangs at work, and I'd understand the need to do what I was doing.

"I told myself that once you were born, I was just going to take off. As long as we had each other, that we would be okay.

"And that's what I did. Only, it wasn't as easy as I hoped for an almost fifteen-year-old and a baby to make a real go of things. I fucked it all up. But I was terrified. Terrified that they'd find you and take you from me."

"Who was he, Jennifer?" I demand, no longer needing Theo's DNA report to put all this together.

I knew the moment Brianna mentioned it in my bedroom earlier; I just didn't want to believe it.

"For obvious reasons, he didn't go by his real name when he thrust himself into my life. But I later found out that his name is—"

"Victor Harris," a deep voice says from the doorway before Theo joins us with a scowl on his face.

"You knew?" Jennifer gasps.

"Based on the information Brianna gleaned from Brad, yes."

As if she knows how serious this is, Brianna trembles in my arms.

"Who is he?" she whispers.

"He was a gang leader in the US. One of the founders of the trafficking ring," Theo explains.

Brianna's gasp fills the air as everyone else falls silent.

"And that's why Brad wanted me. He thought my blood would bring him the power he craved."

"He was tasked to start finding the children that were a part of this whole thing over the past twenty or so years. When he came across evidence that Victor had another heir out there, the mission turned personal," Jennifer explains.

"He found me first. I had no idea he had an ulterior motive. Like I said, I was finally getting my life together, and I thought finding him was another step toward finding myself a life I could be proud of. My next step was finding you.

"I told him all about you, although not those details we just discussed. As far as I was concerned, I was taking that to my grave. All I ever wanted was for you to be safe and to live a good life, and Joanne and Jodie had allowed that to happen for you. Victor was always going to be a risk, but I hadn't heard anything about it for years, so I naïvely lived in the hope that we'd been forgotten.

"He was so encouraging of us reuniting. I thought it was so sweet of him. If I had any clue then—" Her sob rips through the air.

"Mum," Brianna says, making Jennifer's eyes widen in surprise. "You have really shitty taste in men."

There's a beat of silence as that fact hits us all.

"I mean, she's not wrong," Theo agrees.

"What now?" Calli asks.

"Is this Victor guy a threat?"

"Unlikely," Theo offers.

"He's dead?" Brianna asks.

"Yeah," I confirm.

"Good."

Stepping out of my hold, Brianna moves closer to her mother. Jennifer stands, holding her daughter's eyes.

"Is there anything else we need to know right now that might put mine or any of my family's lives at risk?" Brianna asks fiercely.

Jennifer shakes her head. "No. But there is so much I'd like to talk to you about, if you'd be willing."

Silence falls as they continue studying each other.

Without another word, Brianna spins and faces me. Tears fill her eyes, but she fights them.

"Is there somewhere a little more comfortable Mum can stay?"

"Of course, if that's what you want."

"Keep security on her. I don't want her disappearing until we've heard everything. But this... after what she's been through. It's too much."

"You got it, Siren."

"D and I have got it. You three head back upstairs."

Gathering Bri and Calli in my arms, I lead them away from Jennifer's cell.

"Brianna, wait," she calls before we disappear.

Brianna pauses, but she doesn't look back.

"All I ever wanted was to keep you safe. I'm sorry I failed you."

Sucking in a deep breath, Brianna keeps her eyes on the stairs before us.

"Rest assured, I have people around me who can do a better job. And if you were wondering, this is Nico, my boyfriend."

My chest swells at her words.

Boyfriend. Fuck yeah.

"And he'll kill for me without a second thought if I just say the word. Let's go," she says quieter before taking off again.

None of us speaks until we've climbed the stairs and the lift doors close behind us.

"Well, between us, we've had a pretty shitty experience with mothers," Calli says, her hand slipping to her belly. "My girl is never ever going to doubt how much she's loved and wanted."

"You got that right, Cal," I agree as Brianna tenses beside me. "You doing okay, Siren?"

She nods as I press my lips to her head, but she doesn't say a word, making worry knot up my stomach.

It's really not what I need before heading out on this job.

21

BRIANNA

"Do you want me to make coffee?" Calli asks, beelining for the kitchen the second we're in the flat.

"Sure," I mumble. "I just need a minute."

Twisting out of Nico's hold, I walk toward his bedroom.

It pains me to do it, but I just need... I don't know what I need.

His eyes burn into my back as I try to give myself some space. I hate that I'm worrying him, but I don't know what else to do.

Pulling my phone from my pocket as the door clicks closed behind me, I find a message from Jodie.

> Best Bitch: It's in your handbag. Just please really think this through before you do something you can't reverse.

I blow out a long breath before loving her message and stuffing my phone back in my pocket.

Lowering myself to the bed, I drop my face into my hands and just sit there with my head spinning.

I'm not sure what I expected from seeing my mother, but it certainly wasn't to feel sorry for her.

She's a mess. She'll probably always be a mess. But after being groomed and impregnated at such a young age by a man who's planning on selling your child into a trafficking ring? Yeah, I kinda get how that might screw up even the most stable of kids.

But does that all mean I can find a way to rebuild any kind of relationship with her?

She might think she was trying her best, but that doesn't excuse all the events of my past. The alcohol, the drugs, the men.

I try to remember what it was like to be a lost fourteen-year-old. If I were unlucky, would I have fallen into the exact same trap if some guy showed the right kind of interest?

Thankfully, I don't get to answer that question, because there's a soft knock on the bedroom door before Nico pokes his head inside the room.

"Siren?" he says softly, looking totally out of his comfort zone.

When I don't say anything, he slips into the room and slowly closes the space between us.

The second he's in touching distance, I push to my feet and wrap my arms around him, tucking my face into the warmth of his neck.

"I'm sorry, Nico. You deserve so much better."

He tenses at my words.

"Siren, what are you talking about? You're—"

"Your mum," I whisper. "I'm not talking about me. You're stuck with me whether you deserve better or not," I say teasingly, hoping to lighten the mood a little.

"Fuck her, Bri. I don't care about anyone but the people in this building right now. But mostly, you."

His hand slides up my back until his fingers are twisted in my hair, giving me little choice but to look up at him.

"You still want me with this toxic blood running through my veins?"

"Toxic? Babe, that prick in our basement might have been onto something. What you hold isn't toxic. It's power. And you have no idea."

"I don't want power."

"Maybe not. But you have it. And there are going to be people out there who will bow to you because of it."

"Yeah, no. I'm not down for that."

He chuckles, making me frown.

"What?"

"Babe, you're a Hawk."

"The only thing I am is yours."

His eyes soften and a small smile twitches at his lips.

"I fucking love that, Siren."

Dipping his head, he brushes his lips against mine, and everything I've learned in the past few hours melts away until it's just the two of us again.

He walks me backward until the bed hits my legs, and then he's lowering me down like I'm the most precious thing in his world.

He crawls on top of me, his lips never leaving mine as his hands caress my body, being careful of where he knows hurts most.

His gentle touch brings tears to my eyes once more. I'm so used to him being a brutal and rough lover that anything else throws me for a loop.

I fucking love it, though.

Grabbing my hips, he rolls us, putting me on top.

Slipping my hands under the soft fabric of his t-shirt, I glide my hands over his hard muscles, smiling as they jump and pull beneath my touch.

A deep growl rumbles in his throat as I roll my hips against his already hard length.

Reaching behind his head, he helps me out by dragging his shirt off. He barely even lifts his body from the bed; it's like magic.

"Nico," I cry when he thrusts up, hitting my clit just so.

"Get off on me, Siren. I want to watch you come while you're grinding down on my dick."

My temperature soars at his words as I move faster.

"Gonna need to lose some of this, though."

Releasing my body, he pinches the zip running down the front of my hoodie and drags it down, shoving fabric from my arms.

In a rush, I pull it off so I can get my hands back on his body.

"Can't get enough of you, babe. Your body is... fuck," he groans when I grind harder the second he cups both my breasts in his hands.

A door slams somewhere in his flat before voices float down to us.

"We shouldn't be doing this," I confess breathlessly. It's unconvincing as fuck.

"Fuck that; there isn't anything else we should be doing."

"Nico," I gasp when he sits up before me, dragging my tank down and sucking one of my nipples into his mouth. "Fuck."

"Louder. Make sure they all know not to interrupt us."

"NICO," I scream when he sinks his teeth into my

sensitive flesh, sending a bolt of pain through my body that ends at my aching clit.

"Fucking love watching you fall apart."

He switches to my other breast, his hand working the one he abandoned as I keep grinding, building myself up higher with the help of his glorious dick.

What I really want is him inside me but—

"Please," I beg, my mouth overtaking my brain.

"As if you need to ask."

One second, I'm grinding down on him, the next my sleep shorts are pushed aside and the head of his cock is right there. Right where I need it.

"N-Nico," I whimper, my sensible side almost breaking through.

But then he thrusts up, and I forget about everything but our connection.

The scream that rips from my lips as he impales me on his dick is porn star worthy, and I swear the sound of it only makes him harder.

"Fucking love you, Siren," he grunts out between thrusts.

placing my hands on his broad shoulders, I get some leverage to help him out.

Resting back against his bent legs, I ride him like a pro, taking his cock and rolling my hips so that it hits exactly where I need it.

"Fuck, Siren. Look at you."

Ripping my eyes open, I stare into his dark, lust-blown eyes.

"I need you."

"Not as much as I need you. Should have been doing this since the night we met."

I refrain from pointing out that we pretty much have been and focus on my endgame.

"Come on, babe. I want to watch you shatter like a good little whore. Fuck," he groans when my pussy clenches around him. "You fucking love that, don't you? Being my filthy whore."

"Yes. Yours. Only yours."

"Hell yes. Mine. Fuck whatever surname you've got. The only one you need is mine."

"Yes," I cry, not really registering his words as my orgasm gets within touching distance.

"You want that, Siren? You want to be mine? Forever."

"Yes. Yes. Nico, please. You. Always."

The words fall from my lips as pleas as I finally throw myself off the edge and scream out his name as I crash.

His grip on me tightens as he fucks me through my release.

But he doesn't come with me, and I realise why when I'm done and he practically throws me onto my back, straddling my hips and jerking himself in front of me.

"You're mine, Siren. Fucking always," he roars before hot ropes of cum cover my bare chest.

His head drops back as he rides out his high, and I watch with fascination. He's so fucking beautiful when he loses control.

After long seconds, his eyes find me again before they drop to the sticky mess on my chest.

Reaching out, he begins writing something through his jizz. It takes me a few seconds to figure it out, but the moment I do, my breath catches and my heart rate picks up once more.

Mrs. Cirillo.

After getting up to grab some tissue to clean me with, Nico climbs back onto the bed beside me and pulls me into his warmth.

Silence surrounds us for the longest time as our heart rates return to normal and we cling onto each other for support.

The minutes tick by. Voices continue out in his living room, but no one comes to disturb us, and Nico certainly shows no signs of wanting to go and talk to anyone.

Eventually, though, the thoughts spinning around my head get too much, and I have to break the silence.

"Do you want to talk about it?" I whisper. Despite how quiet I am, his body still startles beneath me.

"Depends which part you're talking about. The one where my mother is a lying, cheating traitor or the fact that my girl is part of one of America's most notorious gangs."

I suck in a breath to respond but quickly discover I don't have much I want to say on either topic right now.

"On second thought, I think I prefer the silence."

Gently, Nico rolls me over, untucking me from his side so he can look at me.

"What do you know about him?" I ask, needing something. "Other than the whole fucked-up gang shit," I add.

Nico thinks for a minute.

"The best person to talk to about all of this would be Stella."

My brows pinch.

"Stella, why?" But as that final word rolls off my tongue, I answer my own question. "That's where she lived."

"Galen was there for a bit, helping out with some stuff."

"She knows them?"

"I don't know, but she'll know of them in a way that none of us do. Everything I know is hearsay and gossip."

I nod, understanding why he's probably not all that willing to tell me whatever he's heard.

"Victor has other kids, though. Boys, as far as I know."

My breath catches. "I have brothers?"

"Yeah, babe. You do. I know all of this is a lot to take, trust me, I do. But whatever you want to do with it all, I just want you to know that I'm here for it, okay? If you want to forget it all, then we'll push it all aside. If you want to embrace it, then I'll be right by your side for that, too."

"Mum said that Brad was sent to find the kids involved in all this. I can't ignore it if someone is out there looking for me." Concern covers Nico's features as he considers my words. "Do we know who's behind this?"

He shakes his head. "We can find out. It's all in the past, so hopefully, it's just someone doing some digging and it's nothing to worry about."

As much as I want to agree with that, I think about our lives. Are we really going to be that lucky?

As the silence stretches between us once more, the frown between Nico's brows gets deeper.

"Talk to me," I beg, reaching out to smooth out his worry line.

"I can't believe it was her. And him. I should have seen this coming. She's been nothing but a cold, heartless cow since Dad died. It should have been obvious."

"No, Nico. This isn't on you," I assure him, hating the way he's beating himself up.

"If I didn't lose myself like I did after that night, maybe I'd have seen—"

Leaning forward, I rest my brow against his.

"Nico, this is her doing. Not yours. She sold you all out, not the other way around."

"She killed him, Siren. That whole night only happened because she told them where we were, what we were doing. The ambush on The Manor was because of them. Christos will have heard where you were, and he told her." His grip on me tightens. "He fucking told her and sent them after you all. What kind of woman does that to her children?"

The sight of the tears filling his eyes rips my heart in two.

For almost all my life, I've asked myself similar questions. What did I ever do to make my mother hate me so much that she'd allow me to barely survive like we did?

I understand his pain more than I can probably ever express, and I feel it just as keenly.

"You didn't do anything," I say, brushing my thumb under his eye when a tear finally falls.

Watching him break is fucking painful, but I'm determined to be everything he needs, to keep him upright even while I'm fighting my own shit.

Separately, we both might fall. But together, we're strong. So fucking strong.

"We're stronger than the women who gave birth to us, Nico. We are not the product of their mistakes. We can do good, so much good, and we can be whoever we want to be despite their influence on our lives.

"Family is so much more than blood. It's loyalty and laughter. It's joint suffering and pain, and holding someone up when they look like they're going to fall. Family is what you make it, and you'll probably agree that we've got a pretty fucking epic one. And fuck anyone who threatens them. Who threatens us. Who—"

A soft knock at the door cuts my words off.

"Sorry to interrupt, but we've got a job, Nic," Theo says on the other side of the door.

Nico tenses in my arms.

"This isn't about what's happened in the past. It's about the future we have to look forward to. It's for Calli and your niece, for Theo as future boss, you as his right-hand man. It's for us and whatever the future might look like for us.

"It's for your dad, Nico."

"Fuck, babe," he chokes out, wrapping his arms tightly around me and hauling me into his chest. "I fucking love you."

"I love you too," I whisper in his ear. "Now go out there and finish this. It's time for revenge. Look that motherfucker in the eyes and blow his fucking brains out for the pain he's caused our family."

"You really do have a way with words, Siren," he says, pulling back from the warmth of my neck with a smile playing on his lips.

"I'd hate to disappoint you," I tease.

"Impossible."

"Nico, we need to move out," Theo snaps.

"I fucking heard you. Give me a minute."

"It'll take her longer than that to locate your tiny dick. Give it up until later. If you're lucky, she might even lick it in celebration."

"Fuck you, cuz."

"He got laid before coming here," I say confidently. "He's not usually this chipper."

"Going out to kill members of your family can fuck up even the coldest of arseholes," he says loudly, ensuring Theo hears.

"Two minutes, or you're coming in your boxers," Theo warns.

"Demanding prick," Nico mutters, finally climbing from the bed.

I sit up, watching as he sheds his sweats in favour of his uniform.

The shift in his personality as he dresses is mind-blowing. With each item of black clothing, I swear his presence becomes more dominant, controlling, fierce, and dangerous.

And I'd be lying if I were to say that I wasn't sitting here salivating over my man.

Makes me wonder just how fucked my DNA is to be quite so attracted to a man who's about to go out and—

"Siren?" he says, dragging me from my dark thoughts.

Licking my dry lips, I swallow and look up at him.

"I said your name like four times. Problem?" The smirk on his face tells me he knows exactly what my issue is.

"No, just... hurry back."

"Trust me," he says, stepping up to the bed and grasping my chin in his hand. "I have no intention of being away from you for longer than necessary."

I stare up at him with my heart in my throat.

"I wish I could come," I confess. I hate the thought of sending him to do this alone. Well, not alone. Just... without me.

"I'll be back between your thighs before you know it."

"Is that a promise, Mr. Cirillo?"

"Too fucking right it is."

He pulls me to my feet and makes my knees weak with another searing kiss before he tucks me into his side and heads toward the door to join the others.

22

———

NICO

With her hand tightly in mine, I hold my head up high and march toward where I know the others are waiting for me.

"About fucking time, bro," Alex teases, and it doesn't take him long to notice that he's the only one.

The others get it. They didn't want to leave their girls again to go and take these pricks down. But they don't have a choice.

I just fucking pray that it's going to be the last time.

We will always have enemies out there. People who think they can get the better of us who try their hand. But it's never usually like this. Normally, we deal with our issues and move on with life. Or at least, that's been our experience thus far. Maybe I'm wrong. We've only really been a part of all this for a couple of years. Maybe it's what we should be expecting going forward as we all begin to play a bigger role in this Family.

"You okay?" Toby asks, able to see beneath the mask I pulled on before walking out of my bedroom with my girl at my side.

"I'll be better when it's over and I'm back here."

Tugging Brianna in front of me, I drop a kiss on the top of her head.

"Never thought we'd see the day, man. But she looks fucking good on you," Theo states. "I hope you know what a lucky motherfucker you are."

"I do," I say, fighting a smile when Brianna jabs her fingers into my ribs.

"Can't believe I've lost my wingman," Alex sulks. "Who's going to come out and celebrate our epicness with me tonight?"

"Ant will finally be free; take him," Daemon says, watching his brother closely. "Call Isla if you have to."

"Isla?" Alex barks. "What the fuck have you been drinking?"

Daemon shrugs, but it's loaded with unspoken words that Alex seems to hear perfectly fine.

Weird fucking twin shit.

"Right, well, are we ready to hit this?" Seb asks, rubbing his hands together.

Steeling my spine, I give Brianna one last squeeze before releasing her.

"Yes, let's go."

We came up with a solid plan with the boss earlier.

Theo and I are heading to the meeting place to take out Ricardo with Uncle Damien, Stefanos and Galen.

Alex, Seb, and Ant are heading for the Italian compound where they're going to meet Matteo and Enzo and take out any Italians who are singing from Ricardo's hymn sheet. And Daemon and Toby are going for the hotel where my bitch of a mother is while a couple of others go and intercept Christos, who has obviously been completely kept out of this entire plan.

I just pray that it's enough.

If they're not our only leak and these cunts are waiting for us once again...

A violent shiver races down my spine.

"Don't even go there, Nico," Theo warns. "Tonight, we take back our power, our territory. And you get the vengeance you crave."

I nod at him. All these weeks when I've been thinking about getting my revenge for Dad's death, I've pictured that Italian cunt. But all too quickly, that face has morphed into another. Ricardo might have been the one to make the hit that night and fuck us over so many times since. But *she* was the one who orchestrated it.

I might not know the whole story, but I know she's been the puppet master. And not only is it going to get her killed, but Christos as well.

One face appears in my mind. Jerome and I have never really been friends. We might all have grown up together, but we're very different. He never embraced this part of our lives like we did, and that's kept him on the outskirts of our little group.

"Jerome," I blurt, turning everyone's eyes on me. Focusing on Alex, I explain. "You should take Jerome out tonight. He's going to need it."

"You think he's ever been out to pick up a woman before?" Seb asks with amusement.

"Hell no," I bark. "But tonight might just be the perfect night to discover pussy."

Brianna's hand slapping me in the chest cuts off my laughter.

"You're a pig," she mutters.

"Oh yeah?" I ask, twisting my finger in her hair and backing her into the wall. "I think you love it."

She gasps as I hook her leg up around my waist and grind my semi against her.

"Put her the fuck down, Nic. We need you thinking with your head, not your cock," Theo barks.

"When the hell has that ever happened?" Toby asks.

"Who's that?" Daemon asks when my front door opens. "Ant?"

When more than one set of footsteps make their way closer to us, my heart jumps into my throat and I step in front of Brianna, my hand on my gun at my back, ready to pull it.

It's probably overkill but I'm already in that headspace, and no one is touching anyone I care about tonight.

"Oh hell no," Theo barks a beat before I get to see who's joined us. "No. No. No fucking way."

Four excited faces stare back at us.

Like us, they're head to toe in black and look fierce as fuck.

"Bri," Jodie says, "We brought you an outfit if you're up for it."

"No," Theo says again, seemingly unable to muster up any other word while faced with the force of his wife, Stella, Jodie, and my little fucking sister standing there ready to head to war with us.

"Uh-uh, nope," Emmie says, stepping forward and pointing a finger at her husband. "You're not sidelining us for this one. No fucking chance."

"This isn't just your war," Stella joins. "It's our war. And we're not staying here, or hiding in some fancy hotel like damsels in distress. Not after what happened last time."

"And anyway," Calli adds, "Uncle Damien has already approved it, so there's fuck all you can do about it." She grins, her eyes darting between Daemon, me, and Theo.

Accomplishment is written all over her face, hell, all their faces, because they know we won't go against the boss.

"Fine," Theo says. "I'll go and get extra weapons."

"Wait," I call before he marches off for more guns. "You're not actually considering this—"

"What the fuck do you want me to say, Nic? I thought you of all people would want all the help you can get tonight. I know they can handle it. Seb, Daemon and Toby do too. Do you want Brianna by your side as you put that motherfucker out of his misery, or do you want her here not knowing what's going on?"

Brianna steps around me with the pile of black clothes in her hands, her blue eyes hesitantly finding mine.

She's been through so much recently. I should demand she stays here and rests. Fucking hell, they all should be here, out of fucking danger. But really, this should come as no surprise. They've argued enough in the past; we really should have seen this coming.

"You really want to do this?" I ask, my stomach knotting up and my heart pounding at the thought of her putting herself in danger.

She hasn't been trained like Stella and Emmie, or been putting hours into catching up like Calli and Jodie.

"What? Don't you think I can handle it?" she asks, quirking a brow.

I think about The Manor, about how she protected all of them without a second thought.

"Siren, I know you can handle it. You've got five minutes," I state before slamming my lips down on hers and slapping her arse as she spins.

"Yes," Emmie sings, clapping her hands together excitedly.

"Careful, Hellcat. You almost look like a normal girl,

doing that," Theo comments, rejoining us with an armful of guns that he's stolen from my hidden stash.

"Fuck you, Cirillo. I'm all the girl you could ever need."

"Ain't that the fucking truth. And thanks for all this, but we're already packing."

Emmie pulls the already short-as-fuck hem of her skirt up, revealing a loaded holster.

"Holy fuck."

"Aw look, Theo's orgasm face," Alex pipes up. "You'd better go clean up, man. No one wants to go into a fight with jizz in their pants."

Theo silently fumes while everyone else snorts a laugh at his expense.

"And where exactly are you hiding all yours, Hellion?" Seb asks, prowling toward his girl.

"That's for me to know and you to find out," she teases.

"Okay, I'm ready," Bri announces, striding into the room with more confidence than I think I've ever seen from her.

My mouth waters as I run my eyes up and down the length of her. The black trousers fit her like a second skin, highlighting every one of her sinful curves. And the top emphasises her already insane rack.

"I changed my mind. You can't leave this flat looking like that."

"Hey," Theo quips. "At least I get easy access. Good luck getting into those trousers."

"Easy access?" Emmie taunts. "You'll be so lucky."

He's on her so fast she has zero chance of seeing it coming. Although, as he stares down at her with her chin in his tight grip, all she does is smile back up at him, and I realise it was all part of her plan.

"You're all fucking insane. You know that, right?" Alex

mutters. "And you're all hot as fuck, but that's by the by. Ready to go kill some motherfuckers?" he asks, stalking across the room toward my front door.

I swallow as Brianna steps up to me and runs her palms up my chest.

"You really okay with this?" she asks quietly.

"Having you right by my side while I slay our enemies? Yeah, Siren. I'm more than okay with that. Just... for the love of God, do as you're told."

She looks up at me and bats her eyelashes.

"I promise, I'll be your good girl," she teases, before reaching out and squeezing my junk.

"And that needs to stop unless you're going to blow me in the back of Theo's car on the drive over."

"That will not be happening."

"Don't worry, big man. I can distract him so you can get some," Emmie says, slapping me on the shoulder as she passes.

"Fucking love you, Siren." Tugging on her hand, I pull her into my body.

"Me and you, Nico," she whispers against my lips.

"Fucking heaven, babe. Now let's go and show some motherfuckers hell."

Despite all our joking around, the second we all pile into the lift to descend through the building, a wave of seriousness wraps around our group.

Not a word is said as I hold both Brianna's and Calli's hands tightly in mine.

Looking up, I meet Daemon's eyes. Despite his mask, I can see his worry over this. But he's not going to say anything.

All he's done since getting with my sister is help her

grow. He's helped her discover the woman she always should have been, and as much as I might want to demand she stays behind, locked up in her castle like she always has been in the past, I know it's not my place.

Calli is her own woman. She can make her own choices, and if she needs to be here for this, then who am I to argue?

She lost just as much as I have to Ricardo, and I can only imagine she has a few words she'd like to say to our mother with this new revelation. Who are we to stop her?

She's a Cirillo. She was born fierce, even if we did try and smother it.

'I've got her,' Daemon mouths and I nod, trusting him to put his own life on the line to protect her.

My eyes scan the others, taking in the fierce determination on their faces as a weird mix of emotions rushes through me.

Excitement, relief, pain. All of it collides into one big mess. A mess I have no idea what to do with.

It got the better of me earlier when Bri and I were alone. But I refuse to let it win now.

We're both going to have a lot to work through and process after all of this is done. But I have every intention of doing it together. And if that means she has to witness me break, then so be it, because I have every intention of being there to keep her together when she does, too.

It might not have been so long ago that I'd have considered myself weak for allowing someone else to see my grief, my pain, my anguish. But Brianna is quickly proving me wrong.

Having her beside me, knowing she's fighting for me, with me, makes me stronger.

And I know that I wouldn't be able to do what I'm about to do without her by my side.

The lift dings, announcing our arrival, and as the others spill out, I pull Brianna into my arms and hold her a little tighter.

"You're everything," I whisper before finally releasing her and following the others.

23

———

NICO

I slide into the back of Theo's car right behind Brianna.

Nothing is said as we get ready to head off, but the second my eyes lock on Theo's in the rear-view mirror, I pause.

He doesn't say a word. He doesn't need to.

Sucking in a deep breath, I rest back and close my eyes.

This is it. This is where it ends.

I startle when the warmth of Bri's hand lands on my thigh.

Her support and her love seeps through my skin, warming me from the inside out.

Keeping my eyes closed, I place my hand on top of hers.

Theo rolls out, the tension in the car almost unbearable as we head toward the location of this meeting.

Thankfully, it's not happening in the middle of the city, and he's chosen one of the empty warehouses Mickey uses every now and then for Circuit fights as a safe place to meet this supplier.

It works perfectly for us. And if we're lucky, we can be

in and out before anyone else knows something untoward is going down.

The sun is setting as we head across town, the warmth of the last of the rays heating my skin through the dark window of Theo's car.

The others have headed off in different directions for their own jobs, leaving the four of us to park a few streets over from the industrial estate.

We head around the back, climbing through the old perimeter gate that used to protect this site when it was in use. Now though, after years of abandonment, it's shredded, the ground covered in rubbish, empty bottles, and the odd syringe. Not exactly my ideal location to spend the night with my girl. But it is what it is.

With my hand locked around hers, I lead her toward an old container that's almost been burned to the ground.

It looks unsteady as hell, but it's the perfect place to scope out Ricardo's arrival.

"Here," Theo says, handing me an earpiece.

"What about us?" Emmie asks.

"You're a pain in my arse, Emmie Cirillo," he mutters, passing over another comms device to both his wife and my girl.

"Ah, it's as if you knew," she teases.

"It's not too late to send you back home, you know," he mutters, making her eyes roll. "Watch it, Hellcat. We've got time; I have no problem taking you over my knee and punishing you for the attitude."

Brianna's wide eyes find mine as a smirk curls at her lips.

"You like the sound of that, Siren?" I ask, my cock stirring to life at the image that emerges in my mind.

Her grin gets downright filthy as she watches me.

"Okay, enough," Theo barks. "We need to focus."

"You started it," Emmie mutters. Brianna snorts a laugh but quickly tries to cover it with a cough when Theo shoots her a death glare.

"When I turn this on, we're all business. No one at the other end needs confirmation of how much bigger my cock is than Nico's, or how I leave my girl with weaker knees than Bri." He winks at Bri, making me growl.

"The fact you even need to bring it up just shows how self-conscious you are over your performance, cuz."

"Trust me, it's not just his ego that's that big."

"Hell yes, girl," Brianna laughs, holding her hand up to Emmie for a high five.

"Do we need to take you home, or are you going to figure out a way to be useful?"

"We got it, Boss. Give us our orders," Emmie purrs, looking up at Theo and batting her lashes.

"If this goes wrong, then I'm blaming—"

"It's not going to go wrong," I assure him. "We've got this, right?"

"Right," both girls agree.

"Now, get the comms up and running and let's make this motherfucker our little bitch."

The small device crackles in my ear as it comes to life before Theo starts testing.

When Uncle Damien's voice fills my ear, confirming that they're in place, I relax a little.

Curling herself into my side, Brianna looks up at me, squeezing my arm in support, but like a good little soldier, she keeps quiet, waiting for orders.

"We have word that they're on route. ETA, ten minutes," Stefanos says. "Let them go in, allow them to think all is well, then we take them by surprise. Shoot to kill."

"Ricardo is mine; no motherfucker shoots him," I bark.

"You got it, son," Uncle Damien agrees.

Silence falls as we stand there. My heart pounds in my chest, blood rushing past my ears as I will the minutes to tick by faster.

I've waited a long time for this. I need to look that cunt in the eyes, let him acknowledge all his mistakes before I send him with a one-way ticket to hell.

I focus on my breathing, willing my hands to stop trembling.

I'm never this on edge. But then, a job has never been so personal before.

And I haven't had my girl standing right beside me about to go into a fucking gunfight.

I look to my left, my eyes finding Theo's, and I swear I see the same hesitation written all over his face.

But when I glance at Emmie and Bri, they're both fully focused.

Fuck, I hope we did the right thing here.

"Car," Emmie states, hearing the approaching engine first.

"Got him," Stefanos agrees.

A few seconds later, a black SUV pulls around the building, stopping at the entrance.

I swear time fucking stops as we wait for the doors to open.

As each second passes, the more my fear grows.

What if they've seen us?

What if there's another leak and they know?

What if they're on our comms?

Just before I'm about to say something, I let out the

breath I didn't know I was holding as the back door opens and Ricardo's underboss steps out.

He smooths down his jacket before buttoning it up and checking his gun is secured in his waistband.

"Armed," Theo growls.

"But we outnumber them," I add. "Driver is staying. Targets heading inside," I say focusing on the movement of Ricardo's head that I can just see over the top of the car.

The second the door slams closed after them, Theo moves, pulling his gun from his back and twisting a silencer on the end.

"They're in. Ready?" he asks, his voice cold and calm as fuck.

"Ready," Stefanos confirms.

"On three," Uncle Damien says, but fuck that.

We're doing this now.

"Three," I bark, ripping my arm from Bri's grip and surging forward.

I've fired a bullet through the driver's window before Theo even gets a chance to chastise me for jumping the gun.

He barks orders directly into my ear, but I don't hear a word of it as I storm toward the building and rip the door open.

"So much for being fucking discreet."

"Fuck discreet, this fucker needs to know he's lost."

I push forward, aiming for the room at the very end, and the second I open the door, a fucking bullet bounces off it.

"Motherfucker," I hiss.

Movement behind me catches my eye as Emmie and Brianna follow me with Theo behind them.

"Em, do your thing," he demands before she darts into the room without fucking hesitation.

Guns fire and chaos erupts, and my heart jumps into my throat before I follow her lead with my gun in front of me and a set of eyes in my mind as my target.

Everything around me blurs as I fire at anyone who isn't a member of my Family.

There are more people in here than we were expecting, but it soon becomes clear that they're not all on the Italians' side.

The contacts Ricardo was meeting are very quick to pull their own weapons, and in only a matter of minutes, his underboss is bleeding out on the floor and Ricardo's gun has been kicked out of reach.

"We've got it from here," Uncle Damien says, stepping up beside me as I glare pure hate at Ricardo, who's got more than a handful of barrels pointed straight at him. "Sorry for any loss you've suffered."

"It'll cost you," one of their guys—the boss, I guess—says before several guns lower and men back away.

"It'll be worth it. I'll be in touch."

I don't look away or move an inch as we're left alone.

"Ricardo Mariano, it's been a while," Uncle Damien taunts. "But we knew we'd catch you in the end."

His eyes bounce between mine and Uncle Damien's, but if he's scared of his impending death, then he doesn't show it.

My finger twitches on my trigger, more than ready to just end this now.

I don't need to hear anything from him.

I thought I'd have wanted to hear him scream and plead for his life. But mostly, I just want to leave with my girl on my arm.

But then his eyes shift over my shoulder and a smirk curls at his lips.

"Well, fuck me. You really must be scraping the barrel if you've brought women to fight your battles," he taunts.

I glance to my left as my girl steps up to my side, looking like every motherfucker's wet dream with her skintight black outfit and a gun in her hand.

"I wouldn't underestimate them if I were you."

"I've already doubled my Italian body count tonight," Bri taunts, making pride swell. "Your boy there," she taunts, jerking her chin toward the man bleeding out at Ricardo's feet. "He looks good with my bullet in his chest, don't you think?"

"Not as good as the one last weekend with a champagne bottle impaled in his neck," Emmie counters, completing our circle beside Theo.

"True."

Ricardo's eyes crinkle with amusement.

"Am I actually meant to be scared of these bitch—" His question ends with a roar of pain as Emmie shoots out his kneecap.

"Oh, whoops. Who knew this trigger did that?"

"Fucking crazy bitch," Ricardo roars.

"You would know all about those, wouldn't you? You have been fucking my mother, after all." Honestly, I've no idea if that's true, but it's about the only thing that makes sense after what we discovered today.

His nostrils flaring is his only reaction to my statement, but it's all I need.

"Credit where credit's due, you had us chasing our tails for a bit. But you were never going to win. Especially when you enlisted the help of that bitch. What was the plan, huh?"

"Fuck you," he sneers, blood and spit spraying from his mouth.

"You know, I'd really rather leave that to my mother. She seems to be so good at it, after all."

This time, his jaw tics.

"Aw, don't tell us you went and fell in love with her."

"She's mine," he roars. "She was never his."

"Wow," I laugh. "Is that what all this was? Poor scorned lover takes on the Cirillo empire."

"She only married him because he got her pregnant with you before I could."

I don't react; I couldn't give a fuck about any of this. Although, there is a part of me that hopes he's telling the fucking truth with that.

"You should have done us all a favour and taken her after she had my sister. You could have run off into the sunset together and ruined each other's lives away from all of us."

"And leave you here with all the power? Un-fucking-likely."

"How's the alternative working out for you?" Theo asks.

"She's dead, Ricardo. We've sent guys in after her; they'll have already ended it. What now, huh?"

"No, she's protected. You can't get to her."

The flash of Theo's phone catches my eye as he holds it up for Ricardo to see.

Whatever is on there makes the blood drain from his face.

"Believe us now?"

"You fucked up going after us, Ricardo. Your own men think the same. It's a shame you won't get a chance to face your brothers and hear it from them. They're too busy overthrowing your regime with the men you left behind in your compound."

"No," he cries.

"Aw, who did you think was giving your intel all this time? You should be proud. Matteo will do a fantastic job taking over from you. Ant too. He recovered well, by the way. I'm sure you were just about to ask after his well-being."

I should probably feel smug, pointing out all his failings. But I don't.

I'm bored.

Bored of his face. Bored of having our lives controlled by this twisted fuck. Bored of looking over my shoulder every time I leave our building.

"We should probably keep you and treat you like you did Ant and Daemon. But honestly, I can't even be bothered." I take a step forward, holding his eyes firm. "Dad, this is for you."

The shot pierces through the air, the power of it is making my body jerk back as the bullet finds its home in Ricardo Mariano's skull.

The warmth of his blood sprays down the front of me, covering my face. But I don't do anything. I just stand there as he falls to the floor, his eyes wide open and staring up at the ceiling.

"Rot in hell, you piece of shit," I mutter before wiping my face on my sleeve and turning back to my girl.

Our eyes lock and she lifts her head a little higher, not shying away from what she just witnessed.

"It's over. Let's go home."

She squeals when I sweep her off her feet and throw her over my shoulder.

"Laters," I say with a wave before marching out of that building and leaving that prick where he should be.

In my fucking past.

BRIANNA

"Nico, you brute. Put me the fuck down," I scream, kicking my legs and slamming my curled fists into his solid arse as he carries me from the warehouse. "NICO."

One second, I'm upside down and the next, I'm flying through the air again before my back lands on something hard.

I scramble to get up but quickly discover that it's pointless when Nico captures my wrists and pins them at my sides on the bonnet of the Italians' car.

"There's a dead man right there," I hiss, resisting the urge to look behind me and see him.

"How disappointing for him. He could have watched otherwise."

My lips part to respond, but he steals them with his own before I can form a response.

My body reacts to him without instruction from my brain, my legs wrapping around his length as I kiss him back just as furiously as he claims me.

I forget all about what just happened, the fact he's covered in another man's blood. A man he just shot. In. The. Head. Instead, I lose myself in the man I can't get enough of.

Shifting my arms above my head, he restrains my wrists in one of his giant hands.

The other moves down my body, gripping and teasing wherever he touches until he's palming my arse, dragging my body closer to his.

"Siren," he groans into our kiss, rolling his hips and grinding his length against me. "Need you."

I have no idea how he manages it with one hand, but one second, I'm fully dressed in the outfit that Jodie gave me, and the next, the button of the jeans is undone and being dragged down my legs.

My boots hit the floor with a thud as he spreads me wide for him.

"Fucking knew you'd be wet for me," he mutters, staring down at the soaked lace that's covering my pussy.

"Nico," I groan, watching as he rips his own fly open and frees his dick.

"Hold on, babe," he warns before he releases my wrists in favour of my hips.

He slides me down the bonnet until I'm exactly where he wants me, and then he thrusts himself inside me.

"FUCK," I cry as my body fights to adjust to his size.

He doesn't give me a chance to recover; instead, he fucks me like a man possessed, roaring out in delight as he pounds into me.

I watch him in fascination as he lets go, releasing all the tension and anger that the man inside that warehouse caused him. It's fucking intoxicating to watch.

Then his eyes open, immediately finding mine, and that connection that has always been so potent between us slams into me once more, making my heart clench and my breath catch.

"Get there," he demands. "I need you coming on my cock, Siren."

Without thought, my hand slides down my stomach, finding the sensitive nub between my thighs, and I play myself in a way that has me on the brink of orgasm in only seconds.

"Fuck yes. Fuck. You squeeze me so fucking good."

Panic flares inside me as his cock swells and his thrusts become erratic and jerky.

"Nico, you can't—"

I gasp when his hand releases my hip in favour of my throat.

He squeezes just enough to make my head spin, but it's his next words that make me stop breathing.

"I don't care, Brianna. You're mine. I'm yours. Whatever else happens. I'm here for it. All of it."

He thrusts once more, and that mixed with his promises is enough to push me over the edge and I scream into the silent night around us as he unloads deep inside me.

I can barely catch my breath with the strength of that release, and it's not helped by the fact Nico has collapsed on top of me.

"You two should go into porn, you know," a female voice says in my ear.

When I look to the side, I see Emmie approaching us with her phone in her hand.

"Put your cock away, Nico," she demands flippantly, as if she wasn't blatantly standing there watching us.

"It's exactly where it belongs," he says, thrusting his softening cock inside me, sending aftershocks shooting off around my body.

"Cute," she says, barely sparing him a glance as she pockets her phone and pulls out a tissue. "You're probably going to need that."

"What the fuck else are you hiding in that outfit?" Nico asks as the tissue is waved in front of his face.

"That's for me to know and Theo to find out. Now, put the snake away. We've got work to do."

"Fucking slave driver," Nico mutters, finally pulling out of me and tucking himself away.

"A little help?" I hiss. I might have little shame where owning my sexuality is concerned, but being left spread-eagled on the bonnet of a car with his cum dribbling out of me and one of my closest friends watching, and possibly his uncle and cousin, is a little much, even for me.

He helps me pull my jeans back on before dropping to his knees and sliding my boots into my feet while I abandon the tissue and stand.

"Gross," I mutter, making Emmie snort as Theo emerges from the building.

"They have it so easy, don't they?" she says, rolling her eyes at Theo as he stops beside Nico. "Bet he's already forgotten it happened and you're going to be dealing with the evidence for at least an hour or two."

"Two hours; there was way more than that."

"Way more what?" Theo asks innocently.

"Oh you missed a treat. Don't worry, though; I recorded it for you."

"Emmie," Nico growls, looking part horrified, part intrigued.

"Don't worry. I'll share."

"I should fucking think so."

"Wait," Theo says as he moves closer to the car. "Why is the bonnet caved in?"

One look at Nico's smug face and I can't help myself. I fall about laughing.

Nico follows while Emmie titters beside us.

"Jesus."

"What?" Nico asks through his laughter. "You'd have done the same in my position; don't even try and argue."

He doesn't respond, but we all know the truth.

"Dad's called in clean-up. Let's head out."

Tucking myself into Nico's side, I let him lead me down the dark track that will take us to where we hid Theo's car.

"Is she really dead already?" Nico asks. He doesn't need to say a name; we all know who he's talking about. And despite her turning out to be an even bigger disappointment than my own mother, my heart still twists up for both Nico and Calli. No kid should ever have to go through what they are tonight.

"Nah, Daemon's keeping her warm for you. It wasn't even convincing. Fuck knows how he fell for it."

"Can't you just take us home?" Nico asks, sounding utterly exhausted as Theo goes in the opposite direction to their building.

"No can do, man. You need to see this through. For you, and for Calli."

He blows out a long, pained breath before dragging me over the seat and depositing me on his lap for a distraction.

"It's nearly done," I whisper, cupping his rough jaw and staring into his eyes.

"Give me something else to think about," he murmurs before stealing my lips.

Nico doesn't let me up for air the whole journey to the hotel where Daemon and Calli are holding their mum. Not that I'm complaining. I'll take his lips on mine any day.

"Might want to fix this before you walk into that room. I know you're a little fucked up, but that's a whole new level of—"

My words are cut off as he sucks on my neck, hard enough to leave one hell of a mark while I continue grinding down on his hard length.

"Maybe you should stop doing that then," he growls, his voice deep and hoarse with desire.

A girly giggle falls from my lips as Theo pulls the door open. His brows lift as the sound hits his ears.

"I think I'm drunk," I confess.

"On dick," Emmie helpfully supplies.

"One more job and you can indulge all you like."

Nico lifts me off his lap and climbs out behind me, not bothering to hide as he rearranges himself.

"What?" he asks when he catches us all watching him. "Come on, babe. Let's get this done. I've got other plans for the rest of the night that are going to be way more fun than this."

There are suited men stationed both outside the hotel as well as inside. I have no idea if they're Cirillo or the next generation of Mariano, but as long as they're not trying to kill us, I don't really care.

A few of them nod in our direction as we pass, but most mind their own business.

"Eighth floor," Theo says as the four of us step into the lift.

Reaching out, Nico presses his finger against the button, and in only seconds, we're climbing through the building.

I keep my arm locked around his waist, my other hand resting on his tense abs.

He doesn't want to do this, that much is obvious but at the same time, I know he also needs to.

Just like I need to deal with the situation that I've been ignoring in the basement of their building.

It's time to pull up our grown-up pants and handle our shit.

I want everything Nico has promised me over the past few days, and we're not going to be able to embark on any of that until the demons of our past are dealt with.

The future we can handle one day at a time. We can work together to find a way forward, but this needs to happen first.

I remain at his side as we walk down the hallway toward the room they detained her in.

Two vaguely familiar guys stand guard on either side of the entrance, but neither says anything as Nico throws the door open and marches inside with his head held high, leaving his concerns and apprehension in the hallway.

I'm so fucking proud of him, I can barely contain it.

All of that is quickly forgotten when my eyes land on his mother.

I've never met her, but ruined make-up and messy hair aside, she's exactly what I expected.

She's dressed immaculately, or at least I'm sure she was when she put on her designer dress and tailored jacket this morning.

Her watery eyes find Nico, and she tracks his movement across the room.

The door closes behind us, leaving the seven of us in here with the privacy for what needs to happen.

"Nico," she whimpers. If she thinks he's here to rescue her, then she really needs a fucking reality check.

Nico holds her eyes for a few seconds. There's nothing but contempt and hatred in his stare. It's fucking terrifying how he can turn everything off and become this entirely different person.

I guess it's what they've all been trained for since before they can remember. And as the future underboss of this entire organisation, his training, along with Theo's, is of the utmost importance.

Once she's had long enough to understand just how much her son hates her, Nico turns to the other couple in the room.

Daemon has Calli cuddled on his lap on the sofa opposite where they have Cassandra tied to a chair.

Both look entirely too comfortable, considering the situation.

"How are you doing?" Nico asks, walking over and placing his hand supportively on his sister's shoulder.

"I'm good, Bro. You?" Her eyes drop to the specks of the blood that's dried on his face and neck.

"Yeah. We've solved one problem. Ricardo Mariano is exactly where he belongs."

Cassandra whimpers as he breaks the news.

"Oh, that's right. How long have you been fucking the enemy *and* your best friend's husband, *Mum*?"

"You don't know anything," she wails.

"I think it's probably for the best you spare us the details, don't you? We're all fans of good sex, but I'm not sure any of us would take it in favour of our kids' safety. Calli?"

Her hand slides to her belly, a move that her mother does notice if her gasp of shock is anything to go by.

"Such a shame you're not going to get a chance to meet your grandson."

"Daughter," Calli argues, making Emmie laugh beside me.

"Callista," Cassandra whispers.

"Aw, Mum. It's a little late to try and pretend you care now."

Tears continue to fall from Cassandra's eyes. I might not know the woman, but even I don't buy her bullshit. Even less so when her body stiffens and she changes tact.

"I knew this would happen if she was allowed to run around the city with you and your friends."

"What? That I'd fall in love and get pregnant? Yeah, imagine that. Such a crime," Calli mutters, finally climbing from Daemon's lap and stalking closer to her mother.

"Before I forget, I need to thank you, *Mum*," she sneers, lowering down so she's at the same height. "Thank you for showing me exactly how not to bring up my own children."

Cassandra's top lip peels back when Daemon steps up beside his girl and wraps his arm around her.

"Him? Really, Callista? You could have chosen his twin, at least."

"You can stop, you know. The time when I considered your opinion to matter has long gone."

I look up, taking in how Nico stares at his sister with nothing but admiration and pride. It makes something melt inside me, seeing how fiercely he loves her. It reassures me that all of us will be okay. You don't need biological parents when you've got a family who love each other like we all do.

"Do you really hate us that much, Mum?" Nico asks,

stepping up to me. "We both could have died the night Dad did. You didn't even care, did you? All you wanted was your bullshit happily ever after with the power-hungry cunt you've been selling us out to."

"I've never hated you," she hisses. "I just never wanted you."

"Ouch," he says, lifting his hand to cover his heart as if her words have any impact.

I mean, I'm sure they do deep down. I'm not sure there are many people out there who wouldn't be affected in some way by cutting words from their parents, but there's no way in hell Nico is letting her see that.

"Feeling's mutual though, *Cassandra*. We never wanted you, either. And aren't you lucky? Because unlike most kids, we're not afraid to get rid of you like the piece of shit that you are. We've already sent your boyfriends on a one-way trip to hell. It only seems fair that you join them, don't you think?"

To my surprise, all Cassandra does in response to Nico's threat is laugh.

Clearly, she doesn't know her son as well as she thinks she does, because something tells me that he won't hesitate to put a bullet in her head like he did Ricardo only an hour ago. The fact he hasn't already shut her up is actually surprising me.

"You're your father's son, Nico. He was weak. Weak and pathetic. He knew I never loved him, yet he kept following me around like a puppy, giving me everything I ever asked for. It was pathetic. He thought he was so special, he—"

A shriek rips from my throat as a loud bang pierces through the room a second before Cassandra slumps down in the chair, her eyes wide and terrified as blood begins to soak the pale blue dress.

Looking to my side, I expect to see that Nico's pulled his gun and that I was too lost in my own head to notice, but it wasn't him who couldn't take any more of her rambling, because Calli is the one with the smoking gun in her hand.

"Angel," Daemon gasps, clearly as shocked as me.

"Sorry. No one talks about Dad like that and gets away with it," she says with a shrug as if shooting her mother is an everyday occurrence.

"Cal," Nico whispers.

"Why are you both looking at me like that? We came here to kill her, no?"

Silence fills the room before a gargled whimper comes from the woman slumped in the chair.

"Whoops. Did I miss?" Calli asks innocently.

Daemon can't help himself and the widest, proudest smile spreads across his face as he pulls Calli into his arms.

"Fuck, I love you, Angel," he professes before twisting his fingers in her hair and dragging her head back so he can kiss her.

"Your sister's a bad-arse," I tell Nico as he stares at the two of them in disbelief.

"I can't believe she just did that."

"I can. Calli knows what she wants and she takes it. You really should give her a little more credit."

He looks between me and his sister, who's still being molested by her boyfriend, with confusion pinching his brows.

"So the question is, what do you want? Gonna leave her to bleed out, or are you going to—"

Reaching behind him, Nico pulls his gun out and fires, finishing the job Calli started.

Without looking at her, he grabs my hand and marches toward Theo. "Now, will you take us home? I want to spend the night inside my girl and forget all this ever happened."

"You got it, Boss," Theo says with an uncharacteristic salute to his cousin.

25

BRIANNA

ithout another word, Nico drags me from the hotel room and down the hallway.

I glance back as he presses the button for the lift to find Theo and Emmie, and Daemon and Calli tailing us.

The guys who were guarding the room have gone, I assume slipped inside to clean up the mess.

My stomach turns over as I think about what we just left behind, but I don't feel bad.

Nico and Calli did what needed to be done in order to protect everyone around us. I know the fallout from their actions isn't going to be easy. Everything that's happened in the past few weeks is going to haunt all of us for a while. But we're in this together, and right now, the future is looking brighter than ever.

The door to the lift hasn't even closed before Daemon has Calli backed up against the wall as he growls all kinds of filthy things in her ear. Glancing up at Nico, I find his jaw ticking in frustration, but he doesn't say anything or put a stop to it.

Why should he? Calli might be his little sister, but she's an adult who's able to make her own decisions, just like he said back in that room. She's going to be a mother herself in only a few months, and I already know hands down that she'll do a better job than the woman they just left behind. Hell, she already is doing a better job.

Ignoring them, I twist in front of Nico and rest my hands on his chest.

"How are you feeling?" I ask, loving the way our bodies line up when I lean against him.

He thinks for a minute, his eyes searching mine as if he's trying to find the answer.

"Free," he finally says. "It's... a little overwhelming." The vulnerability in his voice makes my heart ache.

"I'm so proud of you."

He smiles down at me, his eyes glittering with emotion. Lifting his hand to cup my jaw, he runs the pad of his thumb across my bottom lip.

"I love you."

I'm about to return the sentiment, but my words are cut off by a ringing phone.

"Boss," Theo grunts before Damien's deep voice rumbles down the line. "Yes. Yes. Okay, we'll be there. Okay.'

A frustrated groan vibrates in Nico's chest as he predicts what's coming next.

"Boss wants to debrief at the office. Says it'll be quick."

"Everything okay with Matteo, Enzo, and Ant?" Daemon asks, ripping his lips from Calli's for a beat.

"Yeah. They're meeting us there. We did it. The Marianos are under new leadership." Pride fills Theo's voice and butterflies explode in my belly for what they've managed to achieve.

"Fuck, yeah," Nico barks, a wide smile splitting his face, pulling me tighter against him.

"Are you three going to be okay heading back home?" Theo asks, looking between us.

"Sure. I'll drive your car back," Emmie offers with a twinkle of mischief in her eyes.

"Like fuck you will. You destroy every car of mine you touch."

"Calli can drive mine," Daemon offers.

"See, Calli's allowed to drive her boyfriend's car; why can't I drive my husband's?" Emmie sulks. Something tells me that she's gunning for a spanking tonight after what we overheard earlier.

"Don't be a brat, Hellcat. You know where it lands you," Theo warns, taking her by the throat and flipping their positions so she's pinned back against the wall.

"I think that's her plan, cuz," Calli points out, her line of thinking parallel to mine.

"Is that what you want, Hellcat?" I swear she trembles under his firm hand and intense stare.

"You know I do," she breathes.

"Jesus. What is wrong with our friends?" Nico whispers in my ear.

"Oh, because you're any better. Give you half a chance and you'd put me over your knee and teach me a lesson for being a brat."

A groan rumbles deep in his throat. "Now there's an idea."

"After your meeting," I whisper, lifting up on my toes so I can whisper in his ear. He shivers as my breath races over his skin and I smile, loving the power I have over him. "I'll be waiting and you can do whatever you want. No holds barred."

"What the fuck did I do to deserve you?" he groans, his dick swelling between us just from his filthy thoughts alone.

"Nothing, but I seem to have got stuck with you anyway."

"Okay, go home. I want you waiting for me in the sexiest thing you've got. Then, I'm going to spend the evening worshipping every single inch of your body."

"Just remember you've got an exam tomorrow, Bro," Calli points out, eavesdropping on our sex talk.

"Seriously, that's what you're worried about right now?" Nico blurts.

"Just being a good sister. Come on, the doors opened while you were lost in your little fantasy."

Looking up, I find she's right. Emmie and Theo have already left.

We come to a stop beside Theo's car. He's already in the driver's seat, Emmie hovering ready to head home, but Daemon isn't ready to release Calli yet, and it quickly becomes apparent that Nico isn't overly willing to let me go either.

"Go, babe. Do what you need to do. I'll be waiting," I promise.

"Fucking hate leaving you," he groans. "I promised I wouldn't."

"Everything is good. Go do your thing and hurry back."

"Fuck. Yeah, okay."

He slams his lips down on mine in one more knee-weakening kiss before he releases me and climbs into Theo's passenger seat without looking back. Something tells me that if he does, he'll forget all about the boss's orders and take me home instead.

"Come on, sis," Calli says, looping her arm through mine.

"That sounds weirdly good."

"Of course it does. It's meant to be. You two just needed your heads banging together to figure it out."

"It wasn't our heads that were banging."

"Ew gross," she laughs. "I don't care what it was. I couldn't ask for a better sister."

"You know we didn't secretly get married recently, right? He's not Theo."

"Pfft," Emmie scoffs when we finally join her.

"Semantics. This is it for us now. Family. Fuck the ones we're born into; the ones we make for ourselves are far superior."

"Amen to that."

We're all distracted by our thoughts as we climb into Daemon's car that's parked a little down the street. But even while the events of the night run through my head, my eyes don't leave Calli.

I know she's stronger than what the guys have always believed. But what she did tonight... it was huge. And I can't help waiting for her to break any minute.

But as she drives, her hands look relaxed on the wheel and her head is held high.

"Who are you and what have you done with Calli?" Emmie asks, and when I glance at the passenger seat, I find her studying our friend too.

"Have you ever considered that this was always who I was, it was just smothered?" Calli asks calmly.

"Cal, I *know* that is the case. But what you did... Girl, that takes some fucking balls."

"It's Daemon—"

"You stole his balls?" I blurt, unable to bite back the words.

Both of them howl with laughter, and in only seconds, Calli is wiping tears from her eyes.

"I needed that," she confesses when her giggles have died down. "But no, rest assured that Daemon's balls are still where they're meant to be. He just... he gives me the confidence to go after what I want in a way I've never experienced before. It's... freeing."

"Who knew the Devil could be so good for our little Cirillo princess?" Emmie teases.

"He's everything."

"We see it, Calli. The way he looks at you. You are literally the only person he sees."

"I know that look, Bri. I see it on my brother every time he looks at you."

"Stop," I beg, my cheeks heating.

"I'm serious, and he is too," she assures me. "You've changed him. You've..."

"Made him less of a dickhead?" Emmie offers when her words tail off, making me bark out a laugh.

"Something like that," Calli mutters, taking the next left turn.

"Nah, he's still a dickhead. We wouldn't have it any other way," I confess, a fond smile pulling at my lips as I think about my lovable idiot.

I think back over the last few hours, replay the things he said to me when were we fucking in his bedroom earlier. The way he claimed me, owned me, made me promises of forever. It makes my body light up from the inside.

How can I go from never wanting anything serious to getting all mushy over him calling me his and promising to love me forever?

It's bizarre how fast things can change. But then... we've all just witnessed just how quickly it can go the other way.

And when you're living in the fast lane, facing death more often than not, I guess everything is amplified. The hate is ever more toxic and the love... well, that's intense.

"You've got a sappy look on your face, Bri," Calli points out after checking on me in the rear-view mirror.

"I can't help it. That dickhead does things to me."

"I know, I recorded it," Emmie reminds me.

"You what?" Calli gasps.

"Ugh," Emmie groans. "It was hot as fuck. I couldn't help myself." Calli stares at her, her eyes darting between our screwed-up friend and the road as she tries to process her confession. "He was so excited to wipe that cunt off the planet, and he just couldn't wait to get inside you," she says, glancing back at me with heated eyes. "It was mesmerising."

"You recorded my brother fucking my friend?" Calli asks in disbelief.

"Can I have a copy?" I ask, sitting forward.

"Brianna," Calli gasps.

"Oh come off it, like you wouldn't want to watch a video of Daemon railing you like that." Calli's lips part ready to argue, but she quickly thinks better of it. "See. Hot. As. Fuck."

My phone vibrates in my back pocket and I can't resist.

Pulling it free, I open up the video Emmie just sent and press play, turning the volume down to save Calli's ears.

Ears.

That thought hits me like a truck.

We had those comms in our ears. Theo knew exactly what we were doing. I bet the sick fuck listened too.

He came out of that warehouse looking so innocent.

"You heard all of this, didn't you?"

"Yep," Emmie says smugly.

"So Theo, his dad..."

"Probably. Bet they loved it as much as I did."

"Jesus, this Family is fucked up."

"I know, isn't it great? You really need to meet my uncle and his lot. They'll blow your mind."

I've heard all about Emmie's biker background, but I'm yet to be formally introduced. I'd be lying if I said I wasn't a little excited. I might be fully gone for Nico, but I'm more than happy to be surrounded by hot, leather-clad bikers.

Movement on the screen before me drags me from my thoughts and I forget any other man exists as I watch Nico's bare arse as he ruts into me like a man possessed.

Heat surges through me, all of it making a beeline for the clit.

"Told you," Emmie says smugly as she watches me gawp at our little homemade porno.

"Do you think they're gonna be long?" I ask, already desperate to have a go at remaking this.

"Bloody hope not," Emmie mutters. "I'm on a promise."

"So we heard, brat," I tease.

Despite the heaviness of what our night has entailed, we somehow manage to laugh almost all the way back to the guys' building.

And as Calli parks, another car pulls up beside us, and Stella and Jodie climb out.

"Tell us everything," Stella begs.

"The bit where Brianna starred in her own sex tape—"

"Or the bit where Emmie was a brat in the hope of being put over her husband's knee?" I counter, the three of us falling about laughing once more.

"I was more thinking about the demise of our enemies, but sure, you may start with that."

"Stel, you've got blood on your neck," Calli points out.

"Ugh, that Italian was a fucking bleeder. Pussy too. You

should have seen the way he dropped to the floor with just one hit."

My eyes widen. "So things went well then?"

"Yep. Stella beat the shit out of anyone who wanted a pop, and we left Ant, Enzo, and Matteo rounding up what's left of their troops."

"They're confident they have everyone?" I ask. The fear of someone getting missed and coming after us is real.

"Yep, you got the leaders and we took out the rest of their pack. We're good to go."

"Does this mean it's all really over?" Jodie asks as we turn as a group toward the doors that will allow us into the main part of the building.

Two guards watch our every move, reminding us that danger will always be out there lingering just because of the surnames we bear and the love we have for the men inside this building.

But that's okay. It's worth it.

Nico is more than worth it.

Something I never thought I would have said a few months, hell, weeks ago.

But there it is.

"So what now?" Calli asks.

"Showers," Jodie suggests, but as much as I agree with that thanks to what Nico left behind earlier, there's something else I want to do more.

When you've spilled blood all over the city in only a few hours, what's a little bit more?

"I was wondering if you all wanted to help me with something?"

"Oh?" Stella says, bloodlust still shining bright in her eyes.

"We've got access to the basement, right?"

As my eyes scan over the faces before me, I watch as understanding dawns.

"While the boys work, the girls get to play," Stella says, her smile getting wider as she follows my line of thought.

"It's a good job we love you, you fucking savage," Emmie says, wrapping her arm around her friend and leading the way to the hidden entrance to the torture chamber that lies beneath us.

26

———

NICO

I scan the group of men currently filling the boss's office with a sense of pride.

My boys are standing on either side of me while Uncle Damien talks with Matteo, the newly crowned Mariano boss, while Ant and Enzo flank his sides.

The smile on Ant's face is infectious, and I find myself grinning right alongside him.

The past few weeks must have been hell.

He's been ripped away from his family, from everything he's ever known, after taking one serious beating from those who are meant to be on his side before being thrust into our lives.

I mean, I'm sure it's not all been bad. We throw some killer parties, after all. But he has to be craving home.

I sure know I am, and I've only been away from her for less than an hour.

Home. It's no longer a place but a person.

My siren.

The only person I've ever met who's been able to bring both the best and worst out of me at the same time. She makes me crazy to the point I wonder if I should be checking myself into some special kind of clinic, but she also fixes me, all at the same time.

It's a head fuck.

One that I'm no longer going to spend time trying to understand or dissect.

It is what it is. And I never want it to fucking stop.

"Stand still," Theo hisses in my ear as I fidget restlessly.

"I don't want to be here."

"Tough."

The words Uncle Damien is saying to Matteo blur into nothing. I'm sure it's really important peacekeeping shit, but fuck if I care.

We did what we went out to do tonight. The virus that has been infiltrating our side of the city has been eliminated, and it's time to try and remember what life was like before he started trying to take over. Hell, it's time to fucking sleep.

"Uh..." Daemon mutters on my other side. "The alarm to the basement just went off."

"What?" Theo hisses as he pulls his phone from his pockets to see what's going on.

"Oh fuck," Daemon grunts.

"Are you fucking shitting me? What the hell are they doing?"

"Problem?" Uncle Damien barks as Daemon turns his phone so I can see the security feed he's pulled up.

"No, Boss," Theo says, although not once does he look up from the screen.

If Uncle Damien says anything in response, then I don't hear it, because I'm too focused on watching the show before me.

Stella and Emmie lead the way—hardly surprising—as

the five of them descend the stairs and head directly to Brad's cell.

There's movement around me, voices, but I don't register any of it until the giant flat screen hanging on the wall comes to life and a bigger version of what I'm watching appears for the entire room to see.

"What the fu—" Uncle Damien starts but cuts himself off when Stella wakes the cunt up with a fist to the face.

"Holy shit," Matteo gasps as all of us collectively take a step forward to watch the show.

There's no sound, Theo hasn't put it on, but it doesn't fucking matter.

"Ouch," Ant winces as Brianna steps up to the man who tried to take everything from her and slams her knee into his junk.

But while everyone around me arches over as if she just assaulted them, my cock begins to harden as I watch my girl take control.

And fuck, does she own it.

With Stella and Emmie's instruction, she batters the barely conscious man hanging in the centre of the room.

He was already in a pretty bad state before they entered, thanks to Daemon's experiments.

The bellend held his tongue for quite a while. Daemon was almost impressed. Almost.

But in true Daemon fashion, he soon had Brad squealing like a pig, and willingly spilling all his twisted secrets. And once we had all those, there really was only one thing left to do.

I was going to bring it up with Brianna when I felt the time was right. There was no rush; Daemon liked his new pet and was willing to keep him barely breathing a little longer.

It seems that wasn't necessary, because she has it more than handled.

"Ooof," Alex gasps. "Your girl is a savage."

A wide smile spreads across my face as I watch her go to town on him.

"There's definitely Harris blood in there. Jesus," Theo adds.

"From what we heard on the comms earlier, that's not the only DNA inside her," Uncle Damien deadpans, successfully dragging my eyes from my girl. My lips part, but I don't get a chance to accuse him of being a massive creep before he puts his hands up in defence. "I took the earpiece out the second I knew that was happening."

"Didn't stop us hearing her scream, though," Galen mutters.

"Louder than Stella?" Seb asks, risking having his throat cut by her father.

"Don't fucking start," Galen warns.

Silence falls again as we continue watching the girls.

Despite her burst of violence earlier, Calli mostly stands back and watches with a mix of pride and horror on her face as the others let loose.

Blood covers them all as they fight to the death, which has to be close. I mean, he was practically there anyway.

"Uh... where do I find myself one of those?" Matteo asks, his eyes fixed on our girls.

"Not sure they make Italian girls like that, man," Seb offers helpfully.

"No worries. We're all friends now, I'll have one of yours."

"Like fuck you will," Uncle Damien growls. "We might have a truce, but there are limits. None of my girls are going to be Marianos."

A smirk twitches at Matteo's lips. "We'll see."

A few more minutes pass with us watching our girls be the bad-arses we know they are before it becomes obvious to everyone that they've achieved what they went for.

Emmie, Stella, and Jodie back away from Brad's battered body, leaving my Siren standing before him with her top lip peeled back in disgust.

She doesn't say a word—not out loud, anyway. I'm sure there's plenty going on in her head.

We all stand there, barely breathing, waiting to see what she's going to do.

After long silent seconds, her lips part and I swear the words 'thank you' actually fall from her.

My brows pinch in confusion as I watch her turn her back on him and walk out of the cell, followed by the others. The door swings closed behind them as we all continue watching in silence as they climb the stairs and disappear from our live feed.

"Well, that was something," Uncle Damien mutters before turning around and commanding the room once more.

Thankfully, the boss didn't keep us longer than necessary. I think it was pretty obvious where we all wanted to be after that little show our girls put on.

If our faces didn't show it, then the tightness of our already pretty fitted trousers sure pointed him in the right direction.

I've been hard since the moment I first saw my girl standing in front of her enemy, and it's not going to be going down anytime soon. There's really only one way to fix the situation.

"Stop," I demand when Theo approaches a shopping centre that's still open. Although, only just.

"What?"

"Just fucking pull over. I need to get something."

Not giving him a chance to refuse, I reach over and yank the wheel to the left, forcing him to pull into the free space beside us.

"What the fuck, Nico?" he barks, steam threatening to billow out of his ears.

"Pipe the fuck down. I'll be like five minutes, tops."

Total fucking lie, but whatever.

"You want company?" Toby offers from the back of the car.

"Nope," I say, but I'm pretty sure the door is already closed before the word tumbles from my lips.

I take off toward the main entrance. There's a security guard stopping people from entering, seeing as it's closing time, but fuck that.

Knocking his arm out of the way when he tries to stop me, I race into the building in search of what I need.

I head for the first shop that will have what I'm looking for with my heart pounding so hard it makes my head spin.

But nothing will stop me now that I've got this idea in my head.

"I'm sorry, we're closing," a woman says as I push open the door she's trying to shut.

"You can in five minutes after you've helped me with something. It's an emergency."

She stares at me with a raised brow.

"Please," I beg, shooting her my most knee-weakening smile.

"Come on then," she says, proving that despite no longer being on the market, my pretty face can get women to do almost anything. Oh, the power.

Three minutes. That's all it takes to find what I'm looking for, pay, and get the hell out before security takes matters into their own hands.

"Sorry, man. Emergency," I explain when the same guy who tried to stop me on the way in growls at me as I exit. "Have a good night." I know I am.

"What the fuck was that?" Theo asks when I drop back into his passenger seat.

"You can go," I say, nodding toward the road beside us.

"Are you for fucking real? What did you even get?" he asks, his eyes dropping to my empty hands.

"None of your fucking business." I smirk.

"Prick," he mutters before pulling the car out of the space and rejoining the traffic.

"You're seriously going to pull that stunt and not explain?" Toby asks, wrapping his hands around my headrest and leaning forward so he can glare at me.

"Viagra," Alex says. "He needs to give his little guy some extra help tonight," he explains like it's fucking necessary.

"Fuck off, I didn't buy any Viagra."

"Shit, they'd run out? I'm sure if you talk to Theo nicely, he'll share his stash."

"What?" Theo splitters. "Don't fucking drag me into this."

"It's interesting that you bring up this little issue while you're the only one going home with no one to fuck. Jealous, man?"

"Who says I don't have anyone to fuck? For all you know, I've got a flat full of fuck buddies waiting for me."

"Sure you do," Toby teases.

"I have more sex than the lot of you put together," Alex announces.

"Dude, that is physically impossible," I say, more than aware of how often everyone in this group is at it.

"Yeah, well... fuck you all," he sulks.

"Aw, man. It'll happen. You'll meet her."

Alex scoffs.

"Him?" Toby jokes.

"Think he'd take anyone at this point," Theo says, earning himself a slap around the head from Alex.

"I hate you all. I hope you fuck yourselves to death tonight."

The three of us are still laughing as Theo drives into our underground garage.

The second we come to a stop, my door is open, and I'm heading toward the lift.

"Fucking hell, that Viagra must have kicked in fast. Look at him go."

Flipping Toby off over my shoulder, I keep going, heading toward where I know my girl is waiting for me.

Theo, the cunt, manages to shove his hand into the lift just before the doors close.

"Nice try," he grunts as the three of them pile in with me.

No one says anything as we climb through the building. We don't need to. We all know what's going to happen next. It's why Alex is so pissed off.

We spill out onto the top floor of our building which houses both mine and Theo's penthouses, knowing that the girls are hanging out with Bri in my place.

The second the green light shows on my biometric scanner, I throw the door open and storm in.

All eyes turn on me as I race into the living room, looking for my girl.

"Where is she?" I demand, my heart jumping into my throat when I find everyone but my siren.

Panic rises in me faster than I thought possible and crazy, paranoid thoughts slam into me, leaving me weak and vulnerable.

"Waiting for you in your bedroom," Stella says with a smirk.

I take off before she's even finished explaining.

"Enjoy," someone calls from behind, but I'm too far gone to even consider trying to work out who it was.

I almost rip the door handle off as I twist it, throwing the door open to find the one person I need.

My eyes land on her laying out on the bed, and I almost trip over my own feet in my need to get to her.

"Holy fuck, Siren," I blurt as the door slams behind me.

"You told me to be waiting for you, wearing the sexist thing I have."

"Fuck," I grunt as she runs her hand up her naked body, spreading her legs to show me everything.

My jacket hits the floor a beat before my knees do.

Her face, her chest, and her arms are covered in blood.

His blood.

And fuck if I'm not hard as fucking steel, knowing what she did.

"I killed him," she confesses.

"Fuck. I know. I watched. It was magnificent. You're magnificent."

Pressing my hands against her thighs, I spread her wider and lick her from arsehole to clit, my chest puffing out as she screams out my name for the entire world to hear.

27

BRIANNA

"Nico," I scream as he sucks on my clit. My back arches off the bed as my fingers twist in his hair, holding him against me. "Yes. Yes. Yes."

He eats me like a man possessed. Just like I hoped he would.

I have no idea what came over me as I walked into that cell in the basement.

When we returned, I knew I needed to do something. I couldn't go back up to this flat after everything we'd been through, knowing that the man who will have forever changed my life was still breathing a few floors beneath us.

It was a night for cleansing this city of its rats, and he was one that needed to go with them.

I had every intention of walking in there, pulling the gun that was tucked in the back of my jeans and mimicking what Nico had done twice tonight. Assuming I had any kind of aim, of course. I've never fired a real gun in my life, and I'm not sure the water pistols Jodie and I have chased each other around with in the past really count as target practice.

But then Stella stepped up and punched him straight across the cheek, and this violent haze that I only realised I possessed recently just descended over me.

I didn't even think. I couldn't. The only thing in my head was that this man wanted to hurt me, ruin me, utterly fucking destroy me in his need for power and control, and there was no fucking way that he was going to get away with that.

He taught me who I can count on, how much I love the man I watched fight for his family tonight, and he allowed me to finally understand where I came from. And the power that apparently comes with my DNA... yeah, he found himself on the wrong end of it.

And fuck if it didn't feel good to show him just who he went up against.

I guess, in the end, he was right. He didn't need to be scared of the Cirillos. He should have been terrified of me.

I fully believe that even if Nico wasn't there to catch me that day, I'd have rescued myself. I'm just really fucking glad I had him to run into.

"Oh fuck, yeah. Right there," I cry as he pushes two fingers inside me.

With a few more precision licks of my clit and grazes of my G-spot, he sends me crashing into one of the most intense orgasms I've ever experienced.

Even our little session on the bonnet of that car earlier didn't take the edge off.

My body trembles and convulses as he works me through wave after wave of pleasure until I'm a lifeless, sweaty heap on the bed.

Who knew violence was such an aphrodisiac?

Sitting back on his haunches, he wipes the back of his

hand across his glistening mouth before making a show of licking my taste off his lips.

I stare down at him with my chest heaving and my need for more increasing by the second. He's not even naked and I'm practically drooling for him.

"I've got something for you," he says, his voice deep and raspy. "Sit up."

I do as I'm told. I'm too intrigued not to.

Pushing his hand into his pocket, he grabs something and pulls it out.

"What?" I ask with a laugh, still riding high on endorphins.

"You made me promise, and I want to seal the deal."

My brows pinch as I study him.

"What are you—"

"Give me your hand, Siren."

And I do, because hell, I'd throw myself off a cliff if he asked me nicely.

Lifting my arm, I hold my hand out between us as crazy arse thoughts fill my mind about what he's going to do.

Surely, he's not—

"NICO," I shriek as he does the exact thing I was picturing.

"You're mine, Siren. You promised me. Now, let's make it official."

I see him grin in my periphery, but I don't look up. My eyes are locked on the fucking ring he just pushed onto my finger.

My fucking ring finger.

"N-Nico, you can't just—"

"Why not?" he asks, surging to his feet. "Would you say no if I asked?"

"Well... that's not the point. You didn't ask."

With my hand still in his, he cups my jaw with the other and stares down into my eyes.

"Brianna An—Ha—" I shake my head, not willing to go there right now. "Siren, will you marry me?"

All the air rushes out of my lungs as those words fill my ears.

My heart soars, my stomach knots, and emotion burns up the back of my throat.

Time stops—literally fucking stops—as I stare at him.

The gold in his eyes shines bright as he watches me with something akin to amusement while I silently freak out.

Why isn't he freaking out?

He's the ultimate player who never wanted anything serious.

Why isn't he freaking the fuck out?

"Breathe, babe," he says softly, his thumb brushing over my bottom lip.

"Y-you... you just asked me to marry you?"

The most incredible smile curls at his lips.

"Did you... did you mean to?"

His responding laugh makes my toes curl with desire.

"Is that a yes?" he asks, the gold shining even brighter.

My mouth opens and closes like a freaking fish as I stand there like a deer in headlights.

The last few months flash through my head like the fastest movie in the world before I land right back here, standing before the man who, without permission, has utterly stolen my heart and flipped my world upside down, and I realise there really is only one answer to his question.

"Yes," I whisper.

His smile grows so wide it practically meets his ears.

"Yeah?"

"Yeah," I confirm.

"Fuck. Get on your knees; I need your lips around my cock right the fuck now."

"So romantic," I mutter as I allow my knees to buckle beneath me as he pushes against my shoulder.

I land on the thick carpet at our feet and immediately reach for his waistband. But only with one hand. The other begins stroking his more-than-obvious erection that's straining against the fabric of his trousers.

"Been like this since I saw you walk in that cell," he confesses as I loosen his belt and pop the button.

"How did you know?"

"W-we get alerts when the doors o-o-open." His lids lower as I pull his dick free and slowly stroke him.

"And you all watched?" I ask, teasing him by letting my breath race over the head of his cock as I speak.

"Uh-huh," he agrees, twisting his fingers in my hair and trying to drag me forward. "Siren," he warns. "Wrap your lips around me and let me fuck your throat."

"When you ask so nicely." I smile at him, letting him see every single thing I'm feeling for him right now as I lick him, letting the saltiness of his precum coat my tongue.

His deep groan bounces off the walls around us, and my need to hear more has me sinking down on his length.

"Fuck, yes," he growls, his grip on my hair tightening until it hurts as I take him all the way back.

He lets me have control for all of two minutes before his need to dominate the situation takes over and he starts thrusting his hips, forcing himself deeper down my throat.

Relaxing my muscles, I let him take what he needs. Hell if he doesn't deserve it after everything he's done tonight.

"Fuck, Siren. I'm gonna come so fucking hard," he grunts, his eyes never leaving mine. "You ready?"

Gripping his arse harder, I sink my nails into his skin. The pain helps push him over the edge and his cock pulses in my mouth, hot ropes of cum sliding down my throat.

The second he's done, he has me on my feet, carrying me across the room until he presses my front against the floor-to-ceiling windows.

I yelp as the coldness of the glass bites into my heated skin, my nipples instantly hardening.

A violent shiver rips through my body as his knuckles skate down my spine until he palms my arse then dips his fingers between my legs, finding my heat.

"You fucking love sucking me off, don't you, Siren?" he growls in my ear as he teases me, collecting up my juices and spreading them over my clit.

"Yes," I moan. "I love it."

"Dirty, dirty whore," he groans, kicking my legs wider to give him better access.

A whimper rips from my throat when his fingers leave me. The heat of his body presses against my back. It's almost enough to make up for his touch. Almost.

Thankfully, he doesn't keep me waiting, and he pulls me away from the window slightly so he can slide his hand down my stomach to find my clit once more.

"Yes," I moan as he circles me leisurely.

Leaning back, I rest my head against his shoulder and press my lips to his neck.

"Look," he says, startling me with the roughness of his voice.

Following his stare, I find my hand pressed against the window. My hand with my new ring on.

"Mine," he groans, staring at it. "My fucking queen."

I stare at the ring, taking it in for the first time since he slid it on my finger.

"It's a crown," I blurt.

"I know it's not a real engagement ring, but I didn't have many options. I'll get you—"

"It's perfect."

"Babe, it cost like eighty qu—"

"I don't care. It could be a Haribo and I wouldn't care."

"Fuck, you're perfect," he says, nuzzling my neck, grazing my sensitive skin with his teeth.

Tilting my head to the side, I give him better access, my skin erupting in goosebumps from his drugging kisses.

"All that out there," he says, ensuring my eyes focus on the view of the city. "It's going to be ours. You ready for that?"

"Anything. As long as it's with you," I confess.

"I like the fucking sound of that Mrs. Brianna Cirillo."

"Nico," I whimper. Hearing that name roll off his tongue sends shivers through me. I'd be lying if I said I hadn't had something of an identity crisis this week. Discovering that the name I've always know myself as was fake, and that my real surname should be Harris, which belongs to a man I know nothing but awful things about, has been a head fuck.

I never would have thought hearing myself being referred to as a wife would feel right. But it does.

Fuck my past and all the bullshit. It's time to think about the future, and I'm more than ready to take that on, to fully embrace this incredibly dangerous, broken, crazy man behind me and figure out this whole life thing together.

"Fuck me, please."

"It would be my pleasure."

I grind my arse back against him, feeling him hard again.

"You're wicked, Mrs. Cirillo. Fuck, you just gushed over my hand."

"Please," I whimper, my body just about ready to combust from his gentle touch.

His fingers leave me in favour of grabbing my hips so he can position me exactly where he wants me.

"Yes," I cry when I'm almost bent in half and he's rubbing the head of his cock through my juices, spreading them from my clit to my arse.

I push back against him, letting him know what I want.

"Fuck, babe. Do you know how badly I want to take you here?" he groans.

"So what are you waiting for?"

"Later. I need this first."

Thank fuck he's holding me, because he thrusts into me with such force that my arms would have buckled, sending me careening toward the window.

My pussy grips him tight, desperately trying to get him deeper.

"Fucking addicted to this cunt, Siren."

"Move, please," I beg when he just circles his hips, hitting those places deep inside me. But it's not enough.

His grip tightens before he pulls out.

"Ready?"

"So fucking ready. Give it to me. Everything you've got."

"Fuck, yeah," he roars before slamming back inside me, rocking my world in the way only Nico can.

Once he's set a punishing rhythm, he releases my hip in favour of twisting his fingers in my hair.

He drags me from the window and tugs my head back so he can access my lips, which he takes in a filthy, all-consuming kiss.

It's wet and dirty and all tongues and teeth. It's fucking everything.

"Clit," he growls without breaking our kiss. "Now."

Following orders like the dirty whore he accuses me of, my hand slips down my body, but I don't stop when I get to that aching nub; instead, I keep going, wrapping my fingers around his shaft where it disappears inside my body.

"Fuck, Siren," he groans, getting thicker as he tries to hold his orgasm back.

"Get yourself there, or I'm going without you."

His teeth sink into my bottom lip, the pain shooting straight between my legs, forcing me to release him and do as I'm told.

"Shit," he hisses as I pinch my clit, my muscles clamping down on him. "Need you coming, babe. We do this together."

"Always," I promise, pushing myself over the edge I was already riding from his cock and filthy words alone.

"NICO," I scream as the first wave of my release hits not a second before his body stills behind me and he once again spills his seed inside me with zero concern for the consequences.

He kisses me until we've both ridden out our highs, then he slips out of me, scoops me up into his arms and carries me to the bed—thank fuck, because I'm not sure my legs would have taken me there.

He lowers me down gently, then crawls over me, his lips finding mine once more as his hands begin to wander.

"How tired are you?" he whispers.

"I'm not," I confirm. "We can go all night."

"That might be an offer I have to take you up on."

Slowly, one kiss at a time, he works his way down my

body, kissing and nipping me as if we both haven't already had two intense releases each.

When he ends up between my thighs once again, he doesn't bat an eye that his cum is still running out of me and he licks at me again, savouring our combined taste.

It's fucking filthy, and I love it.

"What's wrong, babe? You look jealous. You want a taste too?"

Dipping his fingers inside me, he coats them before offering them up to me.

The second I can reach them, I wrap my tongue around his digits, cleaning him up.

"Fuck," he groans. "I need you again."

NICO

I finally shed my clothes before flipping her over. I drag her arse back against me, grinding into her.

"Please," she whimpers, her desperation going straight to my dick.

I fucking love it when she's like this.

Reaching over, I pull the top drawer of my bedside table open and rummage around for what I need.

"Does my filthy whore need my cock?" I ask, barely able to form the words. I need back inside her too much to think about anything else. Every ounce of blood in my body is in my dick. It doesn't matter that I've already unloaded in her mouth and pussy. I need more. I always fucking need more.

"Nico. Please. I need—" Her words are cut off when I flip the lid on the bottle of lube and dribble it between her cheeks.

She moans like a wanton slut, and it only gets louder when I dip my fingers into the wetness and tease her puckered hole.

"Oh fuck," she groans loudly when I push one finger inside.

I can't help but grunt in response. "So fucking tight."

My cock weeps, needing to be inside her, feeling that ring of muscle strangling it instead of my finger.

"More," she cries, pushing back against me.

"Fuck."

I make quick work of prepping her as she demands for me to give her more. But as much as I want that too, I'm not rushing this. I refuse to hurt her. She might be covering it well, but there's no way she's not still hurting from her ordeal. The bruises might be fading, but there's more evidence littered over her body, and I know it's not going to be leaving her head anytime soon.

The second I'm happy that she's ready, I squeeze another generous amount of lube over my aching length and finally line myself up with her entrance.

"Yes, Nico. Please. Fuck me right fucking now."

Unable to deny her request, I thrust forward.

"Relax, babe. Be a good girl and let me in."

And she does.

"Jesus. Fuck. This arse. Fuck," I bark as her heat surrounds me and her muscles ripple. "I'm not gonna last."

"Nico," she whimpers as I pull out before slowly sliding back in. "Not enough. More. More."

Pulling my hand back from her hip, I crack it across her arse cheek. "Filthy, filthy girl," I bark, taking her harder and faster.

Considering I'm the one who's concerned about crashing too fast, Brianna is the one screaming out her next release in only seconds.

And she squeezes me so goddamn tight that I have no choice but to fall with her, roaring out her name as pleasure explodes from my cock and shoots off around my body.

My body gives out and I collapse on top of her, crushing

her between me and the mattress. She doesn't complain, and even if she did, I'm not sure I'd have the power to do anything about it.

The only thing that can be heard is our ragged breathing as we come down from our highs.

"Fucking love you, Siren," I groan, my voice hoarse.

"Love you too."

I have no idea how much time ticks by, but eventually, I manage to roll my weight off her and tuck her body into mine so I can hold her.

Silence spreads out around us, but it's not uncomfortable. The opposite, in fact.

I have no idea what's rolling around in her head, but I have a feeling that her thoughts aren't all that different from mine.

I hold her a little tighter, my fingers fidgeting with the new ring proudly displayed on hers.

It was a totally hot-headed decision to make Theo stop. But after the promises we made each other earlier in the day, it just felt right to seal them with a ring.

Okay, so the eighty-quid crown ring wasn't exactly what I had in mind to propose with. Or at least, it wouldn't have been if I ever saw myself offering forever to a woman. But the second my eyes landed on it in the shop, I just knew it was the one.

The one for now.

My queen deserves something way bigger and better than that. It'll just take a little more effort than sweet talking a shop assistant to find it.

My lips part to say something, to make sure she's okay, but she beats me to it.

"How are you feeling?"

"Amazing," I confess. "That was—"

"I don't mean the sex, Nico. I mean—"

"I know what you mean," I cut her off before she ruins the moment by naming any of those we dealt with tonight. "And my answer is still the same. Everything we did tonight, we did for us. For our future. And that is the most important thing to me right now.

"Fuck yesterday, last month, last year. It's all about tomorrow, babe."

"B-but you killed—"

"Shh," I breathe, sliding my hand up her arm and wrapping it around the back of her neck so I can tilt her face so she has no choice but to look up at me. "I did what needed to be done to keep you and the rest of my family safe. I'd do it a hundred times over for those I love."

She stares up at me with her big blue eyes, and I swear my heart flips over in my chest.

"Anything for you, Siren."

"Same," she breathes before stretching up to take my lips in an emotion-filled kiss that makes me melt for her.

***

It was long gone midnight by the time we finally stumbled toward the bathroom to wash up. Although, that wasn't all we did in there, and by the time we fell into bed tangled together with sated smiles on our faces, we both sank into our exhaustion.

And I fell into a peaceful sleep, knowing that we've got everyone off our backs and my girl tucked safely in my arm.

Although, that isn't how I wake however many hours later, because when I reach for her, all I find is an empty, cold bed.

With a groan, I flip over to look at the clock, and my groan gets louder when I stare at the time.

I've got a fucking exam this afternoon.

I could really, really do with binning those off.

But I won't. Dad wanted me to do them, and even if I fail after all this, at least I will have tried.

With a sigh, I throw my legs over the side of the bed and pad toward the bathroom.

It's not until I kick the door closed behind me that I realise it's the first time I've woken without her and not immediately panicked that she might have run.

I know she hasn't. After yesterday, I know she's here with me. Even if she has left the flat in favour of hanging out with Jodie and the girls, I know she's coming back to me.

I brush my teeth and pull on a pair of boxers before heading out of the bedroom to start my search for my girl.

The scent of coffee hits me as I progress toward where I hope she is.

I feel lighter than I have in a really fucking long time as I close the space between us, each of my footsteps easier than I'm sure they ever have been. Everything, even breathing, just seems effortless.

But that all comes crashing down when I round the corner and find her curled up on one of the chairs at the dining table, wearing one of my shirts with her phone and what looks like a packet of pills before her.

Her shoulders are slumped, and she's so lost in her own head that she hasn't even noticed me approach.

It's not until I'm standing right beside her that she startles and looks up at me.

"Siren?" I whisper, dragging a chair closer and lowering my arse to it.

My knees bump against her bare thigh as I reach for her hands and take them both in mine.

"What's going on, babe?" I ask gently, hating the vulnerability that's coming off her in waves.

I want to say it's just the effects of the past couple of weeks and what happened last night has finally tipped her over the edge. But I think it's more than that.

She doesn't do or say anything for long, agonising seconds. She doesn't even look up from that white and purple box.

"I thought I'd just take it and everything would be okay," she finally whispers.

I keep my lips sealed, letting her say what's on her mind without interruption.

"I thought I'd made my decision on this years ago. It was never going to happen and I'd do anything I could to stop it. But then, here I am. It's right there, what I thought I always wanted, and I don't know if I can do it."

My head spins, trying to figure out what she's talking about.

"What if this is meant to happen? What if I'm not destined to be like her? What if taking that is the wrong decision and I'll forever regret it?

"So much has been taken out of my hands recently, and weirdly, I've been okay with that. But this... this feels so much bigger than even what I did last night. I... "

She trails off and finally lifts her eyes to mine.

They're bloodshot and full of unshed tears, although from the state of her cheeks, I'm pretty sure she's already let a few fall.

"Babe," I say, releasing one of her hands in favour of cupping her cheek.

The second I make contact, her first tear falls, running down the back of my hand.

"Talk to me. What's really—" I look to the side and my eyes lock on two words on the box she was staring at.

Emergency contraception.

"Brianna, I—"

"He cut my implant out, Nico. And we... w-we've—"

"I know. It's okay, babe. Calm down, yeah?" I say in what I hope is a soft and supportive voice. Hell knows I've never needed to use one before. Not like this, anyway.

"You've just ignored it. I didn't even know for sure if you knew."

"You really think I'd miss anything about you, Siren? Come on. I know everything there is to know about your body."

"B-but—" she sucks in a shaky breath. "I'm not protected. We could have—"

"Yeah, we could."

"And you're okay with that?"

I shrug. Probably not the answer she was hoping for, but it is what it is.

"Babe, if I had an issue with the consequences, I wouldn't have done the actions."

She holds my eyes for a beat before a smile twitches at her lips.

"I'm serious, Nico. This..." she says, gesturing to the box on the table. "It's serious."

"I am being serious. That ring I put on your finger last night, when I told you forever, I was pretty fucking serious."

"You're nineteen," she points out. "You can't possibly want—"

"Unless you're trying to remind yourself of what a hot boytoy you've got, babe, then my age has fuck all to do with anything. I haven't been a kid since I was about eight and started running around with guns and learning how to kill men twice my size with one single punch.

"What we've got... It's everything to me. And I want everything with you. If that's now or in the years to come. I'll never say no to anything.

"If you want to take that and get back on birth control, that's what we'll do. But equally, if you don't want to take it, then I'll be right there beside you."

She bites down on her bottom lip as she studies me, trying to find the lies in my words.

She won't, though.

Yeah, this conversation is fucking terrifying, and I'm in no way feeling prepared for what the outcome could be. But there's no way I'm going to push her into a decision that she's not happy with. While the result could change my entire life, it's not as much as it'll change hers.

"What do you want, Bri? What's really in your heart?"

Her eyes drop to my lips as I run my tongue over the bottom one.

"It's not so much about what I want. It's more what I don't want."

"Okay." I nudge her chin, forcing her to look at me. "Go on."

"I don't want history to repeat itself. I don't want to be my mother and ruin someone else's life."

"You won't. That will never happen," I assure her with absolute certainty.

"And... I don't want to kill anyone else, Nico. Two people have lost their lives because of me."

"They deserved it."

"Not the point. I killed them, Nico. They're done.

Vanished from this Earth without a choice in it. I'm not sure I can do it again."

"Then don't. And yeah, we had unprotected sex, but that doesn't mean anything has happened. Is it even the right time?" I ask with a wince. I'm entirely out of my depth here and starting to wish I paid a little more attention to all this when we did sex ed instead of just focusing on the sex part.

"I don't know," she confesses quietly. "I barely have periods with the implant in. I've long lost track of what's meant to happen when."

"You might be freaking out over nothing," I point out, lifting her from her seat and depositing her on my lap instead.

"Or I might be."

"So, do you want to wait and find out, or do you want to do something about it?" I ask before peppering kisses down the side of her neck, making goosebumps erupt over her skin. "You don't have any knickers on, do you?" I ask when the heat of her pussy practically burns through my boxers.

"Do you take anything seriously?"

"Yes. I take sex with you very seriously. It is hands down the most important thing in my life right now."

"Pretty sure that should be your exams. You do know you have an English lit one this afternoon, right?"

"Of course I do."

Her gasp rips through the air when I slip my hand beneath the shirt she's wearing and cup her breast.

"Wanna help me study? Our sessions were the highlight of my year thirteen experience."

"Nico," she moans when I pinch her nipple. "You need to focus."

"I'm more than focused on laying you out on this table

and eating you until I need to leave for my exam. If you just so happen to give me some information about what I might be expected to write about while I'm at it, then that's up to you."

"You're a nightmare," she says, hopping up out of my reach and walking around the table so I can't get to her. "I'm ordering breakfast, and you..." Her eyes drop to the serious tent in my boxers. "Get rid of that and go and get your books. From here on out, you're going to be fully prepared for each exam you sit."

"As you wish, Mrs. Cirillo."

Her eyes shutter as I call her that, and it does nothing to sink my boner.

29

BRIANNA

"What are you doing?" Nico asks when I follow him through to the bedroom to get changed with him.

"I'm coming with you," I say confidently.

A wicked smile appears on his face.

"As much as I'd love for you to sit next to me while I take this exam, I don't think they'll let you. Teacher or not."

"Ha, cute," I say, pulling open his wardrobe to find something to wear. Almost all my stuff is still at my flat—something else that we need to talk about—but Jodie and Toby did pack me some essentials to tide me over until we make a decision about where I'm going to be living.

Honestly, for the first time in a very, very long time, the desire to have my own space isn't there. I'll be more than happy to just stay here. But while things have moved at the speed of light in the past few days with Nico, I'm not ready to broach the subject of me moving in.

I don't know why I'm shying away from it. He's asked me to marry him; I'm wearing his ring. We just had a whole bizarre conversation about the consequences of our fucking without protection, yet I'm scared to ask if he wants me here.

What if he doesn't?

It's stupid.

Really fucking stupid.

But there is still a small part of me that thinks he's going to wake up and realise that he just freaked out when he couldn't fuck me for a few days and remember that he doesn't want me, or a relationship.

I wish I could squash the doubts and for once believe that I am enough, that I'm not going to be turned away in favour of something new. But that deeply ingrained childhood fear still lingers.

"You don't need to do this yet, you know that, right?" Nico says, dragging me from my own head. "There's no rush. Your place at Knight's Ridge will be there, no matter how long it takes."

"Nico," I sigh.

"No, Brianna," he says firmly. "I know you don't want special treatment because you're one of us now, but you're fucking getting it, okay? School isn't going to kick you out because you've been through some shit. Uni won't, either. Uncle Damien won't allow it."

"I can't—"

"You can," he states, closing the space between us in a heartbeat and taking my chin in his hand. "You are one of us, and we will treat you as such. Teaching is your dream. It's what you were made to do—aside from being my whore," he adds quickly. "And it will happen. Fuck Brad and my bullshit behaviour which stopped you from doing what you needed to do. You will qualify, and you will have a job come September."

My mouth opens, but he doesn't allow me time to argue

with everything he's just said; instead, he makes use of my parted lips by slamming his down on them and plunging his tongue into my mouth.

"Take the help, Brianna. We're a team now, a family. You've helped us, so let us return the favour."

"You don't play fair," I mutter, our lips still connected.

"There's no fun in fair, babe. Now, stop trying to distract me with sex, I've got an exam to get to."

"Me? You were the one who kissed me."

"Yeah, and you're the one that did this," he says, grabbing my hand and pressing it against his hard length that's hidden behind his boxers.

"Did nothing," I purr innocently as I step away and make a show of peeling his shirt from my body.

"Motherfucker," he grunts.

"Exam time, babe. If you kill it, maybe I'll reward you later."

His eyes trail down my body, the gold in them blazing with heat.

I honestly thought he'd freak out when I finally had the courage to say something about the whole maybe-baby situation.

We've been reckless. I knew that. But I really thought he was just being naïve about the whole situation.

Turns out, I was wrong, and he knew exactly what he was doing every single time he's come inside me since he brought me back here.

Nico was knowingly unloading inside me, aware of the chances of me getting pregnant.

That whole statement is utterly mind-blowing.

Nico. Nico Cirillo, the city's manwhore who used to come out in hives if anyone so much as mentioned any kind of commitment or relationship to him, was almost actively trying to get me pregnant while sliding an engagement ring on my finger.

I shake my head as I turn my back on him, barely able to process all of this on top of everything else that happened recently.

"You don't need to worry, babe. I'm gonna smash this exam. From here on out, everything is going our way."

I nod as I pull a floral sundress from its hanger before going in search of some underwear.

We can only fucking hope, right?

It's weird walking back down the hallways of Knight's Ridge College. There's a part of me that feels like I've been away for so long that my time here is nothing but a figment of my imagination, but there's another part that feels like it's just come home.

Nico and his antics aside, I liked being here. I liked teaching here.

I thought I was going to feel uncomfortable around all the rich kids and well out of my comfort zone. But it was never like I feared.

The kids were always incredible, the teachers so welcoming and supportive.

I could do a hell of a lot worse than land myself a job here in September.

Even if I haven't done anything to deserve it.

Everything is quiet as I make my way down toward the office I want. Classes are in full swing, but I know she has a free lesson.

"Come in," a familiar voice calls after I knock on the door.

Pushing it open, I step inside with a smile on my face.

"Oh my gosh, Brianna," Melissa gasps, her eyes wide.

Before I know what's happening, she's on her feet and racing toward me.

She engulfs me in the warmest of hugs before she stills and pulls back.

"Crap, am I hurting you?"

"No, not at all." *Nothing like having a grown-arse man collapse on you after an intense anal session.* "It's good to see you too," I say, finally recovering from my shock and returning her embrace.

"Coffee?" she asks once we move back toward her desk. She nods at her cafetière sitting beside her monitor and the cute stack of mugs.

"Always."

"Awesome. Take a seat and tell me everything. Well, I guess you can't tell me everything, but you know."

I follow her orders as she pours me a mug, studying her and wondering just how much she already knows.

"How well are you connected?" I ask curiously.

"Loosely. But enough to know you've been through some shit."

I can't help but laugh. "You can say that again."

"So, what can you tell me?" she asks, her eyes sparkling in the hope of some juicy gossip.

Unable to come up with anything more exciting than what's adorning my left hand, I lift it above the table and wiggle my ring finger.

"Fucking hell, girl," she gasps, shocking the hell out of me. She's always been so polite, so well spoken.

"Trust me, I know. But—"

"He's a good one," she says softly. "I know he can be the world's biggest idiot, and he's got an ego the size of Mars.

But if you can get beneath all that bravado and macho bullshit, he's got a heart of gold. What?" she asks when I smile at her.

"Nothing. Just wondering if he has any idea that people can see right through him."

"Nope. And don't ruin it. He loves thinking that we all believe he's 'da shit'."

I can't help but snort in amusement.

Our conversation turns toward school, and Melissa happily forgets all about whatever she was doing when I walked in in favour of catching up. She tells me about the classes I should be teaching by now and what some of the kids I already knew by name have been up to. It's nice. Normal. And it gives me a new rush of excitement to get back to it.

Nico was right earlier; no matter what life throws at me next, there's no way I'll ever be able to give up teaching.

A knock on the door startles both of us, and when the person on the other side joins us, Melissa groans in frustration while our new addition squeals in excitement.

"Brianna, I missed you," Rhea cries, launching herself across the room at me. "My stupid dad and brother stopped me from coming to see you. I'm so glad you killed that creepy motherfucker for treating you like that."

My eyes shoot to Melissa, but if she's shocked by Rhea's announcement, she doesn't show it.

"Rhea," I warn.

"Oh, it's cool. You're down with all this, aren't you, Mel?"

Mel?

"That's enough, Rhea," Melissa snaps. "What did you do to end up here in the middle of a lesson?"

"Nothing. Ms. Taylor was being a di—"

"Watch it, young lady."

Rhea throws her hands up, and groans in frustration.

"I just wanted to see Bri. I've been so worried and no one would tell me anything."

"I thought you eavesdropped on everything," I point out.

"Dad found my bug," she confesses.

"I'm sorry. You bugged your father's office? You do know how dangerous and stupid that is, right?"

Again, all she does is shrug.

"Jesus, Rhea. You need to stop before you discover something you don't want to hear."

"Too late." She winks.

"Well, he found it now, I guess," Melissa says, trying to look positively, but the way Rhea grins makes me wonder if she's already hidden a replacement, or at least has plans to. "I assume you're staying?" Melissa eyes Rhea's bag and the textbook she abandoned on the floor when she ran for me.

"Yep. I'll just be over here. Please continue with whatever you were discussing."

"Don't tell me—you already know, because you've bugged me too."

"I'd never invade your privacy like that, Mrs. Hendrix," Rhea says like the innocent teenager she most certainly isn't.

We continue chatting but significantly change topics now we've got ears listening, and when I notice we're only minutes away from the bell, I pull my phone out and shoot off a message.

I didn't only come here to see Melissa. I've got someone else I want to catch up with in the hope of getting some more answers.

"Hey, how's it going?" Stella asks, looking at me with concerned eyes as she approaches her car where I told her I'd meet her.

"It's good. You?"

"Yeah, you know. Not as exciting as yesterday."

"I could probably cope with no day being as exciting as yesterday," I confess as I drop into her passenger seat.

"Where did you want to go?"

"Dunno, anywhere," I say.

"Waffles it is. Good choice."

We chat about everything and nothing as she heads across town to one of her and Emmie's favourite hangouts. In no time at all, we're sitting in a booth away from the other customers getting their sugar fix while Stella studies me from across the table.

"Why are you looking at me like that?" I ask, shifting nervously under her stare.

"I'm just waiting for you to blurt out all the questions you have."

With a sigh, I reach up and comb my curls from my face.

"How bad was he?" I ask. I don't need to say his name; she knows exactly who I'm talking about.

"Bad. Really fucking bad. But you don't need to worry about him."

"His sons are just as bad, then?"

A smile twitches at her lips before she shakes her head.

"No. They're... not like their father. Or at least, not as far as I'm aware."

"You've never met them?"

"No. Their reputations precede them, though. But I can

totally hook you up with a couple of girls who do know them."

"You'd do that for me?"

"What?" she asks, frowning as if me questioning that is the craziest thing she's ever heard. "Of course. Family, remember?"

Her eyes drop to the ring adorning my finger, but she doesn't say anything. It's not unusual for me to be wearing one. I never really bought into the whole it's-bad-luck-to-wear-a-ring-on-your-ring-finger bullshit. I never intended to be anyone's fiancée, so it never fazed me.

But instead of commenting on it, she continues with our previous conversation.

"Harley, one of my girls from Rosewood. Her boyfriend and his brother used to be... connected."

"By connected, you mean, part of their gang?"

"Kane, the eldest brother, was a Hawk, yes. He managed to get out earlier this year thanks to Reid, your eldest brother and the new leader."

I drop my eyes to the table and shake my head.

My brother.

How the fuck did all this happen?

"How many of them are there?"

"Five. The youngest though, he's..."

"He's what?" I ask, leaning forward, totally invested in her answer.

"He tried to kidnap Harley after she got with her boyfriend."

"Why?"

"Long story that isn't important right now. But..."

"But what?"

"I... uh... I might have shot him. A little bit," she adds,

lifting her hand and holding her thumb and forefinger about half a centimetre apart.

"How do you shoot someone a little bit? Like, you missed and grazed—"

"I never miss, thank you very much. Fine. I shot him, okay?"

"He probably deserved it." I shrug. Why should I care if she hurt one of them? Until a few days ago, I didn't even know they existed.

"What are the others like?" I ask.

"I think that's something you probably need to find out for yourself," she says helpfully.

"Do they know about me?"

"I have no idea. I haven't said anything to Harley. I can totally get one of their phone numbers though, if you'd like to—"

"What the hell is this? How dare you cheat on me?" a familiar voice bellows across the café.

"Oh Jesus. Who let the riff-raff in?" Stella teases as Emmie and an embarrassed-looking Calli march toward us.

"I can't believe you'd do this to me, Stel. I thought this place meant something to us."

Stella rolls her eyes at our friend as the two of them slide into the booth.

"Did we interrupt something?" Calli asks, looking between the two of us.

"No, you're good. Stella was just filling me in on some of my relatives. Apparently, she shot one of them."

"No, shit. Did he deserve it?"

"Obviously," Stella mutters as our server heads over to take Emmie and Calli's order.

"So, do you want to meet them?"

"How many are we talking?" Emmie asks.

"Five brothers."

"Christ. Talk about not doing things by halves."

"Well, it could be four. The one Stella shot is MIA," I explain.

"Why?"

"Because he's a dick who tried to kidnap and hurt my friend, that's why."

"Ah, it's good to hear other's lives are as dramatic as ours," Emmie muses.

"Why do you think I fit in so well here? It's like home away from home."

"We all need to go back to your old home to meet these people," Calli says. "You've talked about Harley and Poppy so much, I feel like I know them."

"And Seb's met them all and we haven't. That's hardly fair," Emmie adds.

"Let's get these exams out of the way, and we'll see what we can do. A vacation sounds like a fucking solid idea."

"Amen to that," I say, lifting my hot chocolate and tapping it to Stella's. "Where's Jojo?" I ask, feeling her absence.

"She's taken Joanne to see your mum," Calli explains.

Selene, Nico's aunt, and Joanne moved her after I requested she had a more comfortable place to recover from her ordeal. Although, they never told me where she went, just that she was out of the building.

I'm still undecided if I want to make time to try and rebuild our relationship—if there even is a relationship to save, that is. I've spent too many years hating the woman for everything she inflicted on me as a child.

Things might be a little different now I know the truth, but it doesn't lessen the pain of what I experienced. The loneliness, the neglect.

Right now, I want to focus on Nico and our future, and our new family. I didn't realise I was missing out on so much until this incredible group of people dragged Jodie and me into their lives and showed us what having a big family was really like.

It's everything. Literally everything. And no matter what happens with my lack of birth control or my mother or anyone else who wants to come and try and rip us apart, I know they won't succeed. The love shared by this family is too strong to let anyone sever it.

"Umm... is there something you need to tell us, Bri?" Calli asks, her eyes locked on the rose gold crown ring that sits on my finger.

"Oh, what? This?" I ask, holding my hand to my chest.

"Oh my God, he didn't?" Emmie gasps while Stella smirks.

"You're going to be my sister?" Calli squeals, her eyes brimming with tears.

"I am," I cry, wrapping my arms around her when she leans in for a hug.

"Mrs. Brianna Cirillo," Emmie says, trying it out for size. "Not bad, cuz." She winks.

All three of them fall into excited chatter, asking me a million questions about how Nico proposed and my ring, which they all think is fucking epic.

My heart is so full, surrounded by them, and I can't wipe the smile off my face as they begin questioning me over wedding plans, as if I've even thought about it among the rest of the shit I've had going on.

I'm so lost in our own little world that I don't notice the atmosphere of the entire café change—nor do I notice the six devastatingly handsome men heading our way with Jodie tucked into her boy's side where she belongs.

Calli is the first to notice, quickly followed by the rest of us.

"Look out, we've been tracked," she teases.

"Ladies," Daemon greets, dragging Calli from the booth to allow Nico to slide in beside me.

"What do you lot think you're doing, stealing my fiancée? I was on a promise after smashing my exam," he complains.

"Oh, pipe down," Emmie says, throwing a marshmallow at him, which he catches and pops into his mouth.

"Wait a minute," Seb says, pausing halfway to Stella's lips. "Did you just say fiancée?"

"Yep," Nico says proudly before he holds my hand out for the guys to see. "She's gonna be my queen. Bought her a crown and everything."

Disbelief ripples through the guys before their pride begins to shine through.

"Congrats, cuz. That's fucking epic."

"Nice one, man," Daemon says, clapping Nico on the shoulder.

Seb and Toby offer up their congratulations while Jodie smiles happily at me. Obviously, she already knows. I'd messaged her a photo of the ring before I went into meltdown mode over the pregnancy situation this morning.

Calli might become my sister by marriage sometime soon, and I might have half-brothers on the other side of the pond, but Jodie will always be my sister, my ride or die, my forever best bitch through it all.

"I can't believe this," Alex grunts. "You two are already married." He points at Emmie and Theo. You two are reproducing, and even the manwhore is getting fucking hitched, and here I am, barely getting my dick wet."

"At fucking last, he's confessing to his lack of action," Seb barks way too loudly.

"Aw, Bro," Daemon says supportively. "Now your new bestie is a free man once again, he can take you out on the pull."

"He's gotta be pretty fucking desperate after being locked up in our building all this time. Surprised he hasn't resorted to fucking you," Toby teases.

"Leave him alone," Nico says, for once not making the situation worse for Alex. "House warming slash engagement party at ours Friday night."

"House warming?" Stella asks. "You've been living there months."

"Yeah, but Brianna hasn't, and we need to celebrate her moving in."

"W-what?" I blurt.

"You really thought I would let you go back to your flat? Siren, didn't you get the memo? You're mine now. Forever."

He stares down at me with nothing but love and devotion in his eyes. It's a far cry from the way he looked at me only a few weeks ago. Or... is it? Was it always there and were we just too stupid to acknowledge it?

My life changed the night I met him in that dive bar. I just never could have appreciated how big an impact he would have on me and how he would turn my world upside down in the best possible way.

"Yeah, I got it," I say, holding my hand up. "Husband."

His eyes flash with heat before he leans forward, his lips brushing my ear in a way that sends a shiver racing down my spine.

"I love you, Siren."

"I love you too. Hey," I complain when I discover the

reason he moved so close when he steals what's left of my waffle and stuffs it into his mouth. "Such an idiot."

"Some things never change," Theo says, watching us closely.

"I really hope they don't," I say to myself with the widest, happiest smile splitting my face.

This really is what dreams are made of. Friendship, laughter, and love. What more could any of us want?

EPILOGUE

Brianna

Siren,

My siren.

I had a meeting with a shrink tonight and amongst other things, she asked me what I wanted. What I really wanted.

I could only think of two things that were worthy of telling her.

1. I want to prove my right to step into my father's footsteps. Whether that is next week, next month, or in ten years, I want it.

2. You.

My pulse rate picks up just like it did the first time I opened this letter.

Only, it hits differently now.

Then, I thought he was joking. Saying anything he

could to get back into my knickers. I mean, yeah, I'm sure there was an element of that. This is Nico we're talking about. But now, as I sit here twisting my engagement ring around my finger, I know that there was a whole lot more truth in his words.

I don't need to tell you that I never wanted anything serious. You understand that just as well as I do.

We're the same, me and you, Siren.

Both are terrified to trust someone enough to hand our hearts, our lives to another in the way those around us have done.

I thought it was a myth that when the right person came along, it would be like second nature.

I fought it. I fought it so fucking hard. You know I did. You've got the scars to prove it.

But I don't want to fight anymore.

I need you, Brianna.

I need you in my life. In my bed. In my heart.

I'm done fighting, I'm done pushing you away.

I'll do whatever it takes to prove to you how serious I am.

I miss you, Siren, and I have no fucking idea how to get you back.

I don't deserve your forgiveness, I know that. But I'm going to do everything I can to make it happen, because I can't imagine my life without you by my side.

I want everything with you, Brianna.

EVERYTHING.

But mostly, right now, I just want the chance to talk to you, to tell you how sorry I am. To tell you how much I love you.

Because I do. And I really want to show you just how good we could be.

I'll wait for you, Brianna. I don't care how long it takes.

I'm here. And I'm yours.

Always.

I blow out a long, slow breath as I read those words for what must be the hundredth time since he first pushed this letter under the door of Toby's guest room. Tears fill my eyes as I think back to how things were between us then.

It wasn't all that long ago, but honestly, it feels like a lifetime after what we've been through in the past couple of weeks.

Back then, I wasn't even talking to him. Now, I'm wearing his ring and have officially moved into his penthouse.

Nico's bachelor lifestyle is no more. And I've never seen him happier.

With the Italians under new control, the leak exposed and my truth uncovered, he's got a new lease on life.

He reminds me of the Nico I first met before he lost himself in grief. But he's not just that Nico. He's an even better version of himself.

And I never thought I'd say it, but I fall in love with him a little harder every time I see him.

The warm breeze blows my hair around my face as I stare out at the city beyond.

The flat behind me is in silence. Nico and the guys are all at school, but they won't be for much longer.

Next week is half term. A reprieve from real life that everyone desperately needs before they sit their final few exams and then embark on their summer.

I, however, will be heading back to Knight's Ridge College full time next Monday to continue my training and then become a permanent member of staff in September.

Accepting the position when I've done nothing to deserve it goes against everything I believe in. But sometimes, you've just got to let things slide. And right now, I could do with a little bit of easy in my life. After all, what's the point in being engaged to one of the most influential men in this part of the city if you can't use it to your advantage every now and then?

I rest back, closing my eyes and making the most of the peace.

I've spent all week packing up my flat and moving in here. I've discovered every inch of this place and fully thrust myself into Nico's life. Not that he's complaining. I swear he has a permanent smile on his face, and it's contagious.

It's weird being so happy after what we've just been through. Anyone on the outside looking in would think we're certifiable, I'm sure. But it is what it is.

The minutes tick by as I clutch his letter to my chest. When Jodie picked it up off the floor that day, I never could have imagined what I'd find hiding inside. It's become one of my most treasured possessions. The moment Nico finally owned up to what he felt. The beginning of us.

I'm so lost in my own head, thinking about times gone by, that I don't hear the front door or the heavy footsteps approaching. His voice, though, flows through me like liquid gold, making butterflies erupt and my skin prickle with desire. Something I hope never ever changes.

"What are you reading?" he asks, joining me on the balcony with his school shirt undone at the collar, his tie hanging loose and his sleeves rolled up, exposing his corded forearms.

Fuck, my man is hot.

My mouth runs dry as I stare at him.

When I don't respond, a smirk curls at his lips.

"Missed me, Mrs. Cirillo?" he growls, taking a step closer.

My heart rate picks up as heat floods my core.

"Had to go into the library today," he confesses. "Wasn't the same without my favourite teacher."

As he gets closer, his intoxicating scent fills my nose and it makes my mouth water.

"Nico," I whimper as he reaches out and plucks his letter from my hand. His brows shoot up as he opens it, finding his own handwriting staring back at him.

"You really did miss me, huh?"

"I found it in one of the boxes," I explain.

Lowering it to the table, he tucks it under my empty glass so it doesn't blow away and drops to his haunches in front of me.

"I meant every word."

"I know."

He quirks a brow.

"Now. I know now," I add.

"Fuck, I love you."

Taking my face in his hands, he brushes his lips over mine in the sweetest of kisses. Something I didn't think he was capable of only a few weeks ago.

"How was your exam?" I ask.

"Already forgotten about," he murmurs, kissing down my neck. "I finished early and spent the rest of my time planning what I wanted to do when I got home."

"Oh yeah?" I ask as his hands begin wandering over my curves.

I'm only wearing a tank—sans bra—and a pair of booty shorts so I almost feel his touch as potently as if I were naked.

"Yeah. Want me to show you what I was imagining?"

Before I get a chance to answer, his fingers are around the hem of my tank and he's peeling it up my body, exposing me to him and the rest of the city. Not that they can see us this high up. Doesn't stop an extra shot of lust from shooting through me, though.

I glance over, looking through the glass barrier to the city beyond.

"You love it, you filthy whore," he groans, sliding his hands beneath my thighs and lifting me from the sofa as if I weigh nothing more than a feather.

We don't move far. All he does is twist me around and lay me out on the outside coffee table before peeling my shorts down my legs, leaving me bare for him.

"Beautiful, and exactly what I imagined. Fucking love this tan on you," he says, trailing a finger down my body, appreciating my lack of tan lines thanks to the privacy of this balcony.

He circles my nipple and a shudder of desire rips through me.

"Please," I whimper, spreading my legs in invitation.

"Fuck, yeah," he grunts, dropping to his knees and latching onto my clit. "This is a welcome home I can get on board with."

With his hands spreading my thighs wide, he eats me like he hasn't had the chance in months. The reality is that he woke me with his face between my thighs this morning. But I'm not fucking complaining.

He doesn't come up for air until I'm screaming his name and coming all over his face. Then he sits back, drops his trousers low enough to expose his hard length, and fucks me over the table with such force we end up at the other side of the balcony once we're both spent.

"Shower," he states, pulling out of me and scooping me up into his arms. "I'm not done with you yet."

"When you invited us to celebrate, we thought you'd both be joining us," Toby's amused voice booms through the flat as I snap my bra into place, much to Nico's irritation.

"Who's idea was this?" he sulks, watching me get dressed with heated eyes.

"Uh... yours," I point out.

"I'm such a fucking idiot."

"Something we can agree on."

Pulling my dress over my body, I take his hand to pull him from the room to join our friends.

By the time we get out into the living room, Alex has already got the music booming and Jodie and Emmie are in the kitchen, making sure the drinks are flowing.

"To the newest member of the building," Jodie says, handing me a cocktail.

"Why thank you," I tease.

We still don't know the outcome of my absent birth control, and I still don't know what I want the result to be. Whatever happens, I'm going to roll with it. But until I get an answer, I'm planning on enjoying life in my new home with my incredible family.

As the drinks start to go down, Seb and Stella appear. Not long after, Calli and Daemon show their faces with a few extras in tow. Isla and Ant immediately join in the party as if they belong, which they sort of do, but Enzo and Matteo look a little awkward.

Theo and Nico soon put any of that to bed by taking them beers and dragging them deeper into the flat.

After everything they've done for us, they deserve this. We can only hope that it's a truce that will last, because having the two Families working together is much more powerful than them being against each other.

I'm busy dancing with the girls when a pair of hands slide around my waist and I'm pulled back against a hot and hard body.

"You look sinful, dancing like that in this little dress," he growls in my ear.

"I guess you should think yourself lucky that you get to peel it off me later then."

A filthy moan falls from my lips as he sucks on the sensitive skin beneath my ear while his hands begin to roam.

"Well, if that's the way this night is going, then I don't mind if I do," Seb says somewhere close before Stella squeals in delight.

I shouldn't really be surprised; our parties always end

up taking this kind of turn. It's inevitable when you've got five couples who are unable to keep their hands off each other.

Toby's arm brushes mine as he moves in front of Jodie, twisting his fingers in her hair and crashing his lips to hers. I have no idea where Theo and Emmie, or Daemon and Calli are; I'm too lost in Nico's burning touch and the way his hard cock grinds against my arse as we move in time with the music.

"Can't get enough of you, Siren," he groans in my ear.

"Good, because you aren't getting rid of me now."

Alex

"For the love of God," I mutter, as one by one the couples in the room begin to pair off.

I'm happy for them all, I really fucking am. But for all that's fucking holy, I'm fed up with this shit.

"Ah, time for the orgy to start," Isla jokes.

Ant laughs along with her, but Enzo and Matteo's eyes widen in surprise.

"So this is why you've been happy living here?" Enzo asks, elbowing Ant in the ribs. "Live porn."

"It's not all it's cracked up to be," I murmur.

It was all fun and games when it was just Seb and Stella, and even Theo and Emmie. But one by one, I've lost my boys. And it fucking sucks.

If it weren't for me inviting these lot, I'd once again be alone while they all enjoy themselves.

I'm trying not to be bitter about it. But some days it's harder than others.

"So you two aren't going to join them, then?" Matteo asks, his eyes shooting between me and Isla.

"I don't fucking think so," Isla grunts, looking downright disgusted.

"Hey, I don't remember you saying that the last time when we—" Her hand clamps over my mouth, shutting me up immediately while her eyes narrow dangerously in my direction.

"Oh, I sense a story there," Enzo says, rubbing his hands together. "Do tell."

I raise my brows at Isla, not missing how Ant squirms beside her.

Ah, good times.

"I'd rather not. I've done my best to bleach the memory from my mind."

"Pfft, it was the best night of your life and you know it," I tease.

"In your dreams." She stomps off, leaving the four of us watching her arse sway in her ridiculously short shorts that show off more than they hide.

"Damn, bro. She really hates you."

"Didn't stop me tapping that, though," I deadpan.

Ant rolls his eyes but otherwise chooses not to get involved.

"We need to take this one out on the pull. He's been locked up here for way too long," Enzo says, throwing his arm around Ant once Isla is out of sight. "I bet it's so underused it's about to fall off."

"Fuck you, man."

"I'm up for it if you want to head out. This lot are going to be boring really fucking fast."

"Shots," Isla announces, suddenly popping back up in our group with a bottle of Grey Goose and five shot glasses.

"Hell yes," Enzo says, immediately taking the bottle from her, or more so trying.

"Excuse me," she snaps. "This little lady is more than capable of pouring a few shots."

"Never said you weren't," Enzo says, holding his hands up in surrender.

"Down the hatch, boys," she says before throwing her shot back and immediately pouring us all another. "So, where are we going?"

An idea that's been festering away in my mind for a while surges forward.

"Fancy taking us to Paradise?" I ask.

"Paradise?" Matteo asks, intrigued.

"Seriously? You wanna spend the night in a strip club?" Isla barks.

"Problem? I thought you'd enjoy it just as much as us. A hot dancer is a hot dancer, right?"

"You're a dickhead," she sneers, making Ant laugh.

"What the fuck did I say?" Isla shakes her head and throws back another shot. "So, are you in or what?"

"Yeah, I'm fucking in. Paradise has the best dancers in the city, and it's been off-limits for too fucking long."

My point exactly. I need inside that place, because if my suspicions are correct, then I'm going to find exactly what I've been searching for.

"Awesome, let's go," I announce, ignoring all my friends behind me and throwing my arms around both Isla and Ant.

"Careful. This is feeling very déjà vu-y," Isla warns, making Ant tense. "That night was already more than you could handle."

"Shut your mouth, pest," I mutter teasingly. "Best night of your lives and you know it."

"Do we have to?" Ant whispers.

"Sorry, man. Let's go find you some willing pussy."

"In a strip club full of men?" he asks curiously. "I'm sure you can cope."

Excitement stirs within me as we leave the building and pile into an Uber I called on the way down in the lift.

I've been to every strip club I could safely access in the past few weeks on my hunt, but I've come up empty. There are a couple on Italian territory that I haven't been able to step inside, but Paradise is by far the best, and it makes sense for her to be there.

The rest of the bottle of vodka vanishes between us as we drive. But despite the buzz I've got going on, I'm fully focused, and the second the Uber pulls to a stop, I'm out of the car and heading toward the bouncers, aware that they'll let me in the second they see who I'm with.

"Jesus, you're desperate," Matteo calls. I look back just in time to see him give the nod of approval to the bouncers.

I don't respond, mainly because he's right. I am desperate.

I head into the club, my eyes darting about everywhere.

But I don't bother looking for her red hair. I already know I won't find it. So instead, I search for the blonde she tries to hide behind.

And before long, I discover that I was right.

She's right here. Hiding in plain sight. Just like I knew she would be.

Look out, Vixen.

I'm coming for you.

Are you ready for our final Knight?
ONE-CLICK SINFUL KNIGHT NOW

Do know already know who Brianna's biological father is? If the name Victor Harris is new to you, then you're going to want to head over to my Rosewood High & Maddison Kings University series. We'll be heading back there next year for a new series!

Need to discuss all things Knight's with other addicts? Head over to my reader group TRACY'S ANGELS now!

ABOUT THE AUTHOR

Tracy Lorraine is a *USA Today* and *Wall Street Journal* bestselling new adult and contemporary romance author. Tracy has recently turned thirty and lives in a cute Cotswold village in England with her husband, baby girl and lovable but slightly crazy dog. Having always been a bookaholic with her head stuck in her Kindle, Tracy decided to try her hand at a story idea she dreamt up and hasn't looked back since.

Be the first to find out about new releases and offers. Sign up to my newsletter here.

If you want to know what I'm up to and see teasers and snippets of what I'm working on, then you need to be in my Facebook group. Join Tracy's Angels here.

Keep up to date with Tracy's books at
www.tracylorraine.com

<u>Trick You</u> #2

<u>Defy You</u> #3

<u>Play You</u> #4

<u>Inked</u> (A Rebel Ink/Driven Crossover)

<u>Rosewood High Series</u>

<u>Thorn</u> #1

<u>Paine</u> #2

<u>Savage</u> #3

<u>Fierce</u> #4

Hunter #5

Faze (#6 Prequel)

<u>Fury</u> #6

Legend #7

<u>Maddison Kings University Series</u>

<u>TMYM: Prequel</u>

<u>TRYS</u> #1

<u>TDYW</u> #2

<u>TBYS</u> #3

<u>TVYC</u> #4

<u>TDYD</u> #5

<u>TDYR</u> #6

<u>TRYD</u> #7

<u>Knight's Ridge Empire Series</u>

<u>Wicked Summer Knight: Prequel</u> (Stella & Seb)

Wicked Knight #1 (Stella & Seb)

Wicked Princess #2 (Stella & Seb)

Wicked Empire #3 (Stella & Seb)

Deviant Knight #4 (Emmie & Theo)

Deviant Princess #5 (Emmie & Theo

Deviant Reign #6 (Emmie & Theo)

One Reckless Knight (Jodie & Toby)

Reckless Knight #7 (Jodie & Toby)

Reckless Princess #8 (Jodie & Toby)

Reckless Dynasty #9 (Jodie & Toby)

Dark Halloween Knight (Calli & Batman)

Dark Knight #10 (Calli & Batman)

Dark Princess #11 (Calli & Batman)

Dark Legacy #12 (Calli & Batman)

Corrupt Valentine Knight (Nico & Siren)

Ruined Series

Ruined Plans #1

Ruined by Lies #2

Ruined Promises #3

Never Forget Series

Never Forget Him #1

Never Forget Us #2

Everywhere & Nowhere #3

THE REVENGE YOU SEEK
SNEAK PEEK

Chapter One

Letty

I sit on my bed, staring down at the fabric in my hands.

This wasn't how it was supposed to happen.

This wasn't part of my plan.

I let out a sigh, squeezing my eyes tight, willing the tears away.

I've cried enough. I thought I'd have run out by now.

A commotion on the other side of the door has me looking up in a panic, but just like yesterday, no one comes knocking.

I think I proved that I don't want to hang with my new roommates the first time someone knocked and asked if I wanted to go for breakfast with them.

I don't.

I don't even want to be here.

I just want to hide.

And that thought makes it all a million times worse.

I'm not a hider. I'm a fighter. I'm a fucking Hunter.

But this is what I've been reduced to.

This pathetic, weak mess.

And all because of *him*.

He shouldn't have this power over me. But even now, he does.

The dorm falls silent once again, and I pray that they've all headed off for their first class of the semester so I can slip out unnoticed.

I know it's ridiculous. I know I should just go out there with my head held high and dig up the confidence I know I do possess.

But I can't.

I figure that I'll just get through today—my first day— and everything will be alright.

I can somewhat pick up where I left off, almost as if the last eighteen months never happened.

Wishful thinking.

I glance down at the hoodie in my hands once more.

Mom bought them for Zayn, my younger brother, and me.

The navy fabric is soft between my fingers, but the text staring back at me doesn't feel right.

Maddison Kings University.

A knot twists my stomach and I swear my whole body sags with my new reality.

I was at my dream school. I beat the odds and I got into Columbia. And everything was good. No, everything was fucking fantastic.

Until it wasn't.

Now here I am. Sitting in a dorm at what was always my backup plan school having to start over.

Throwing the hoodie onto my bed, I angrily push to my feet.

I'm fed up with myself.

I should be better than this, stronger than this.

But I'm just... I'm broken.

And as much as I want to see the positives in this situation. I'm struggling.

Shoving my feet into my Vans, I swing my purse over my shoulder and scoop up the couple of books on my desk for the two classes I have today.

My heart drops when I step out into the communal kitchen and find a slim blonde-haired girl hunched over a mug and a textbook.

The scent of coffee fills my nose and my mouth waters.

My shoes squeak against the floor and she immediately looks up.

"Sorry, I didn't mean to disrupt you."

"Are you kidding?" she says excitedly, her southern accent making a smile twitch at my lips.

Her smile lights up her pretty face and for some reason, something settles inside me.

I knew hiding was wrong. It's just been my coping method for... quite a while.

"We wondered when our new roommate was going to show her face. The guys have been having bets on you being an alien or something."

A laugh falls from my lips. "No, no alien. Just..." I sigh, not really knowing what to say.

"You transferred in, right? From Columbia?"

"Ugh... yeah. How'd you know—"

"Girl, I know everything." She winks at me, but it

doesn't make me feel any better. "West and Brax are on the team, they spent the summer with your brother."

A rush of air passes my lips in relief. Although I'm not overly thrilled that my brother has been gossiping about me.

"So, what classes do you have today?" she asks when I stand there gaping at her.

"Umm... American lit and psychology."

"I've got psych later too. Professor Collins?"

"Uh..." I drag my schedule from my purse and stare down at it. "Y-yes."

"Awesome. We can sit together."

"S-sure," I stutter, sounding unsure, but the smile I give her is totally genuine. "I'm Letty, by the way." Although I'm pretty sure she already knows that.

"Ella."

"Okay, I'll... uh... see you later."

"Sure. Have a great morning."

She smiles at me and I wonder why I was so scared to come out and meet my new roommates.

I'd wanted Mom to organize an apartment for me so that I could be alone, but—probably wisely—she refused. She knew that I'd use it to hide in and the point of me restarting college is to try to put everything behind me and start fresh.

After swiping an apple from the bowl in the middle of the table, I hug my books tighter to my chest and head out, ready to embark on my new life.

The morning sun burns my eyes and the scent of freshly cut grass fills my nose as I step out of our building. The summer heat hits my skin, and it makes everything feel that little bit better.

So what if I'm starting over. I managed to transfer the

credits I earned from Columbia, and MKU is a good school. I'll still get a good degree and be able to make something of my life.

Things could be worse.

It could be this time last year...

I shake the thought from my head and force my feet to keep moving.

I pass students meeting up with their friends for the start of the new semester as they excitedly tell them all about their summers and the incredible things they did, or they compare schedules.

My lungs grow tight as I drag in the air I need. I think of the friends I left behind in Columbia. We didn't have all that much time together, but we'd bonded before my life imploded on me.

Glancing around, I find myself searching for familiar faces. I know there are plenty of people here who know me. A couple of my closest friends came here after high school.

Mom tried to convince me to reach out over the summer, but my anxiety kept me from doing so. I don't want anyone to look at me like I'm a failure. That I got into one of the best schools in the country, fucked it up and ended up crawling back to Rosewood. I'm not sure what's worse, them assuming I couldn't cope or the truth.

Focusing on where I'm going, I put my head down and ignore the excited chatter around me as I head for the coffee shop, desperately in need of my daily fix before I even consider walking into a lecture.

I find the Westerfield Building where my first class of the day is and thank the girl who holds the heavy door open for me before following her toward the elevator.

"Holy fucking shit," a voice booms as I turn the corner, following the signs to the room on my schedule.

Before I know what's happening, my coffee is falling from my hand and my feet are leaving the floor.

"What the—" The second I get a look at the guy standing behind the one who has me in his arms, I know exactly who I've just walked into.

Forgetting about the coffee that's now a puddle on the floor, I release my books and wrap my arms around my old friend.

His familiar woodsy scent flows through me, and suddenly, I feel like me again. Like the past two years haven't existed.

"What the hell are you doing here?" Luca asks, a huge smile on his face when he pulls back and studies me.

His brows draw together when he runs his eyes down my body, and I know why. I've been working on it over the summer, but I know I'm still way skinnier than I ever have been in my life.

"I transferred," I admit, forcing the words out past the lump in my throat.

His smile widens more before he pulls me into his body again.

"It's so good to see you."

I relax into his hold, squeezing him tight, absorbing his strength. And that's one thing that Luca Dunn has in spades. He's a rock, always has been and I didn't realize how much I needed that right now.

Mom was right. I should have reached out.

"You too," I whisper honestly, trying to keep the tears at bay that are threatening just from seeing him—them.

"Hey, it's good to see you," Leon says, slightly more subdued than his twin brother as he hands me my discarded books.

"Thank you."

I look between the two of them, noticing all the things that have changed since I last saw them in person. I keep up with them on Instagram and TikTok, sure, but nothing is quite like standing before the two of them.

Both of them are bigger than I ever remember, showing just how hard their coach is working them now they're both first string for the Panthers. And if it's possible, they're both hotter than they were in high school, which is really saying something because they'd turn even the most confident of girls into quivering wrecks with one look back then. I can only imagine the kind of rep they have around here.

The sound of a door opening behind us and the shuffling of feet cuts off our little reunion.

"You in Professor Whitman's American lit class?" Luca asks, his eyes dropping from mine to the book in my hands.

"Yeah. Are you?"

"We are. Walk you to class?" A smirk appears on his lips that I remember all too well. A flutter of the butterflies he used to give me threaten to take flight as he watches me intently.

Luca was one of my best friends in high school, and I spent almost all our time together with the biggest crush on him. It seems that maybe the teenage girl inside me still thinks that he could be it for me.

"I'd love you to."

"Come on then, Princess," Leon says and my entire body jolts at hearing that pet name for me. He's never called me that before and I really hope he's not about to start now.

Clearly not noticing my reaction, he once again takes my books from me and threads his arm through mine as the pair of them lead me into the lecture hall.

I glance at both of them, a smile pulling at my lips and hope building inside me.

Maybe this was where I was meant to be this whole time.

Maybe Columbia and I were never meant to be.

More than a few heads turn our way as we climb the stairs to find some free seats. Mostly it's the females in the huge space and I can't help but inwardly laugh at their reaction.

I get it.

The Dunn twins are two of the Kings around here and I'm currently sandwiched between them. It's a place that nearly every female in this college, hell, this state, would kill to be in.

"Dude, shift the fuck over," Luca barks at another guy when he pulls to a stop a few rows from the back.

The guy who's got dark hair and even darker eyes immediately picks up his bag, books, and pen and moves over a space.

"This is Colt," Luca explains, nodding to the guy who's studying me with interest.

"Hey," I squeak, feeling a little intimidated.

"Hey." His low, deep voice licks over me. "Ow, what the fuck, man?" he barks, rubbing at the back of his head where Luca just slapped him.

"Letty's off-limits. Get your fucking eyes off her."

"Dude, I was just saying hi."

"Yeah, and we all know what that usually leads to," Leon growls behind me.

The three of us take our seats and just about manage to pull our books out before our professor begins explaining the syllabus for the semester.

"Sorry about the coffee," Luca whispers after a few minutes. "Here." He places a bottle of water on my desk. "I know it's not exactly a replacement, but it's the best I can do."

The reminder of the mess I left out in the hallway hits me.

"I should go and—"

"Chill," he says, placing his hand on my thigh. His touch instantly relaxes me as much as it sends a shock through my body. "I'll get you a replacement after class. Might even treat you to a cupcake."

I smile up at him, swooning at the fact he remembers my favorite treat.

Why did I ever think coming here was a bad idea?

Chapter Two
Letty

My hand aches by the time Professor Whitman finishes talking. It feels like a lifetime ago that I spent this long taking notes.

"You okay?" Luca asks me with a laugh as I stretch out my fingers.

"Yeah, it's been a while."

"I'm sure these boys can assist you with that, beautiful," bursts from Colt's lips, earning him another slap to the head.

"Ignore him. He's been hit in the head with a ball one too many times," Leon says from beside me but I'm too enthralled with the way Luca is looking at me right now to reply.

Our friendship wasn't a conventional one back in high school. He was the star quarterback, and I wasn't a cheerleader or ever really that sporty. But we were paired up as lab partners during my first week at Rosewood High and we kinda never separated.

I watched as he took the team to new heights, as he met with college scouts, I even went to a few places with him so he didn't have to go alone.

He was the one who allowed me to cry on his shoulder as I struggled to come to terms with the loss of another who left a huge hole in my heart and he never, not once, overstepped the mark while I clung to him and soaked up his support.

I was also there while he hooked up with every member of the cheer squad along with any other girl who looked at him just so. Each one stung a little more than the last as my poor teenage heart was getting battered left, right, and center.

With each day, week, month that passed, I craved him more but he never, not once, looked at me that way.

I was even his prom date, yet he ended up spending the night with someone else.

It hurt, of course it did. But it wasn't his fault and I refuse to hold it against him.

Maybe I should have told him. Been honest with him about my feelings and what I wanted. But I was so terrified I'd lose my best friend that I never confessed, and I took that secret all the way to Columbia with me.

As I stare at him now, those familiar butterflies still set flight in my belly, but they're not as strong as I remember. I'm not sure if that's because my feelings for him have lessened over time, or if I'm just so numb and broken right now that I don't feel anything but pain.

It really could go either way.

I smile at him, so grateful to have run into him this morning.

He always knew when I needed him and even without knowing of my presence here, there he was like some guardian fucking angel.

If guardian angels had sexy dark bed hair, mesmerizing green eyes and a body built for sin then yeah, that's what he is.

I laugh to myself, yeah, maybe that irritating crush has gone nowhere.

"What have you got next?" Leon asks, dragging my attention away from his twin.

Leon has always been the quieter, broodier one of the duo. He's as devastatingly handsome and as popular with the female population but he doesn't wear his heart on his sleeve like Luca. Leon takes a little time to warm to people, to let them in. It was hard work getting there, but I soon realized that once he dropped his walls a little for me, it was hella worth it.

He's more serious, more contemplative, he's deeper. I always suspected that there was a reason they were so different. I know twins don't have to be the same and like the same things, but there was always something niggling at me that there was a very good reason that Leon closed himself down. From listening to their mom talk over the years, they were so identical in their mannerisms, likes, and dislikes when they were growing up, that it seems hard to believe they became so different.

"Psychology but not for an hour. I'm—"

"I'm taking her for coffee," Luca butts in. A flicker of anger passes through Leon's eyes but it's gone so fast that I begin to wonder if I imagined it.

"I could use another coffee before econ," Leon chips in.

"Great. Let's go," Luca forces out through clenched teeth.

He wanted me alone. Interesting.

The reason I never told him about my mega crush is the fact he friend-zoned me in our first few weeks of friendship by telling me how refreshing it was to have a girl wanting to be his friend and not using it as a ploy to get more.

We were only sophomores at the time but even then, Luca was up to all sorts and the girls around us were all more than willing to bend to his needs.

From that moment on, I couldn't tell him how I really felt. It was bad enough I even felt it when he thought our friendship was just that.

I smile at both of them, hoping to shatter the sudden tension between the twins.

"Be careful with these two," Colt announces from behind us as we make our way out of the lecture hall with all the others. "The stories I've heard."

"Colt," Luca warns, turning to face him and walking backward for a few steps.

"Don't worry," I shoot over my shoulder. "I know how to handle the Dunn twins." I wink at him as he howls with laughter.

"You two are in so much trouble," he muses as he turns left out of the room and we go right.

Leon takes my books from me once more and Luca threads his fingers through mine. I still for a beat. While the move isn't unusual, Luca has always been very affectionate. It only takes a second for his warmth to race up my arm and to settle the last bit of unease that's still knotting my stomach.

"Two Americanos and a skinny vanilla latte with an extra shot. Three cupcakes with the sprinkles on top."

I swoon at the fact Luca remembers my order. "How'd you—"

He turns to me, his wide smile and the sparkle in his eyes making my words trail off. The familiarity of his face, the feeling of comfort and safety he brings me causes a lump to form in my throat.

"I didn't forget anything about my best girl." He throws his arm around my shoulder and pulls me close.

Burying my nose in his hard chest, I breathe him in. His woodsy scent mixes with his laundry detergent and it settles me in a way I didn't know I needed.

Leon's stare burns into my back as I snuggle with his brother and I force myself to pull away so he doesn't feel like the third wheel.

"Dunn," the server calls, and Leon rushes ahead to grab our order while Luca leads me to a booth at the back of the coffee shop.

As we walk past each table, I become more and more aware of the attention on the twins. I know their reps, they've had their football god status since before I moved to Rosewood and met them in high school, but I had forgotten just how hero-worshiped they were, and this right now is off the charts.

Girls openly stare, their eyes shamelessly dropping down the guys' bodies as they mentally strip them naked. Guys jealousy shines through their expressions, especially those who are here with their girlfriends who are now paying them zero attention. Then there are the girls whose attention is firmly on me. I can almost read their thoughts—hell, I heard enough of them back in high school.

What do they see in her?

She's not even that pretty.

They're too good for her.

The only difference here from high school is that no one knows I'm just trailer park trash seeing as I moved from the hellhole that is Harrow Creek before meeting the boys.

Tipping my chin up, I straighten my spine and plaster on as much confidence as I can find.

They can all think what they like about me, they can come up with whatever bitchy comments they want. It's no skin off my back.

"Good to see you've lost your appeal," I mutter, dropping into the bench opposite both of them and wrapping my hands around my warm mug when Leon passes it over.

"We walk around practically unnoticed," Luca deadpans.

"You thought high school was bad," Leon mutters, he was always the one who hated the attention whereas Luca used it to his advantage to get whatever he wanted. "It was nothing."

"So I see. So, how's things? Catch me up on everything," I say, needing to dive into their celebrity status lifestyles rather than thinking about my train wreck of a life.

"Really?" Luca asks, raising a brow and causing my stomach to drop into my feet. "I think the bigger question is how come you're here and why we had no idea about it?"

Releasing my mug, I wrap my arms around myself and drop my eyes to the table.

"T-things just didn't work out at Columbia," I mutter, really not wanting to talk about it.

"The last time we talked, you said it was everything you expected it to be and more. What happened?"

Kane fucking Legend happened.

I shake that thought from my head like I do every time he pops up.

He's had his time ruining my life. It's over.

"I just..." I sigh. "I lost my way a bit, ended up dropping out and finally had to fess up and come clean to Mom."

Leon laughs sadly. "I bet that went down well."

The Dunn twins are well aware of what it's like to live with a pushy parent. One of the things that bonded the three of us over the years.

"Like a lead balloon. Even worse because I dropped out months before I finally showed my face."

"Why hide?" Leon's brows draw together as Luca stares at me with concern darkening his eyes.

"I had some health issues. It's nothing."

"Shit, are you okay?"

Fucking hell, Letty. Stop making this worse for yourself.

"Yeah, yeah. Everything is good. Honestly. I'm here and I'm ready to start over and make the best of it."

They both smile at me, and I reach for my coffee once more, bringing the mug to my lips and taking a sip.

"Enough about me, tell me all about the lives of two of the hottest Kings of Maddison."

"Okay... how'd you do that?" Ella whispers after both Luca and Leon walk me to my psych class after our coffee break.

"Do what?" I ask, following her into the room and finding ourselves seats about halfway back.

"It's your first day and the Dunn twins just walked you to class. You got a diamond-encrusted vag or something?"

I snort a laugh as a few others pause on their way to their seats at her words.

"Shush," I chastise.

"Girl, if it's true, you know all these guys need to know about it."

I pull out my books and a couple of pens as Professor Collins sets up at the front before turning to her.

"No, I don't have diamonds anywhere but my necklace. I've been friends with them for years."

"Girl, I knew there was a reason we should be friends." She winks at me. "I've been trying to get West and Brax to hook me up but they're useless."

"You want to be friends so I can set you up with one of the Dunns?"

"Or both." She shrugs, her face deadly serious before she leans in. "I've heard that they tag team sometimes. Can you imagine? Both of their undivided attention." She fans herself as she obviously pictures herself in the middle of a Dunn sandwich. "Oh and, I think you're pretty cool too."

"Of course you do." I laugh.

It's weird, I might have only met her very briefly this morning but that was enough.

"We're all going out for dinner tonight to welcome you to the dorm. The others are dying to meet you." She smiles at me, proving that there's no bitterness behind her words.

"I'm sorry for ignoring you all."

"Girl, don't sweat it. We got ya back, don't worry."

"Thank you," I mouth as the professor demands everyone's attention to begin the class.

The time flies as I scribble my notes down as fast as I can, my hand aching all over again and before I know it, he's finished explaining our first assignment and bringing his class to a close.

"Jesus, this semester is going to be hard," Ella muses as we both pack up.

"At least we've got each other."

"I like the way you think. You done for the day?"

"Yep, I'm gonna head to the store, grab some supplies then get started on this assignment, I think."

"I've got a couple of hours. You want company?"

After dumping our stuff in our rooms, Ella takes me to her favorite store, and I stock up on everything I'm going to need before we head back so she can go to class.

I make myself some lunch before being brave and setting up my laptop at the kitchen table to get started on my assignments. My time for hiding is over, it's time to get back to life and once again become a fully immersed college student.

"Holy shit, she is alive. I thought Zayn was lying about his beautiful older sister," a deep rumbling voice says, dragging me from my research a few hours later.

I spin and look at the two guys who have joined me.

"Zayn would never have called me beautiful," I say as a greeting.

"That's true. I think his actual words were: messy, pain in the ass, and my personal favorite, I'm glad I don't have to live with her again," he says, mimicking my brother's voice.

"Now that is more like it. Hey, I'm Letty. Sorry about—"

"You're all good. We're just glad you emerged. I'm West, this ugly motherfucker is Braxton—"

"Brax, please," he begs. "Only my mother calls me by my full name and you are way too hot to be her."

My cheeks heat as he runs his eyes over my curves.

"T-thanks, I think."

"Ignore him. He hasn't gotten laid for weeeeeks."

"Okay, do we really need to go there right now?"

"Always, bro. Our girl here needs to know you get pissy when you don't get the pussy."

I laugh at their easy banter, closing down my laptop and

resting forward on my elbows as they move toward the fridge.

"Ella says we're going out," Brax says, pulling out two bottles of water and throwing one to West.

"Apparently so."

"She'll be here in a bit. Violet and Micah too. They were all in the same class."

"So," West says, sliding into the chair next to me. "What do we need to know that your brother hasn't already told us about you?"

My heart races at all the things that not even my brother would share about my life before I drag my thoughts away from my past.

"Uhhh..."

"How about the Dunns love her," Ella announces as she appears in the doorway flanked by two others. Violet and Micah, I assume.

"Um... how didn't we know this?" Brax asks.

"Because you're not cool enough to spend any time with them, asshole," Violet barks, walking around Ella. "Ignore these assholes, they think they're something special because they're on the team but what they don't tell you is that they have no chance of making first string or talking to the likes of the Dunns."

"Vi, girl. That stings," West says, holding his hand over his heart.

"Yeah, get over it. Truth hurts." She smiles up at him as he pulls her into his chest and kisses the top of her head.

"Whatever, Titch."

"Right, well. Are we ready to go? I need tacos like... yesterday."

"Yes. Let's go."

"You've never had tacos like these, Letty. You are in for a world of pleasure," Brax says excitedly.

"More than she would be if she were in your bed, that's for sure," West deadpans.

"Lies and we all know it."

"Whatever." Violet pushes him toward the door.

"Hey, I'm Micah," the third guy says when I catch up to him.

"Hey, Letty."

"You need a sensible conversation, I'm your boy."

"Good to know."

Micah and I trail behind the others and with each step I take, my smile gets wider.

Things really are going to be okay.

DOWNLOAD NOW TO KEEP READING